SPOT
THRU THE
HART

Lou L Berthelson

The sale of this book without its cover is unauthorized. If you purchase this book without a cover, you should be aware that neither the author nor the publisher received payment for the sale of this stripped book.

This book is a work of fiction. Any references to historical events, real people, or real places and events are the products of the author's imagination, and any resemblance to actual events or places or persons, living or dead, is entirely coincidental.

Copyright © 2019 Lou L. Berthelson
All rights reserved, including the right to reproduce this book or portions thereof in any form whatsoever.

ISBN 978107769501

Dedication

To my grandsons, who are the coolest people on the planet. They are so gifted, creative and off the charts smart. Most of all, they are extremely funny dudes whom I love to hang with.

In loving remembrance of Canine Sergeant Molly Malone, formerly of the Los Angeles Drug Enforcement Unit.

Artwork

Book cover by Amelia Blanco
www.ameliabdigitalartistry.com

Chapter One

Day One
9:12 pm
Lil' Pine Cabin
Front gates
Jonesborough, TN

As John Hart past through the gates leading to his little pine cabin, he quickly stopped and turned off his lights. There were lights on in the cabin, but no cars in the driveway. There wasn't a breach alert on his phone.

John opened the console of his Polaris and reached for his gun; it was in his lab with his other weapons. He had spent the day rehabbing, and cleaning them, then left them on the table and went to dinner; not smart.

He looked around and realized his nearest weapon was under the tabletop of the island in the kitchen. Continuing his weapon inventory, he let out a long sigh; he had a substantial pocketknife in his right pocket. Gibbs rule 9, "don't go anywhere without a knife." He had a small square box he used to carry micro-SD chips in his left pocket. He had been carrying it around for a week trying to figure out what to do with it.

John checked his phone; the house security was still armed. He began to think that maybe a light was left on. Maybe it was a new upgrade that made it appear that someone was home. He called Glenn. No such upgrade, but Glenn verified that someone was in the house, but had not tripped any sensors.

Glenn was John's first friend and was now in charge of the Hart Group's technology. Having the threat verified, John's heart rate began to ramp up.

Soon after John blew up the Hart Compound, some sixteen months ago, strange, cult-like, dark-minded people had flooded the area. They felt his actions had closed a portal to hell that disrupted the fulfillment of one of their cult's critical prophesies. The fans of darkness were not happy; John had told his people to be careful.

Kat, John's girlfriend, was with her sister Makayla at the compound; they were leaving for training early in the morning. Kat and Makayla had his German shepherd Molly with them. Sims was meeting John at the Coffee Hole in the morning. John realized he had a problem.

John figured that he could use his phone's countermeasures to get into the house, but either way, he would have to fight his way to a weapon. He thought about having to go hand-to-hand, he was a surprisingly better fighter since his dreams had stopped.

John was no wimp at six foot two inches tall, lean and strong. Chris Sims, a former Master Sergeant, his friend, and trainer, had made him quite dangerous. Combine this with his being raised in the Foster Care system and you have a hardened character.

He moved the Polaris into the shadows just inside the property to ensure that it could not be seen. He reached under the seat, found his binoculars and switched them to night vision mode.

John watched the house for several minutes, he finally he saw movement in the shadows, but he could tell it was light reflecting from the back of the house.

He figured they had come in the back way. Not many people knew about the back path that led through the hills and around the back to The Town with No Name. This was a local or someone who had spent a great deal of time working out how to get to him.

John made up his mind. It was time to go. John left the Polaris, moved way right of the front door, around to the side windows of the dining room and looked inside. The light was still flickering from the back to the front.

He went onto the back deck and slipped into Molly's doghouse, which had access to the house through a rear doggie door. Molly, his highly trained German shepherd, was a big girl, so the opening was large enough to allow him to enter quietly.

As John stood up in the kitchen, he could hear the intruder pulling open drawers in the master bedroom. John needed to get a look without losing the element of surprise. He thought of retrieving the gun from under the table but felt the sound of the Velcro would alert the intruder; he found a silver tray by the sink. He carefully picked it up.

John positioned himself where he could use the tray as a mirror to see down the hall into the bedroom. He had to wait several minutes until the intruder moved across the entry of the room.

One look was all he needed, he knew that jacket; he was in trouble. John began to sweat he was confused and afraid. He knew it was not a rational fear, he had faced the Kabala's worst creatures, hacked the Pentagon, but now he was paralyzed by fear.

John had a little chat with himself; he could not wait any longer. He decided to go in hard, use the advantage of surprise and hope the outcome would go his way. He reached into his left pocket and headed down the hallway.

As he came to the door, the intruder had their back to him. He did not hesitate; he launched himself at his target ready to engage using a full leg sweep. Just as John was about to slide, his mark turned leading with a left elbow that caught him square on the jaw.

John went down hard; it was all he could do to swipe with his left hand before he hit the floor. There was a loud shriek and Kat was on his chest pinning his arms down with her knees. She had the ring out of the box already and was trying it on, the whole time saying, "Yes, Yes, Yes!"

John was no longer afraid, he felt his entire body relax; he couldn't stop smiling. He tried to get up but his captor was having none of it, "Oh, you are not going anywhere mister. I am not done with you yet."

Chapter Two

9:12 pm
Nick Hart's House
Newark, NJ

Nick got up from his oxblood leather-smoking chair, picked up his three fingers of Jack Daniels and moved to the back of his house. The Jersey house looked quite common from the street but inside was another story; modifications had been made.

As he came to his closet in the master bedroom, the doors automatically opened as he touched the antique pulls. Inside he reached up and slid the handgun safe to the right; the back of the closet opened from the middle outward in both directions. The smell of cigars and humidors filled his mind with memories great and regrettable.

He entered the 14 by 14 room, which had more of the oxblood chairs and a bench along the back that matched. The room was begging for a poker or pool table as the middle portion of the room was empty. Nick had a pool table and a poker table suspended in the attic mechanisms, but they were not the choice for this evening.

This was an anniversary of sorts; a ceremony Nick performed each year. He went to the small bar on the left side of the room, pulled down the lever of an old grocery store style cash register. When the cash drawer was fully extended, the ceiling pulled away and a six-foot round black table with gold inlays descended from the rafters. As the table came to rest, it revealed several ashtrays set in a circle following the outer edge of the table.

Each was around eighteen inches apart, twelve in all with a small clear glass ashtray in the middle. In the field of the ashtray was a logo, The San Dimas Inn, in red letters.

Nick walked over to the desk in the left-back corner of the room, pulled open the right-hand side upper drawer and took out the ashtray he received when Sim's had dealt with Zhang Jei in Beijing. He placed it on the table and rearranged the others making room so the circle remained unbroken.

All of the ashtrays represented actions taken to protect the group. Their type of problems could not be litigated, let alone understood by local law enforcement. Some of the actions had been strategic moves to either send a message, clear the board or keep a promise. Whoever completed the action would signify success by sending an ashtray from the hotel where they had stayed.

The ashtray in the center of the table was the first and was only displayed when Nick was alone. Not even John knew of this particular action, the one that changed Nick and justified all further actions in his mind.

It took place in 2009, just after they hacked the Pentagon. Later they became highly valued defense contractors. They went on to make billions from the technology they used during the hack.

All through his school years, John had been tormented by students and deadbeats. As his brother, Nick felt he needed to protect John.

Of all the people who bothered John, one was by far the worst. He was a red-headed kid, barely stood five-foot-tall, a true sociopath; his name was Bryan. Every day Bryan would go out of his way to make John's life miserable.

Bryan went to live with his grandparents after his father was killed in a police shootout. Bryan bragged about how he beat, tortured and stole from his grandparents. People in the neighborhood were afraid of the mad midget. They would find a slaughtered cat or dog on their doorstep if they ever called the police, or talked about him.

While Nick was working the plan for the Pentagon, he heard from one of his high school friends that Bryan's grandparents had died. They had been trapped when their house caught fire.

He said that Bryan made it look like he got home just in time to save most of the house, but the grandparents had died from smoke inhalation.

Bryan's drug buddies said that he was with them when he got a call the house was burning. After the investigation, he and the druggies moved into the house. Bryan received sixty thousand dollars from the grandparent's estate. After hearing this news, Nick decided Bryan must die.

When John hung up on the big wigs at the Pentagon and the hack was complete, Nick told John to get out of town. Later, Nick headed to the airport and flew into Ontario, CA, and then took a bus to the San Dimas Inn.

Two days later while waiting for his flight home, he bought the local newspaper. He learned that

Bryan had been found in the ashes of his grandparents' home. He had been tied to a chair and gagged. The source of the fire was in the back of the house and Bryan had been found in the front living space.

The report went on to say Bryan's chair had been bolted to the floor and that the home's landline phone was placed six-feet in front of him. The Police ruled the fire arson and Bryan's death a murder.

Nick followed the investigation, but it only lasted a week; nobody cared so everyone moved on. Nick's friend called him with the news; they both agreed it was a nasty business and that karma was a bitch.

Nick sat down in another oxblood leather chair, lit an expensive cigar. This anniversary was about looking back at what had taken place. Since John had been awarded sixty-three million dollars in an abuse suit against the California Forster Care system, things had really changed.

They had met Craig Battle and Jess Williams right after they came out of MIT. Craig had the ideas and Jess could build the systems to make them viable. John gave them everything they needed to bring Craig's idea to life.

Craig was getting close to solving the last of the problems preventing him from developing perpetual energy when he lost his battle with Meth addiction. Jess stepped into the lead and after four months working with the supercollider in

Switzerland, she found what Craig could see, but could not explain.

She watched the various tests conducted on the collider until one day in frustration she just stood staring through the glass. She noticed that it took an extremely long time for of the particles to stop. They continued on their momentum without applied power. Kind of like a speedy hamster jumping off the wheel. Jess created a type of conductive fabric, or mesh, which captured all the byproducts of the moving electrical current.

The first working application of her discovery was with cell phones. They used the prototypes to hack the Pentagon and force General Rouse into awarding them an open-ended contract to develop the most important energy technology in history.

Nick was proud of how refined their process had become. They could next day deliver the gun closet, fly anywhere in private Jets. With Glenn, possibly the world's best cyber tracker-hunter, they could reach anyone anywhere.

His mind drifted back to the group's newly refurbished headquarters in Jonesborough, TN. The closer they came to finishing the rebuild, the more weird, Goth type people showed up in the area. He and John had discussed it; they decided to be careful, but not worried. They increased the level of security for everyone in the Hart Group.

Chapter Three

3:30 am
Darkest Night
Jonesborough, TN

He had not been flying in the darkness for some time. It felt good to be out of the cramped confines humans forced him to deal with. He was finally able to fully extend his limbs and stretch out the entire span of his being. In the darkness, he was invisible. If he did not move or rustle around, you would never know he was there.

His coloring had changed from its former brilliance, all his time in the black spaces of time had slowly brought him to this. For many thousands of years, he had existed in various forms.

First, he had been a great force used to protect the master's handiwork. He had been a warrior and a leader. He had also spent eternities in banishment; suspended in complete sensory deprivation, alone, unable to move, left with only his memories and guilt.

Then the messenger who had supervised the terms of his punishment returned to tell him about the great reconciliation of all things; he was released. He was pledged to terms of servitude, and restrictions of his abilities.

At first, he was assigned only the most menial tasks. Most of which did nothing but add to the crushing guilt caused by his previous debauchery.

Many, disregarding their redemption, had fled into the darkest regions of the earth. They were ungrateful and full of the hate that vents from fire. They took great pleasure in creating chaos and division on the earth; for it was there, he had led them to iniquity.

Now his mission was clear, as long as their kind's blood was flowing within some humans he would be tasked to identify them and protect as many as possible.

He had enjoyed getting back into the moonless night's sky, soaring and listening to the spirits that filled the earth. He was in tune with all spiritual beings. While soaring quietly and listening he could monitor the violent and disruptive beings that were dispatched to wreak havoc.

This particular night he had been gliding high above the town of Jonesborough looking and listening. He was angered by voices speaking of revenge and death. They were voices he had not heard for hundreds of years. He knew their master, and their current location meant that was someone was going to die.

His first inclination was to swoop down and separate their minds from their bodies; but he was restrained. He had to consider the innocent being's they inhabited, and he needed consent to kill other beings like himself.

Regardless, he had to find out what his former employee had to gain from the proposed actions. Was it just revenge for the incident at the compound? He could understand those feelings; either way, he needed to figure this out quickly before they ended John Hart.

Chapter Four

5:50 am
Lil' Pine Cabin
Jonesborough, TN

Kat's sister Makayla had to pick up Kat so they could travel together. The Hart Group had moved their training facilities to Virginia in the hills above Bristol. This was going to be MaKayla's first session.

John felt for some time that MaKayla should join the group. She and Kat's parents had passed. She was Kat's only family and now would be John's family as well.

John having been raised in foster care never knew his real parents; the only person he called family was Nick. He and Nick had the same foster mother, and they had grown up like brothers. John liked the idea of acquiring a real family.

Kat had taken care of John and Molly, after the psychological stress they went through during the siege at the compound. She had slowly brought them back to a normal existence. Kat had always insisted that John continue his morning sessions at the Coffee Hole. She made it a house rule; it worked wonders for John and Molly's recovery.

John secured the house and logged out. He and Kat headed out the front doors, said their goodbyes and John headed for the Polaris. He caught himself looking for Molly to join him, but she was with Makayla.

The Polaris was just inside the gates right of the house pointing toward the hills behind the house. They led to the back way to The Town with No Name. He knew it would be tight at some points, but he was up for it. It was a mile and a half of moguls caused by run-off.

The dawn light was threatening to break, so his lights were needed, but were not very effective; like driving at sundown. The first part of the path was almost straight up the back hill that started at their patio.

John adjusted the suspension settings for the terrain, used the seventy yards to the house to build his speed, and then he blasted up the hill. John was focused on the fall-off to his left and failed to see two men dive into the ravine to avoid being seen. They had been watching the John Hart Group for the last two weeks and never dreamed John would come out the back.

They were pretty beat up after they rolled down the two hundred feet. Now they had to drag their asses back up the hill to where they hid their truck.

They got to the truck and called their other team which was covering John's regular route into town. They, in turn, called their master. Word came back that the two cliff divers were to follow John to the Coffee Hole and delay him if he tried to leave before 6:30 am.

John came flying out of the woods onto the road just north of the gas station; he had to veer to avoid hitting a street sign, then skidded to a stop in the middle of Main Street. One hundred yards ahead on his left was the Coffee Hole and the Diner across the way.

Looking at the vehicles he could tell Hoss, Little Joe (Lil' Joe), and Adam were there. Phu, the owner of the Coffee Hole, was the chief instigator, and Sims had not yet arrived. The boys would be bummed Molly was not with him, but they could enjoy all of their donuts for a change.

He had met the boys the first time he went looking for coffee west of Jonesborough. Being the stranger, they grilled him good. He enjoyed it and ended up coming for coffee most days after that; it was Molly's favorite place. Later he learned that Hoss was working for General Rouse.

John had to drive by the Coffee Hole then swing back into a spot next to Hoss' monster truck. He looked at his dash clock, 6:05 am.

When he came in they were all staring at him, "Where the hell did you come from?" Adam said into his coffee. John looked back at the Polaris, "I came the back way." Phu laughed, "What back way, what are you talking about." John had reached the coffee, "You know, the little walking path that starts at the gas station." Phu's mouth fell open, "That little path is a pain in the ass, branches everywhere always slipping down the side hill…you are nuts?"

Lil' Joe stood up and looked out at the Polaris, "You didn't roll it; that is amazing. I took my dirt bike back there once; I was always sliding down the side hill…cracked my nuts bad; not doing that ever again." Phu leaned toward Lil' Joe, "Shit, you almost crack your nuts every time you sit down." Adam grinned and Lil' Joe nodded his head and carefully sat back down.

John looked around, "Where's Hoss?" Adam pointed at the restroom; John's eyes grew wide with fear. Adam held up his hands, "It's ok; he said he was just taking a piss." John took his first sip of coffee; his eyes were still on the restroom door.

John went over and sat next to Adam and Lil' Joe, "Maybe I should take a good look at the Polaris to see if I messed it up any?" Phu moving to the back, "Take the right way home. No one will find you back there if you crash...wise up son."

Hoss came back from the restroom everyone was staring at him as he approached; when he got in range, they smelled soap; everyone relaxed. They told Hoss about John's little ride on the back trail.

Hoss laughed, "Hell if I was in that thing we wouldn't have made up the hill. If I was driving, I woulda scrapped about a hundred pounds off my ass in the first fifty yards." Hoss was a huge individual.

They all laughed and continued to talk back and forth; Phu was mostly in the back. John was thinking of Kat being at Jake's picking up snacks and medical supplies, ready to head on out to Virginia. He was impressed with how much better she became with each training session.

John started to tell the boys about his engagement proposal when the front doors burst open, and two male strangers walked in. There was a tall guy, about six foot four, and his shorter sidekick, maybe five foot two. The short guy seemed to be the alpha and the tall guy just looked mentally jacked up.

The tall guy had extremely large ears that stuck out from the side of his head three to four inches but narrowed to his head at the nose line of his face. They had lobes that hung down as if they had been stretched by piercings. The top of his ears were somewhat pointy in a mule type of way.

His nose was like a snout or a foot. It came from between his eyebrows all the way down to his mouth. He had a sizable overbite and thin lips.

The shorter guy was wearing an old-time pilots leather helmet with the fur ear covers that bikers used to wear. He had a small round face with beady eyes and bucked teeth. He was fidgety, twitching all over with a Joe Pesci vibe. He stood next to his friend rocking back and forth; the tall guy was gazing into space.

Phu had heard the bells from the door and came around to the counter. Hoss and John moved left and Adam and Lil' Joe move right revealing the new customers. Phu leaned over the counter looked at the two strangers then back at his friends; he busted out laughing, "Holy shit, look at these guys. Where the hell is Natasha? You two mutts look like Rocket J. Squirrel and Bull Winkle Moose.

John instantly saw the resemblance, as did the others. They all turned away covering their mouths laughing out of control. Their two new guests had not expected their reaction. They believed they were intimidating looking badasses.

They served the Master they could not take this shit from anyone, let alone some backwoods townies. The shorter one (Rocky) stepped forward, raised both his hands over his head and yelled, "Silence!"

Hoss and the crew turned around. It looked like Rocky was about to take off and fly just like in the cartoons. Adam moved toward Rocky, "Are you trying to take off? Are you gonna fly?"

The laughter got worse. Bull Winkle had had enough and started to move toward Adam. John stepped between them and squared up in Bull Winkles face.

Sims came into the Coffee Hole speaking rapidly, "I have been following a couple of guys from the main road…" He stopped and came around to where John was standing. He looked into John's eyes and then back to Bull Winkle, "Holy shit are you guys looking for Boris Badenov?" Phu chimed in, "Rocky and Bull Winkle right, you see it too."

Sims came to the Hart Group via Glenn. They had been in Afghanistan together; Sims was his Master Sergeant. Sims lost his way after he returned home and Glenn brought him to John. Sims had turned John into a proper soldier.

Bull Winkle started to reach for Sims' arm when John reached across Bull Winkle's body grabbed his off-shoulder and spun him around away from both of them. Sims stepped back, moved to the counter and sat on a stool. He motioned for everyone else to sit down.

Rocky started to move toward John but Hoss grabbed him by the back of his shirt one-handed and put him in a chair. Sims quietly, "John we got to be back to the compound soon, don't make us late."

Bull Winkle stood still a bit confused then he remembered what he was going to do, "I am going to kill you then cut your heart out and eat it." John slowly smiled and then he winked at him; Bull Winkle lunged at John.

John stepped under the left-handed haymaker and came up with his right hand cupped as if he was carrying water and slapped it full speed on Bull Winkle's left ear. It made a popping sound, like a Champaign cork. Bull Winkle screamed, grabbing his ear. He fell to the ground as if he had been shot. Rocky was at his side hissing at John and the others like a pissed-off cat, "He better not be deaf; you're all dead men."

Hoss walked over to Bull Winkle, picked him up by his belt. He looked at Rocky and said: "Exit stage left Snaggle Puss." Rocky fell in line as Hoss carried Bull Winkle outside behind his truck, and tossed him in the street.

Phu was excited, "Whoa that was insane. It was like boom, sit boy!" As Hoss came back in he said, "Phu, Sims calls that shot the Helen Keller." John turned to Sims who had a smile on his face, "I am proud of ya boy." John had another coffee while Sims enjoyed his first cup.

Sims and John discussed their upcoming trip to Canada to meet with Jess about a battle suit they were working on. Sims asked if Glenn was going to be there. John told him Glenn had been using all his time and their resources tracking down someone he felt was looking for him and the group.

Rocky and Bull Winkle worked their way back to their car and checked in. They learned that the follow crew had left the compound and were tracking the target. Rocky and Bull Winkle could relax they had completed their mission; it was 6:50 am and John Hart and Chris Sims were still hanging out at the Coffee Hole.

Chapter Five

6:15 am
Lil' Pine Cabin
Jonesborough, TN

Kat was amazed that John actually cleared the back hill in his Polaris. She felt he was extremely happy or a little bit crazy; she decided she didn't have to choose. She looked down the driveway for Makayla.

Makayla was sixteen months older than Kat, but they were almost twins. If you saw them together you could make them out, but seeing one of them on the street, you would have to guess who was who.

Makayla finally showed up and vacated the driver's seat, "I am done with driving in this state. I get lost every time I drive by myself." Kat got in, petted Molly good morning and asked, "Have we got all our stuff onboard?" Makayla nodded in the affirmative. Kat smiled, "Well, I am so glad you agreed to pick me up," she held out her hand showing her engagement ring.

Makayla's mouth fell open, she was stunned, "Holy shit, look at that rock, my God it looks like your gonna marry Elvis. Tell me everything right now!" Molly was getting more excited as the two women talked, shrieked and laughed.

As Kat told her story, Makayla was firing questions non-stop, "Why did he think you were an intruder?" Kat said, "When you dropped me off I realized my house keys were packed in my suitcase back at the compound. I snuck in through Molly's doggie door so there were no intrusion alerts."

When Kat reached the part where she punched John out, Makayla started to giggle, "You smacked his ass good and snatched the ring before he hit the ground; that was some Lucy Liu, Kill Bill shit sister. I can't wait for my training." Kat noticed as they settled down Molly fell to sleep on the back seat.

After they transitioned off the TN-81 on to W. Jackson Blvd., they swung into the parking lot of Jake's Grocery and Tackle, which was on the North corner of W. Jackson right before the Wetlands Water Park. It was now 6:35 am and they were late.

Jake's didn't open until 8:00 am, but Jake was one of John's contractors. His job was to supply the group with everything tactical it needed, support logistics and supply of all training sessions, plus the occasional off the books operation.

Kat pulled into the parking lot and Molly was finally awake. Jake waved to them as he opened the automatic doors, and then headed for the back of the store. Makayla hooked on Molly's leash and took her to the trees at the east end of the lot to pee. Kat went through the open doors and yelled to Jake, "If you need some help with that order, Makayla and I can give you a hand." There was no answer so she went to see if Jake was back in the freezer area.

Kat had reached the pass-through to the freezers when she saw Jake rolling on the floor with blood coming from the side of his face. As she moved to help him, a hand covered her mouth and someone grabbed her so strongly she could hardly breathe. Kat was not old enough to have ever smelled ether, so she could not recognize the smell that brought on the darkness.

Makayla put Molly back in the car and headed for the store. She came through the entry doors and saw Jake staggering toward her. He was bleeding from his face yelling, "Run, they have Kat, run!" She started to move toward him when he was struck in the head again; he went down hard.

Makayla turned to go and ran straight into a large man. She bounced back, "Molly help me. Molly!" She reached in her purse for her pepper spray when her face as covered by a foul-smelling towel. She dropped her purse and was out.

The two men took Makayla past Molly to their car and loaded her in the back. The man who grabbed Kat had both of their purses; he threw them in the back with Makayla. He turned to the other man, "I have the other one in my car I will meet you at the warehouse now go. Go!" As they drove out of the lot, they saw Molly clawing at the windows and trying to bite the glass; she was pissed.

As Jake started to come around, he realized he had been out more than an hour. It took him several minutes to clear his head and finally stand up. He saw Kat's car in the lot and staggered to it as fast as he could. He looked inside, saw Molly and called the Police.

When Sheriff Jeffery Barlow arrived on the scene, one of his deputies was working on Jakes' head and the other was putting up crime scene tape. As he approached Jake, his deputy pointed at Kat's car and gave him a shooing motion so he would go there first.

Jeff had been Sheriff long before John and his minions had ransacked the land west of town. Jeff was forty, with sandy brown hair. He was five foot ten; his hairstyle was 1950's lawman.

The Sheriff took one look inside the car, then threw open the door. He got down on his knees then looked back over his shoulder, "Get an ambulance here now!" Jake answered, "I don't need an ambulance, Sheriff." Barlow was pissed now; he stood up, "Get me a fucking ambulance now. Do it now!"

Jake worked with the two deputies giving his statement while Barlow stayed with Molly. He took a piece of paper from his tactical folder and made a sign he placed under Molly's collar, it read, Do Not Destroy, in big bold letters.

When the ambulance finally pulled up it went toward the store away from the car. Barlow got them squared away and told them to get Molly to the Johnson City Veterinary Hospital on the hop.

The driver started to argue that he was a people ambulance, but Barlow got in close with both EMTs, "Listen you are wasting time this dog does not have." One of them sarcastically said, "Must belong to someone pretty important."

Barlow had had it with these guys, "Hey listen up, if this dog dies and it is determined that this little chat we are having was the cause, her owner will buy up your ambulance service, your homes, your families homes and burn them to the ground. He will make sure you never work in this state again; you feelin' me?"

They looked at each other, the driver's eyes widened; he turned to Barlow, "Is this Molly?" Barlow just nodded. The other EMT's chin hit his chest, "Shit, we got to go."

Barlow turned away from everyone; he checked the time and dialed the State Police to start the search for Kat and Makayla. These bastards had a good hour head start.

Chapter Six

8:50 am
Nick Hart's House
Newark, NJ

Nick stayed in his oxblood chair drinking way too late. He opened his eyes just enough to see it was light out. That little glimpse caused his headache to come out of hiding; he was hungover. His next visual experiment was risking a look at the bedside clock, "Ouch 8:50 am; ah shit, this is not ok."

Nick's phone buzzed from across the room. He was in no mood. Nick went into the restroom to leave some of last night behind and gain the benefits of a toothbrush and mouthwash.

He headed for the kitchen, to his surprise he had loaded the coffee maker and set the timer last night. He had fresh coffee. He would survive.

The phone buzzed again, it had only been a couple of minutes; not a good sign. Nick shuffled into the living room picked up the phone; it showed eleven missed calls, not good. He checked and they were all from the same number in Jonesborough, even worse.

He did not want to respond. Nick's guts were churning, he had only a couple of sips of coffee and he was in no shape for bad news.

Nick highlighted the number and hit send. Before it even rang, "Hello Nick, this is Sheriff Barlow are you there?" Nick slowly slouched into the sofa, "Yes Jeffery, what do you need?" "Kat and Makayla have been abducted, and I put Molly in an ambulance heading to the Johnson City Veterinary Hospital."

Nick fell silent. Barlow, now yelling into the phone, "Nick, are you there? Did you hear what I said?" Nick held up his hand as if ward off the pressure, "Yes, Yes I am here, tell me what happened."

Nick listened carefully now gulping coffee. He took a more strategic position, by standing next to the coffee maker. He was pouring his second cup when Barlow finished with Molly's situation and the actions the State Police were taking.

Barlow was finishing, "I have no idea where John is, he is not picking up at the home number he gave me." Nick sighed, "Just as well, it's 9:15 am and he is in the air flying to London, Canada to meet with Jess Williams. He should be over halfway there right now. I will contact him and get him back home."

Nick reluctantly, "Do we need the General on this, I don't want to overstep, just tell me if you need help; we can make it happen." Barlow, "No let's give it some time, we may find them right away and if that is not the case, we will need to hit it hard." Nick agreed and signed off wondering how he was going to tell John.

He refreshed his coffee and went back to the sofa, he was not even sure he could reach John. Dom's plane was not equipped to do cell to cell; he needed Glenn to find a way to contact John without getting General Rouse involved. Nick had flown in that plane many times, and he couldn't remember anything other than the radio.

Nick could do something for Molly right now; he went through his phone and found the emergency number for Doctor Peters. Peters was Molly's special Vet, he helped her when she was injured or out of whack mentally. It was hard doing what Molly did for John and sometimes she needed to spend time with Dr. Peters.

Molly was part of John's recovery from the abuse he suffered in foster care. The abuse led to a series of gruesome nightmares that came in groups of three. Molly would revive him if he passed out, help regulate his heart rate and breathing and protect him in times he was incapacitated. After Molly's first year on the job, John bought the LAPD several dogs to replace Molly and kept her on as one of his closest friends.

Peters picked-up on the third ring. He was in the field with several dogs working for the LAPD, "Nick, what do you need?" Nick didn't mince words, "You in Johnson City, TN as fast as you can get here. Molly is in really bad shape; almost killed herself trying to defend Kat and Makayla."

Peters was quiet for a second, "I can get there by 6:00 am tomorrow. I have a dog with a gunshot wound that won't make it if I don't cut on her right away. So tell them to keep her alive, and I will get there sooner if I can."

Nick was quiet, "Do me a favor, call the people at the Johnson City Veterinary Hospital, and see if they need any advice. You probably know more about this type of thing then they do. They can tell you just how bad they think it is as well." Peters letting out a long sigh, "I will call them right now."

Chapter Seven

9:40 am
Marco's Plane at 12,000 ft.
Destination London, Canada

Sims left his SUV at the Coffee Hole and road with John to Hoss' wheat farm. The group used his wide service road as a landing strip for small planes they would contract to get around unseen.

Their pilot was Dom Carbone. He was the older brother of Marco who had died saving Sims life in the tunnels under the compound.

Dom had learned to fly so he could carry on Marco's commitment to the group. Dom, now a good pilot, had always been a top-notch member of the group's security team.

They got John and Sims on board and took off without a hitch. The plane was a small prop-driven, dual-engine model, with seating for two up front and four passengers in the back. Top speed was not great, but the ability to fly without flight plans offset any limitations of the plane.

Sims was filling in John about Jess' ideas on how to combine the shock-absorbing gel and the outer fabric of the battle suit. She felt they could capture the energy emitted from a bullet strike into the gel and merge it with the energy already flowing in the mesh.

The concept is to create a matrix of mesh cells to act like the human body's nerve cells. The human nerves cells relay all things feelings or sensory to the brain. The mesh cells channel all things energy to the conversion cells and then into the batteries.

Sims stretched his arms out and yawned, "The use of static electricity to power the suit is genius. Jess has a working prototype that shows how static electricity is converted to usable power, same as lightning conversion.

"The kicker is with the treated fabrics worn by the suit's pilot. It rubs against the lining of the suit creating static charges. Every time they move, the fabrics rub together creating static synapses of electricity. It is grabbed by the mesh then onto the ever-charging batteries.

You can create up to thirty thousand volts by sliding across your car's seat. You do that then touch someone and snap; that spark is how we power the suit. The more the battle increases, the more power is generated. When the enemy runs out of power and needs downtime we will be at one hundred percent. Game over, we win."

Dom turned and yelled, "We are about two-thirds of the way there; we got another forty minutes until touch down. As he turned back, a loud voice came out of the entire plane as if it were a speaker, "Aircraft Victor Tango 1784, this is a military emergency ban message as follows, "Gimli, call the Wizard. Use the Radagast Protocol. End of message. FA Eagle out."

They were all freaked out. Dom turned back to find Sims and John looking at him with expectant faces. John slid forward near Dom, "So let's get the protocol going so we can find out what the hell is going on."

Dom nodded as if he knew what that was. He grabbed the flight notebook and opened it up. He was surprised to find it. He had never heard of it, but there it was.

John was looking over his shoulder, "Ok I will hold the book, you carry out the protocol. Dom selected the right frequency, opened up the speakers so all could hear, picked up the handset and hit the talk button three times and started, "Radagast this is Gimli, I repeat Radagast this is Gimli. I have Elrond what is your emergency, over."

Glenn's voice came over the speakers, "Dom, give John your headset and make this transmission private. Dom did so, and now all eyes were on John. John heard Glenn's voice again, "John I have no idea what is going on. I have Nick patched in so you and Nick will be on a private line; Go ahead, Nick." At first, Nick's voice sounded like he was talking in a tin can, but after the first twenty words, it didn't matter.

John's face told a story of confusion, followed by worry, sadness and then anger. He listened for a good three minutes then, "How do I get back from here." Nick laid it all out for John.

First, he had to land as planned they were too far to turn around. Nick would have a private jet on the runway waiting to bring John back to Tri-Cities Airport. An SUV, with security, would take him to see Barlow for the latest information.

John slowly gave the headset back to Dom and sat back down across from Sims. He didn't say anything for what seemed like forever, "Someone has kidnapped Kat and Makayla, and Molly may have killed herself trying to stop them. The State Police are looking for them, and Molly is in an animal hospital.

John started talking with the speed of desperation, "Sims you need to head up the team to take these assholes down. Glenn should be able to help track them or something. If he has to hack the NSA that's fine, we need a lead on these guys. They had an hour head start on Barlow and crew. This is not looking good.

"I have Nick working on all the possible ransom scenarios he can think of. I want Dom to fetch Trish and Jess and take them to the compound. Call Hoss and tell him we have to lock that place down. Get Sammy and Bev to see to all the support and comfort elements."

Sims reached across and touched John on the knee, "John you need to focus your mind and make it quiet. Get yourself ready to solve this thing; you are the girl's best bet, so stay locked in."

John didn't answer, he just leaned back in his seat and exhaled long and slow. Then he whispered to Sims, "At least I got to pop one of those mongrels this morning."

Sims understood what John was saying, "I will start with that kid." John nodded then acted as if he was sleeping. In his mind, he was already tracking several of the Goth assholes he had seen in the last several months.

He decided he couldn't think about Molly right now. The weight of both his girls being taken from him was too much; he would focus on Kat and let Doc Peters bring Molly back to life.

After Nick finished with John, he worked to arrange a private flight to Colorado to meet with Glenn. Glenn would be the key to tracking down Kat and Makayla.

Nick refocused, now that John knew he could tell the people arriving for the training what had happened. He would contact Trish Baltran, aka Tbal, to break the news and expedite John's wishes as to how everyone should be involved.

Chapter Eight

11:45 am
Jackson Street
Jonesborough, TN

Corwin O' Caheil (ah-ka-heel) was tighter than normal stretching on his front porch. He was prepping for his daily run. He was a very fit five-foot-eleven, 175lbs with dark brown hair and charcoal eyes. He came to Jonesborough via the EU. He was born in Northern Ireland, lived in London, trained and fought all over the world.

He had caught General Rouse's eye in Pakistan. Neither of them was supposed to be there and soon neither of them had a way out. Together they remedied the situation and O'Caheil had worked for Rouse ever since. General Rouse had brought him to Jonesborough to keep an eye on all the strange people who were flooding into the area. General Rouse was responsible for the Hart Compound Black Site.

Corwin had become accustomed to people murdering of his last name. Those who fought with him grew to call him Corwin Kill-heel. While working with the American units he picked up the American Indian handle Cor-heel. Rouse called him Kill-Heel. The Celtic translation of his actual name was, "Great in Battle."

When he felt loose enough, he zipped up his black hoodie, checked the manpack belted around his waist, started the stopwatch in the pocket of his dark forest camouflage pants and started running south on Walton Street to Blount.

Blount would eventually horseshoe back North toward E. Main Street. Once to E. Main Street, he would usually turn west to complete the circle. To make it a two-mile run he would continue past the entrance to his housing area and continue down to the Corner Cup where Boone St. intersected E. Main and his morning coffee.

His usual run needed to be extended to increase his endurance, so today he was going to try turning east on Main and continue to Jackson Street and go North. He had not been down Jackson St. before and was looking forward to it.

This would make his run two and a half miles and coffee an even greater reward. This was going to be an extreme challenge, seeing he hadn't slept.

He didn't like getting a late start to his day, but he had worked late. He spent most of the night and early morning following two weird-looking dudes of darkness. They led him to a turn-off about five miles west of Jonesborough. He knew where they were going but he could not follow. He couldn't risk being recognized by someone in The Town with No Name.

As he traveled on past the turn-off, he noticed a car without its lights on turned in. Someone was following him follow Rocky and Bull Winkle.

He was about a hundred yards from Jackson St. when an ugly old van exited Jackson St. turning east; moving away. When Corwin turned onto Jackson St., it was 11:45 am, and the sun had achieved a very aggravating angle where it was bright as hell and cutting into his left eye.

He already had a headache and this was not helping. The west side was very cool and shady; it was heavily wooded. Corwin savored the shady portions that allowed him to look east to get the lay of the land.

He was now running slightly downhill and trees gave way to open fields with a few warehouses about fifty yards off the east side of the road. He also saw that the street ended about six hundred yards past the last building. This meant the first stage of his return trip to his precious coffee was uphill.

As Corwin came closer to the buildings, he felt that they might have been leftovers from the once-booming tobacco trade; maybe drying lofts.

When he came upon the first building, he was glad it blocked the sun. He noticed that the last third of the building's height was all dirty glass windows with a thin tin roof, designed to allow the tobacco to dry faster in the sun. He also noticed something else that stopped him dead.

It took him a moment to figure out what he was looking at; then he realized he was looking right into the sun. Corwin changed his angle and looked up again.

He was looking at the silhouette of a woman that had been suspended from the building's roof system. She was horizontal with her head west and her feet east dangling from cords secured at her feet, knees and middle back; her face looking to the roof.

Corwin turned away; he was trying to get his head around this entire thing. He had seen this display before. He moved his pack to the front and retrieved his phone. Corwin bent over, removed his small Beretta from its ankle holster and headed for the building. He was in contact with the local police's desk officer by the time he reached the main doors to the building.

He asked for Sheriff Barlow. The desk officer said that he and all of their available units were at Jake's Grocery and Tackle store responding to a suspected abduction. Corwin decided not to report the details yet; he had to think it through.

Corwin's mind kept flashing back to the country of Wales, dark wet caves in jagged mountains, and the victims of a serial killer they called, "The Druid." He opened the door slowly and knelt in the opening scanning with the Beretta.

The warehouse felt lifeless, no movement and no feeling of anyone inside. Corwin realized he was hesitating and whispered to himself, "You still Kill-heel or not?" He focused and steeled his nerves and moved in, clearing the area as he went. As much as he wanted to look up, he realized that if anyone was waiting to move, it would be when he raised his eyes.

When Corwin was sure he was alone, he walked around the entire warehouse to look for recent activity, other exit points or anything that could have been left behind. All he could find were footprints and marks on the floor. It appeared they were made moving the huge drying racks into position to display the body. Many of the footprints went through a blood pool on the floor.

It was time for him to focus on the victim. Corwin looked up at a white female with shortish blond hair. Her body had been segmented by the killers and then put back together like a marionette. She was draped in gold silk fabric that covered her like a sheet. He took several photos with his phone and after a considerable internal debate; Corwin decided to climb up the drying rack so he could get a look at her face.

As he reached the top, he could see her face had been removed. Her purse was lying on her chest and all her bindings were twisted into a single cord.

Within the cord was what looked like a shiny silver cable; together it all looked like an exotic drapery pull. It ran from the top her neck down the drying rack; it was tied off on the right side. Corwin stared at the silver cable, then shook himself and continued his work.

Corwin took several more pictures. He had to evaluate the scope of his responsibilities concerning what he should or shouldn't do. He was tasked with the safety of the John Hart Group when they were in the town of Jonesborough and keeping track of the Goth types that were frequenting the area. This situation had nothing to do with him.

Only three people knew who he was, Glenn, Sheriff Jeffery Barlow, and General Rouse. Rouse started as a grunt in Viet Nam and was now overseeing several top-secret projects, like the protection and advancement of the John Hart Group.

Corwin went down his list of responsibilities. Sims and John were slated to be in Canada later in the day, and Kat and her sister were on their way to Virginia with the dog. Glenn was in one of five locations, Nick was taking time in New Jersey and Trish Baltran was leading the training.

Corwin was trying to think, but he could not get past the nature of the murder. He knew it had something to do with those satanic wannabes; he needed to look in her purse.

He didn't have gloves, so he would have to leave only partial prints. Corwin wanted to be invisible and leave everything untouched, finish his run and report to General Rouse.

Trying to be very careful, Corwin tried to move the purse so he could reach inside using only his fingernails; that went poorly. He decided he would put his index finger under the small strap and lift it slightly to get to her wallet. The next thing he knew he was involved in a vintage Three Stooges moment.

The weight of the purse pulled the strap in the wrong direction, and it slipped off his finger. The entire purse started to slide off the body heading for mid-air; he tried to grab it, but he hit it instead.

The purse was starting to fall, he tried to gain control of it but he just launched into the air and it spun around with everything exiting the purse. The cherry on top was when it landed in the blood pool below, so much for being invisible.

Corwin could not fetch the purse without stepping into the blood pool. He didn't need to set himself up as the killer so he left. He would let Sheriff Barlow figure out this one.

Having finally reached the Corner Cup, he went through everything that he had seen with a freshly caffeinated mind and made his first good decision of the day; at 1:15 pm, he contacted General Rouse.

Chapter Nine

1:05 pm
Tri-Cities Airport
Blountville, TN

John's return flight had been a blur of activity. Sims and John worked the abduction forwards and backward. John knew Nick was having conversations with all of the members of the Group.

Sims could feel it; the John Hart Group was moving, breathing and acting as a single organism. They had trained for these situations and they were reacting to that training. The overwhelming feeling was that they would get Kat and Makayla back, Molly would live and the people who dared to mess with them would be dealt with.

It was 1:05 pm when the jet landed. It took them another fifteen minutes to clear the airport and another fifteen to get back to the compound.

When they were settled, they contacted the Sheriff's office. There was no change in the situation. The State Police had told the Sheriff they could be anywhere by now and luck was required. John turned to Sims, "This is not what we wanted but it is what we expected them to say."

John knew that running into town wouldn't help anyone, the girls were not there. They were probably in a place where the kidnappers would have the advantage of time. If they could stay hidden, they could take their time and stretch this out to maximize the ransom.

Sims left the room and set up in the widow's suite. With new construction, every technical tool that they could need was available, no working from a laptop.

When he went in he was impressed and then depressed, great layout but no Molly. At 2:38 pm, Sims logged on and decided to take a crack at Glenn. He wanted to see if they could find a way to track these guys from Jake's to where they were holding Kat and Makayla.

As Sims was waiting, he could not help but think that Rocky and Bull Winkle's actions were a bullshit tactic to keep them away from town. He could hear Boris Badenov now, "Once again we underestimate Moose and Squirrel."

Chapter Ten

1:20 pm
O' Caheil's Bungalow
Jonesborough, TN

Corwin O' Caheil walked back to his bungalow and waited for General Rouse's return call. When it came Rouse started, "Kill-heel glad you called. Are you looking to help us with the kidnapping? Corwin was quiet for a second, "Sir, I was doing recon the whole night and just finished my run. What are you talking about?"

Rouse's turn to pause a second, "Where are you right now?" "In my quarters Sir." Rouse continued, "Just after sun up today John Hart's girlfriend Kat and her sister Makayla were abducted at Jakes Grocery and Tackle. By the time the owner of the store regained consciousness and called it in, the bastards had a seventy-minute head start."

Rouse was in the middle of a breath when Corwin cut him off, "Jack, listen to me, I think they're already dead. That's why I called you. A white, blond female's body has been mutilated and is hanging from the roof inside an old warehouse near the end of Jackson Street; I found her on my run."

You could hear the anger in Rouse's voice, "Could you tell if it was Kat or her sister? Shit, sorry, they would look almost identical to anyone who hadn't spent time with them."

Corwin tried to slow the conversation down a bit, "I took lots of pictures, checked the entire building for evidence; no sign of a second body. I climbed up to take a look at the woman's face, but it had been removed.

Her purse was in reach but trying not to contaminate the evidence I caused the purse to fall to the floor. At that point, I made my way here and called you straight away."

The General cleared his throat, "I have not talked to John yet, he just landed at Tri-Cities and is heading to their compound. I have been working with his brother Nick."

Corwin could feel the General thinking, "Mission change Kill-heel. First, I need you to get last night's brief to Glenn ASAP, and then I want you to go full tactical and secure the crime scene; guard that site with your life; am I clear? Corwin stood while receiving his orders, "Understood Sir. How will I know, Sir?" Rouse replied, "Code phrase Elrond lives. Now get there son."

Corwin cut in again, "Jack do you remember Wales and The Druid; well it is just like that, all fucked up." Rouse just let out a long sigh then hung up.

Minutes later Rouse was conferencing with Sheriff Barlow and the Commander of the State Police. He was taking over the investigation as a matter of National Security.

Rouse let them know he was dispatching his finest crime scene investigators and trackers to the warehouse. The Sheriff and State Police were to continue their efforts and report every hour to the command center.

General Rouse's next call was to Hoss. Hoss Cartwright was a big man and was the General's Master Sergeant in Afghanistan. Rouse explained the situation then he told Hoss to activate the entire Town with No Name. Hoss was in command of all actions from the town to the two-mile safety zone around the compound.

Rouse wanted everyone weapons hot, on alert. He needed the town secured and then all personnel were to report to the compound. He put Lil' Joe, Adam, and Phu on sniper reconnaissance. They were to start working the hills and trees between the town and the compound. He wanted video, sound, and bodies if need be. Search, surveil and capture. Rouse knew many of these creeps were living in the woods.

Rouse switched lines and called to activate his command personnel, "Sergeant Mitchell, I need your air militia to bug out to Jonesborough right now and support local command as needed; this is a top-end classified defense of a black site; understood? All Rouse heard was yes sir and the phone disconnect.

General Rouse sat down and took stock of all the firepower he had just unleashed. His mind flashed back to Wales and The Druid. Kill-heel had killed him and cut off his head like a snake; no one complained. If it was like that then Rouse figured Corwin was right; the girls were dead. Now he needed evidence to track the murderers.

Rouse and Corwin had been working with Glenn for the last three months plotting the activities and movements of the weird Goth people around the town; he hoped Glenn could use that information to pull a miracle out of his ass.

Glenn was six foot three, his long brown hair and beard gave him a biker look, but his walk screamed stoner. Glenn was an exceptional hunter, highly skilled and stealthy. Glenn's greatest asset was the fact he had no reputation in the cyber world. No one knew who he was. He had never held a related job, didn't attend a big school and his military service was as boring as it could get. In all his hunting, no one he had tracked had even felt he was there, let alone catch him.

The General stood up again and looked at the clock in his office it was 2:33 pm he felt tired already. He needed to make sure John did not get to the warehouse before they had cleared it; he called Hoss back on an emergency number they set up but had never used.

Chapter Eleven

2:45 pm
Widow's Suite
Hart Compound
Jonesborough, TN

Glenn was having trouble focusing as he talked with Sims. They had been discussing the kidnapping and Sims felt Glenn was having trouble dealing with the situation. In the middle of their conversation, Nick called and Glenn made it a conference call.

Nick wanted to ask him if he had any leads, "Glenn, were you able to get anything off of surveillance footage or traffic cams around town or at Jake's store?" Glenn hesitated, "I haven't started that yet. I have to close out some of my existing work before I can get on it."

Sims reacted poorly, "What the hell are you talking about; you've got a higher priority?" Nick chimed in, "Glenn you can't be screwing around with some other project; you got to get on this shit now!"

Glenn was John's oldest friend. He and Nick were friends when John was placed with Nick in Foster Care. The three of them were brothers, "Screw you guys, you think I would do that? I don't expect you to understand what I am doing, just like I can't fathom half of the shit you guys do. So trust me or fuck off."

The line was quiet for a long time, then Nick, "Explain it the best you can so we can tell John how you are gonna find these assholes." Glenn really subdued, "You need to talk to General Rouse. I have been working with him on some new surveillance algorithms that we hope will increase our ability to find and track individuals of interest."

Sims was going insane listening to this, "Give us something now so we can get started then you can go play with your new toy." Glenn's anger came through the phone, "I need to work this then I can give you everything, so call Rouse if he wants me to back off I will." Sims right back, "How about I call John and tell him you are playing for the other side on this one?"

Nick broke in, "Both of you just chill. We have work to do and this ain't helping. I will talk to General Rouse. Sims you stick with John. Glenn, I called to tell you I am coming to you. Sims, tell John we are working this as hard as we can."

Nick settled everyone down and ended the call. He headed to the fridge, and grabbed a beer and sat on the couch to think. It was now 3:30 pm. and he had to approach the General in a way that he would want to share with him. Nick would chew the General's ass for freelancing with Glenn at another time. Now he had to catch a plane.

Chapter Twelve

4:12 pm
West of Hart Compound
Jonesborough, TN

Hoss settled into the cab of his truck. He had enough technology jammed in there to run a small war. He had positioned his people around the property without John knowing. He was to wait for the General to call John.

Impatient, Hoss picked up his radio and hailed General Rouse. Rouse's Head of Operations came on the line. Hoss needed to know when the crime scene people would arrive and at what point John Hart would be told of the General's involvement.

Operations assured him that all assets would be on-site and active before 5:30 pm. They also told Hoss the site had been secured and military personnel were controlling the area, which meant that Corwin, an army of one, was waiting for reinforcements.

Hoss told them that he would have his recon crew in the trees at dusk and he was monitoring thermal images to aid them. Hoss was identifying small clusters of campers camping where there were no camps. Three such images were bothering him right now. He decided to send the boys out early.

Hoss contacted Marine Lieutenant Phu Nguyen and gave him the coordinates of three campers he wanted dealt with before the evening was over. It bothered Hoss that these three targets were in the exact same place that Semjaza's snipers were when the siege of the compound began almost two years ago.

Phu responded, "We will be slipping into nowhere in fifteen minutes. We will work from behind the Coffee Hole to the east, then work under and back around to the town's main entrance. We will be SAT green on your monitors. Did we get any word as to why we are going mission hot?" Hoss lied, "Still waiting on the General to give me the details, but it is all about the Black Site Protocol."

Phu signed off then looked at the location of the three targets. They had to walk four miles to get to them. With the terrain factored in, they could get to them in less than two hours.

Phu turned to Adam and Lil' Joe, "We have a priority clean up four miles out, above the compound. Sergeant Cartwright is annoyed by these particular campers.

Adam shook his head, "They should know better than to poke the bear." Lil' Joe stood up, "I hope it is Rocky and Bull Winkle; it'd be cool if we could get a shot at his other ear."

At 4:30 pm, the three snipers started into the trees; in less than a hundred feet, they were no longer visible from the lot behind the Coffee Hole.

Chapter Thirteen

4:50 pm
Warehouse Crime Scene
Jackson Street
Jonesborough, TN

Corwin O' Caheil did not like working in open daylight. He was in full view much of the time he was setting up his surveillance gear. His first action was to break several additional holes in the warehouse glass so the smell of death could escape the building.

He placed motion detectors encircling the warehouse and set up his sniper hide in the front of the warehouse. It was up high so he could see everything from Main St. down to the warehouse.

Corwin was indeed an army of one. He had no idea when he would be joined at the site. He was comforted by his enhanced sniper rifle, the 9mm pistol, the compact Israeli machine gun slung over his shoulder, and a box of things that went boom. He also had several hand-to-hand weapons for slicing and dicing.

Having arrived at 2:30 pm, he had achieved threat detection and total lockdown of the site in a little less than two hours. Corwin was scanning Main St. with his rifle when the old van, from earlier in the day, parked at the top of Jackson Street; it was facing the warehouse.

He felt they were the Druid's crew and they were checking to see if anyone had found the body. Corwin set the scope to HD, pushed the record button and zoomed in on the van's license plate; it came in crystal clear. He zoomed out, switched to photo mode and took several photos of the van.

Corwin moved the images to his phone, sent them to Glenn with a text of explanation and at 4:50 pm forwarded it all to Operations(Ops). He radioed the command site and asked for General Rouse code phrase "Elrond Lives." In less than thirty seconds, Rouse came on the line.

Corwin speaking slowly, "General I have a van in my sights that I dismissed during my run as regular traffic. It is parked at the top of Jackson St. and I'm thinking these shit heads performed the ritual. I would like a green light to blow the shit out of the van."

The General calmly, "How would you deal with the occupants?" Corwin replied, "Send the police who are two miles away, and I will keep them in the van dead or alive." I have sent photos and license to Glenn and Ops already." Rouse asked Corwin to hold a second.

Rouse turned to the head of operations, "Where are Mitchell and the choppers?" "They are staged on Sergeant Cartwright's service roads alternating requests from the State Police and Sheriff; we have Mitchell and one other bird available right now."

When General Rouse returned to Corwin's line he heard gunfire, "Kill-heel what the hell are you doing?" "Sorry Sir, they started to leave so I put a round through the engine block and now I am keeping them in the van." Rouse turned to the head to Ops, he responded, "Mitchell is already in the air and on his way; ETA six minutes."

Rouse back to Corwin, "You have to contain them for six minutes then a chopper will be on top of you; try not to kill everyone." Corwin nodding, "Yup, it would be nice to get one right today... Out."

Corwin decided he would take the van himself. He hit record on the rifle and fired eight more rounds into the van in areas he knew should not be occupied. Now he had to hurry; he jumped down from his hide and sprinted out the door with his machine gun out in front of him. He turned on his body camera and set the machine gun to single shot.

He was moving fast while in a controlled run, shooting at whatever tried to exit the van. One brave soul rolled out onto the road then jumped up to run. Corwin took out his legs and down he went. It got real still in the van after that. Corwin continued with intermittent fire until he was around thirty yards in front of the van, "Crawl out of the van and stay on your face; do anything else and you are dead. Do it now!"

One by one, three others crawled clear and stayed on their faces. Every one of the passengers was dressed in black, wearing leathers with weird symbols on their tee shirts.

Corwin took his phone and made each of them show their face so he could get pictures for Glenn and the General. Mitch and his crew landed, cuffed the prisoners, and loaded them in the chopper.

Corwin turned to Mitch to say thank you when Mitchell interrupted, "Where did you start shooting from?" Corwin pointed to the warehouse down the hill. Mitchell just shook his head, "Shit brother that's quite the walk; uphill too. Shoulda waited I coulda given you a lift." Corwin laughed; "These assholes woulda loved it if you came sooner." Mitch extended his hand and Corwin shook it. Mitch winked, "I think you will work out just fine."

Corwin started down the hill as two more choppers landed on the street. The crime scene unit, the trackers and several Military Police types had arrived.

As he uploaded his live footage, Corwin realized his hands were shaking; he smiled and whispered to himself, "Wow, time to breathe."

Chapter Fourteen

6:15 pm
Hart Compound
Jonesborough, TN

John Hart was staring a hole through the wall running ransom scenarios through his mind. His thoughts kept being interrupted by the fact that Glenn had nothing to add. Nick seemed to think things were fine but Sims was pissed about something.

Nick should call him soon; he figured he had arrived in Colorado at 5:00 pm. CST. He had to factor in the convoluted route required to get to Glenn's top-secret location.

As time rolled on the pressure on John mounted. He knew the longer they didn't hear from the kidnappers the more dire the circumstances. His last update with the Sheriff didn't go well, Jeffery seemed distant and uninvolved; almost resolved the matter was out of his hands.

John stood up, looked at Sims, "Screw this, let's go look the Sheriff in the eye; something ain't right." Sims gave him a weird look, "So you thinking all of the do-nothings by Glenn and the response from Sheriff adds up to the fact that maybe they have nothing to do?"

John turned to go, and then spun back to Sims, "Shit, that is not what I was thinking, but what if that is it? What if they believe they are dead already?"

Sims put up his hand defensively, "That is not what I meant. I was thinking that General Rouse had butted in, but now you say that it's messing with my mind." John's eyes changed, not in a good way, "Damn it, let's get into town and get some answers."

Sims and John kept looking at one another all the way to the Polaris. They took the tunnel to the three-way junction, took the middle tunnel and came out in front of Sims' house.

John slammed on the breaks just in time to avoid running over Jimmy, the owner of Jimmy's Gas and Lube in The Town with No Name. John looked at Sims, "That's Jimmy. What the hell is he doing here?" Sims shrugged his shoulders; they both turned to look at the sixty-five-year-old gas station owner.

The Lieutenant Colonel US Army retired, held out his hand in a stop motion. He was over six feet and in great shape for a geezer. His gray hair high and tight made him look the part, "John, the General doesn't want you leaving the compound until he has a grip on the bad guys."

Sims leaned over toward Jimmy, "What about finding Kat?" Sims was thrown back into his seat when John stomped on the gas pedal; Jimmy dove into Sims' landscaping.

John was on the main road heading into Jonesborough before they could try to stop him again. Jimmy picked himself up off the ground and spoke into his radio, "Sergeant Cartwright, Elrond has left the building."

Sims turned and looked behind them, he saw several cars parked around the entry and others way up on the road west of the compound. Sims turned to John, "They got the whole compound surrounded and locked down." John looked up surprised, "Who? Jimmy and who else, what is going on?"

When they arrived at the Sheriff's office John told Sims to go in, and get Jeffery to come outside. Sims looked puzzled, "Jeffery knows who I am you know." "Yes, but the new aid doesn't."

Sims approached the reception area, "I need to speak with Sheriff Barlow." The new girl motioned westward, "They are all down at the end of Jackson St. working on some murder. You need to talk to him that's where he is."

Sims knees felt weak for a second, his mind went numb and he moved to the wall to stabilize himself. He turned so his back was on the wall, he looked out the window; he didn't want to go back to the Polaris and John.

He started looking for some other logical explanations; maybe Rocky and Bull Winkle had gotten themselves killed. Maybe an officer was killed approaching a suspect who knew where the girls were.

Sims returned to the girl, "How long have they been at Jackson St." She flipped over her call sheet, "The military locked it down at 3:00 pm." Sims eyes flashed with anger, "You need to contact the Sheriff and tell him John Hart is on his way down. If you don't do this right away and John gets there before the Sheriff knows he will fire your ass in a heartbeat, cuz I will tell him I told you to warn him. Are we clear?" The girl picked up the phone.

Sims gathered himself then shook off the anger of not being told. He returned to the car and jumped in, "The Sheriff and everyone else is at the end of Jackson St. The receptionist said there was some major problem down there. Maybe they found something."

Sims hated himself for not telling the whole truth, but he did so hanging on to his last fragment of hope. John looked around and then at Sims. In the increasing darkness, Sims could see John's eyes glass up, a precursor to tears. Sims felt his own core darken as he looked out his window.

Chapter Fifteen

6:06 pm EST
5:06 CST
Somewhere in Colorado

Nick had never been to the Colorado location. As he entered, he saw a large picture window across the room that had an amazing view with unlimited visibility of the area below them. Nick turned to Glenn, "So, no one can find you even with this giant window reflecting in the morning sun?"

Glenn walked over to a console and half of the window became a monitor. It showed what Nick felt was the rocky confines of the area around the facility, "What am I looking at?" Glenn zoomed in and then back out, "This view is from the camera that looks directly into this window from the outside. It's the greatest faux image ever; and no reflection."

Glenn went into the kitchen area and came back with a beer for each of them; they sat on a couch across from the view.

Glenn took a drink, "We have a major problem that has been in the making for several months. Someone is trying to find us, me, the group, and they are not your usual bad guy hackers. I believe that they have access to or are with the NSA." Nick held up his hand, "Glenn, not this shit again. I know you hate these guys but now's not the time to go chasing ghosts."

Glenn didn't lose his cool. He put his feet on the coffee table, "There is a guy or a group of people that have been buying up companies we have investigated to bring on as suppliers for the upcoming Battle Suit production. They are trying to find a way to our technology."

Nick, now more interested, "Explain." Glenn put his feet down and leaned forward turning his eyes to Nick, "The only people on the planet that know anything about what we do are in our group or have some access through our relationship with the NSA." Nick looking a little confused, "So what?"

Glenn continued, "Well, we usually buy companies and convert them into the supplier we need. No one realizes they are not still doing what they used to do; airtight right?" Nick impatiently nodded. Glenn knew he had him, "So the second you submitted the names for vetting to Rouse, this group proceeds with hostile takeovers of three of them."

Nick sat up, "How did we come to find this out; another corrupt source?" Glenn a little sheepish, "Well no, it came from my own research. It is the tracking I have done since my mother died four years ago." Nick looking surprised, "What were you looking for?"

Glenn very uncomfortable, "When my mother died of cancer, she had been on the road to recovery when her doctor was murdered. His methods and my mother's hopes died with him. Glenn nodding, "I remember."

When his colleagues searched his house, it had been trashed and all his notes were gone. After that,

I tried to find anyone who could or would continue his path, but I couldn't put it together in time."

Now Nick was uncomfortable, "Sorry that is strange; so that led to what exactly?" Glenn's eyes narrowed with focus, "Afterward I started monitoring his colleagues and found these guys were scared to death of being the next one to die.

All these doctors believed the cure for cancer was obtainable. The problem was that anyone who got close to a cure was killed or died strangely and their research disappeared. So, I decided to find who was doing the killings."

Nick finished his beer and headed to the fridge to get another, "So how do you find these guys when the attacks happened in different countries all over the world?" Glenn looked up at Nick, "Well that is where General Rouse comes in.

I arranged a meet at the Epic Smokehouse and I told him I could track anyone all over the world, plot their patterns and sort suspects from actual bad guys, all I needed was a satellite." Nick's eyes widened, "And he went for it?" Glenn just nodded.

Nick flopped down into a stuffed chair to Glenn's left, "I think that is genius. So, now can you tell me what the hell this has got to do with right now?" Glenn held up his right hand, "Listen just a second more, I'm using a model developed to track cancer cells in the body. They can tag a cell or group of cells and the software can follow and locate them. The software will guide the electron microscope, probe or whatever to the cells.

I figured if the software could talk to the probe why couldn't it tell a satellite where to look. All I had to do is manipulate the code. We changed the search structure from the human body to the earth; it works."

I programmed the parameters of targets I wanted to be tagged then searched and tagged all the airports nearest to the various murders. After two years of tagging and sorting, I came up with sixty possible suspects, I had eighteen repeaters and a solid five that were always in the area when a murder took place. Soon I will have all their previous movements and possibly who they report to. I am tagging NSA people now. I will let them tell us who is talking about our vendors. Nick rotating his hands, "And?"

Glenn caught himself, "Yes, we have been tagging the creeps that have been circling the compound for the last three months and we are adding to their movements each day; a little more info and I should be able to pinpoint their hangout."

Nick said, "That is amazing stuff; so, when can we get this thing pumping out information." Glenn stood and walked to a large half-circle desk that wrapped around him when he sat down.

He started working on two different computers, "I was picking you up, so I didn't get last night's briefing from Rouse's man analyzed yet, let me get it." Nick was watching Glenn calmly work when Glenn jumped up, "Nick get over here and look at this shit."

Nick raced over as Glenn sat back down and started the replay of Corwin's encounter with the van full of suspects. Nick leaned in, "That looks like the video is being shot from the gun's scope; a great shot of the license plate."

The video jumped to the van in the rifle's scope as rounds were being fired. Glenn, "Holy shit this guy is knocking the hell out of this van." The image jumped again and showed Corwin's bodycam footage. Nick, "This guy is taking down the van on foot, he is hitting everything while on the run; what do ya think a half-mile uphill?"

Glenn zoomed in, "No dude stay in the van. Ah shit, cut his legs out. Rouse said this guy was lethal." Nick stood up straight, "Rouse wasn't kidding, those poor assholes didn't even get a chance to return fire."

They watched as Corwin took shots of his prisoner's faces, Glenn immediately went to work on the facial recognition and the license plate. Nick started to walk away from the desk, then turned back, "Glenn go back, back it up." Glenn said, "Which one?" Nick pointed, "Right at the end of the last frame of the last one." Nick put his finger in the upper right corner of the frame, "Tell me what the hell that is doing there?"

Glenn was surprised to see a chopper approaching from the east. He checked the numbers on the chopper. Nick waited, Glenn turned to Nick, "That was Sergeant Mitchell's chopper."

Nick went and sat down, "Anyway to tell where all of this went down and when?" As Glenn began to check he turned and looked at Nick, "Nick this must mean…" Nick cut him off, "Don't say it!"

After a minute or so Glenn had an answer, "I used the coordinates from the rifle's scope video, it all went down on Jackson Street in Jonesborough, starting at 4:20 pm their time. Come over here I am bringing up a live satellite view of the area."

As the satellite image was zoomed in, they could make out two choppers in the middle street and various cars and vans at the front entrance of an old warehouse. Glenn noted that the satellite first picked-up the choppers at 5:30 pm their time, "We were on the road."

Nick went to the kitchen cabinet next to the fridge, found a new bottle of Jack Daniels, twisted the top off and found two glasses, "Start identifying the vehicles and read them off." Glenn accepted a glass from Nick, "We got Rouse, the Sheriff, med techs and shit, we got MPs and all the crime scene boys." Glenn looked back at Nick whose eyes were filled with new tears and an old rage Glenn had not seen in a decade. Nick drank his whiskey in one big swallow then threw the glass against the kitchen wall; the glass evaporated on impact. When he turned back, Glenn was staring out the big picture window, seeing nothing.

Chapter Sixteen

Day Two
7:03 pm
Jackson St. Warehouse
Jonesborough, TN

Sheriff Jeffery Barlow stood just inside and to the left of the entry to the Warehouse. He was watching all the activity and wondered, *what in the hell is all this for; why can't we get that poor woman down and show some respect?* His phone rang. He just answered it without thinking; not expecting what he was about to hear.

"Sheriff, this is Jenny at headquarters, Chris Sims told me I should let you know that John Hart is on his way to see you right now. He left here about thirty seconds ago."

Barlow hung up without thinking. After several minutes, he found himself staring at General Rouse and he was struck by how much respect he had lost for the man. Barlow was going to tell Rouse John was on his way, that he and his men were leaving, and Rouse was going to have to explain himself to John.

The General saw the Sheriff heading his way and wondered what he would have to add if anything. Corwin O' Caheil watched from his position as Barlow started talking to Rouse pointing at the body above and then at Rouse. The Sheriff turned and motioned to his men and they began leaving the scene.

Corwin could tell Barlow was upset about how things were being handled. Barlow made eye contact with Corwin and started across the room. Corwin hoped he was coming to say goodbye.

There was a commotion at the entrance and Corwin followed Barlow's eyes to see John Hart and Sims looking in horror at the woman hanging from the roof. "John screamed, "Kat, Kat! Damn it, take her down. Get her down!"

Corwin turned his head just enough to see Barlow moving to untie the cords and lower the body. He had to make a quick decision; he knew what would happen if the cord was untied without securing the silver line first.

He couldn't reach Barlow in time, but he could save John from a fate worst then death; he bolted toward John. Barlow untied the cord and moved his hand to remove the last of the cord from the drying rack.

Corwin could hear the singing sound of the silver cord as it was released. It flew away from the cord releasing the body's parts to fall independently. He lowered his head and plowed into John's chest all the time screaming as loud as he could, "No, No."

Corwin kept screaming until he knew the body had hit the floor then he backed off John. John jumped up in a rage swinging and pummeling Corwin with punches. Corwin took as many as he could then he spun John around and grabbed him from behind and held him until he was perfectly still.

Corwin leaned in next to John's right ear, "You did not want to hear that lad. You would hear it forever; every day of your life." Corwin pushed him away and prepared for the next attack. John looked at him then at the pieces of her on the floor and headed toward the scene.

Sims had seen the whole thing; he began to move toward Corwin. Corwin knew who Sims was and did not want to defend himself again. Sims stopped about three feet in front of Corwin, nodded then went to help his friend.

Corwin looked over at Rouse and when their eyes met, they both knew that somehow the Druid was still alive. Corwin had been without sleep way too long. It was 7:26 pm and he had done his part; he was going home.

Chapter Seventeen

10:00 pm
Jackson St. Warehouse
Jonesborough, TN

John had gone numb, he had cried his eyes out, vomited several times and now was just staring into the void. His anger level had gone all the way to calm, and that was not good. When John got quiet, people died.

On the evening of the compound detonation almost two years ago, he had calmly lied to his attackers. He made them believe that he would not try to stop them from carrying out their prophetic nonsense. He withdrew to Sammy's Diner and then with the sound of millions of people screaming while being burned alive, he pressed the detonator.

John literally blew the compound and his attackers back to hell. Three days later, he was debriefing with General Rouse.

The difference between then and now was that John was confused as to why those maniacs wanted his compound; he blew them up to spite them; it was his compound. Now this, this really tore his psyche. His heart was in ribbons, shredded to its core; he wanted those who killed his wife dead. John would have his revenge. It would be sweeter if Molly were with him.

He left the warehouse, found the Sheriff's car and climbed in the back. John laid down hands and hoodie over his head. Barlow and his deputy returned to his car at 2:00 am, they saw John in the back, stood silent for a few beats and then got in.

Barlow had agreed to take John home; Sims had taken the Polaris to Hoss' service road to pick up Trish and Jess. He started the car and headed for the Hart Compound.

John sat up and looked into the review mirror. Barlow looked up and made eye contact. In the eerie darkness and the passing pockets of lite, he could see the buffy, wetness around John's eyes, but his pupils' coal-black swimming in blood-red sockets.

Barlow's entire body shook, *where had Hart gone; this was another animal altogether.* "John, you alright, do you need to go to the emergency?" Hart was quiet for what seemed like a minute, "No I just need to get home. When will we know something?" Barlow swallowed, "Rouse's people and the investigators are slowly wrapping up now. Everything is going to Johnson City; they will be working with their experts from Knoxville.

They won't start until they all see..." He stammered and hesitated trying to avoid hurting John. John leaned forward and hissed, "Until they see the whole pile that was my wife?" Barlow cleared his throat, "Sorry, yes."

Barlow switched it up, "I noted you refused sedatives for sleep before you left." John half smiled and fell back in the seat, "I got my own doctor and I won't be sleeping. God help them, I won't be sleeping for quite a while."

Barlow's memory flashed back to screams of burning people, the compound looking like a nuke had hit it. There were pieces of weird creatures everywhere.

He was glad he had been ordered to leave the site that night. He knew what level of hell Mr. Hart could bring to bear. He could only hope it would not all go down in his town.

While staring out the window, John could feel himself slipping back in time. He was regressing to what he was before. Before he was liberated from being the drug-addled, retard from San Dimas.

Then the darkness of hateful revenge would take disgusting twists and turns in his mind. The scary part of being him now was he had all the resources he needed to carry out any actions he conjured up.

When they arrived at Sims house, John climbed out, "Thanks Jeffery, keep on their asses for me, I will see you later today." Barlow leaned over, "Don't like leaving you alone up here."

John started to say, "I am not alone I have Molly," then literally swallowed his words they felt like lava going through his chest. John turned to the deputy, looked him in the eyes, thanked him, turned and walked to Sims' front door.

As they were backing out of the driveway, the deputy looked at Barlow, "Did you see his eyes?" Barlow looked away, "Might be a bit before John Hart returns." The deputy's head snapped around looking at his boss, "He is…ah…oh shit," he dropped his head and was quiet all the way back.

John got to the door and leaned into it with his forehead. He took out his phone and used both hands to control his movements. He finally got the numbers right and turned so his back was in the corner between the door and the right side of the wall.

John allowed himself to slowly slide to the ground and was sitting when Nick answered, "Where are you, John?" "Sims' place; about to go up to the main house." John finally got his courage up, "Tell me."

Nick took a deep breath slowly letting it out, "Molly is a mess. She might have killed herself trying to get to whoever took the girls. She broke her front jawbone that was holding her top front teeth, and the teeth are gone. She cracked her skull on the windows and she has no front claws left.

We will know when Doc Peters gets here if she broke her neck or not, but she is still breathing. He will be here at noon today. Barlow had her moved to the Veterinary hospital in Johnson City. They say she may not make it until Peters gets here."

John was stunned by the amount of damage Molly had inflicted on herself, "I bet you she would have eaten those guys if she had gotten out of the car." Nick was quiet, "Peters said knowing Molly he was afraid that when she is fully recovered she might blame herself for what happened. He is worried she might figure out what happened to Kat.

John started crying, "A lot of that going around. Sims?" Nick stayed in character, "He is working with Jess and Trish on a possible hush mode sniper response if we find where they are hiding."

John asked, "Any word on MaKayla?" Nick sighed, "She is nowhere. We have no clue where she could be." John let out a groan that sounded like a wounded animal, "Shit, shit, shit! Damn it, this is too much. Nick, I gotta go. Get a plan together, we need to kill these beasts and we got to do it quickly."

Nick butted in, "John, have a couple of beers and sit down on Sims' couch and think. When you wake up I will have a better idea of what has happened." John was gone.

John staggered into the house, went to Sims' fridge and took out two beers. He drank the first one standing with the fridge door open then took out another and headed for the couch. He finished the next beer in two swallows.

John looked at the clock on Sims'stove as he finished the third beer; it was 2:24 am. John let out a long sigh then tried to stand up; he didn't make it. He just rolled over, with his face into the couch and was out.

Chapter Eighteen

11:23 pm
Woods, West of Hart Compound
Jonesborough, TN

The woods were pitch black, Phu, Lil' Joe and Adam had been busy rousting the riff-raff between The Town with No Name and the compound. They used the darkness and their tactics to freak out every group of campers they had come across.

They had spent two tours in Iraq and Afghanistan creeping in the deathly quiet of the darkest nights on earth. They were elite hunters sent to kill those no one had been able to kill. Now they protected the owner of most guarded secret in the USA.

The people they came across were mostly wanna be power of darkness geeks. They arrested the serious ones and tied them to a tree. They tagged the campers with GPS buttons, so the other townies could herd them to the compound for questioning.

As promised, they were now moving on the group Hoss had wanted checked out. They refocused for the task and moved into position with complete silence. Their faces now covered, they were just a mile above the Hart Compound. They set up with each of them observing from equally different angles, a deadly crossfire for those inside the triangle.

These campers had sidearms, automatic weapons and lots of technology to keep them safe in the dark. Phu decided they needed to get facial recognition on them. Phu whispered, "Let's get close enough to get a face on each one of these mutts.

Lil' Joe moved to his right and in several yards, switched his night scope to video and smiled, "I got da, Moose." Phu zoomed in on the shortest of the group and whispered, "Positive for Squirrel."

Adam was last, with an all-business tone, "I got someone new; real spooky-looking, he looked right at me, his eyes flashed red, but then he decided I wasn't there. We should run him first. Oh, by the way, humans' eyes don't do that shit in the dark; you feelin' me?"

Phu thought for a second, "Let's just video them for a while, take some stills of the weapons and gear, and let Hoss find out who they are. This new character seems to be the boss man."

After several minutes Hoss came on the line, "We got plenty of info on Moose and Squirrel, but this new guy is supposed to be an owner of a leather goods store in Johnson City. Go ahead take them, and bring them to me."

Phu raised his eyebrows, "You heard the man. Let's shoot the shit out of their automatic weapons then move in using bursts to keep them together. Adam, you take the new guy with a drug dart." Phu waited for thirty seconds, "On three, two, one…"

Their suppressed weapons sounded like spits as the campers' weapons shattered next to them. Adam hit the Boss Man in the chest with the tranquilizer dart; he spun around and went down.

There was what they later described as a sonic pulse, followed by a wash of complete darkness.

After a moment to get his bearings, Adam could still see the Boss Man lying on the ground. As Phu and crew entered the camp area, Rocky and Bull Winkle were laughing and twitching around. Bull Winkle stepped forward, "He split man, you can't catch him he's the devil man...poof he gone." Adam slapped him on his left ear. The Moose went down screaming just like he had that morning, "How can you let me hit you on the other side? Now your ears match."

After they got Bull Winkle on his feet, Phu started walking around the two, whispering in what sounded like another language. After the third time around, he leaned into Rocky and whispered, "He is right there, yes?" Phu was pointing at the shop owner passed out on the ground. Rocky was gritting his teeth while smiling and rocking back and forth, "No, this fool will wake up wondering how he got here. The Master is gone..." Bull Winkle yelled, "Shut up man. You say nothing. Nothing!"

Phu stood looking at the scene thinking, then raised his hand over his head in a lasso type motion, "Get them up, tag their gear for pick up; we've got to walk them down to see the Sergeant. That is when the fun begins."

Phu nodded to Lil' Joe. Lil' Joe spoke into his radio, "Big Dog, all secured. We're coming to you. See you in an hour."

Adam used smelling salts to wake the shop owner. As predicted he had no idea where he was or how he got there. The last thing he remembered was helping a man with white hair into a nice jacket.

When Phu and the boys arrived at the compound they turned their campers over to Jimmy and reported to Hoss. When Hoss heard about the sonic wash of darkness he looked at the time, 2:30 am, he picked up the phone and called Nick and Glenn.

Hoss took the boys into John's private lab in the tunnels and told them about Kat and that John was on his way back to Sims house. Hoss asked Phu if he could keep his cool while he interrogated the Moose and Squirrel. Phu nodded, "I am going to make it look like I have lost it and I am going to kill both of them without a second thought." Lil' Joe chimed in, "Body bags?" Phu nodded, "Could you get it set up in the rec room while I fill in Hoss?" Adam and Lil' Joe left.

When Phu entered the rec room, Rocky and Bull Winkle were tied to folding chairs facing the main doors. Phu walked in, looked at Rocky, then punched him across his right jaw so hard the chair and Rocky went over backward.

Bull Winkle yelled, "You can't do that, we got rights!" Phu got in his face, "I am a private citizen. I am under no obligation to give a shit about your rights. After I found out you pieces of shit cut up my friend, I decided I wanted to kill you myself."

Rocky still lying on his side, "Bull shit, that is murder, and you will fry. When the Master finds out he will skin you." Phu looking at Adam, "Get the squirrel up and get a bag for the Moose." Adam looked at Bull Winkle, "We should use the pan as well, yes?" Phu, "Good thinking."

Lil' Joe stood next to Phu and handed him a silenced 9mm pistol. Phu checked it, showed it to Rocky then chambered a round. Adam came back with the requested items and laid them down in front of the Moose. Bull Winkle's eyes showed nothing but fear, "That's a body bag. What are you crazy?"

Phu stepped back, "Bag the Moose." Adam and Lil' Joe grabbed the struggling Bull Winkle. Both Rocky and Bull Winkle were yelling at them to stop. Phu put the gun to the Moose's head, "Get in the bag." Bull Winkle submitted. When he was in, Lil' Joe put what looked like a bedpan under the bag where the Moose's head was.

Rocky was looking at the body bag squirm back and forth as he heard Bull Winkle beg to get out. He asked what the pan was for, Adam said, "Zero clean up."

Rocky yelled, "Don't worry Ken they ain't gonna do shit. They're trying to scare us." Phu walked over to the body bag pointed his gun where Bull Winkle's head was and fired twice; the bag stopped squirming.

Phu turned around and stood directly in front of Rocky and put the gun an inch from his nose, "Now I am going to ask you a question, you are going to answer it, or we will put you in this." Phu turned to his left as Adam laid out another body bag. At that point, Rocky wet himself.

By 3:30 am, Phu had everything Rocky had to give. He threw him in the makeshift brig; he landed next to the Moose who was quite alive. The Moose and Squirrel realized their Master was going to kill them both.

Chapter Nineteen

1:46 am
Lil' Pine Cabin
The Town with No Name, TN

Sims had picked up Jess Williams and Trish Baltran from the service road of Hoss' hay farm. Dom Carbone had flown them in after spending the day at Jess' company in London, Canada.

Jess had brought along three large crates that made it interesting getting everything to John's house. After flying under the radar at 200lbs over max weight and some well-timed help from Sheriff Barlow's men, they were home safe.

Nick had told Dom to stay at Hoss' service road, gas up the plane and await his orders. Dom would be their emergency evacuation option.

The ride back to John's was heartbreaking as Sims detailed what they thought had happened to Kat and MaKayla. He hadn't even asked about the crates until they had to unload them.

Sims made some remark about Jess packing light; she looked at him with her bloodshot eyes, "This is what is going to kill the bastards that messed with us."

Jess wanted the crates on the back patio to allow room to spread out and assemble all the gear. She had brought the prototype battle suit and a toy nobody knew she had been working on.

After Barlow's men had left, Trish opened the crate housing the newest toy and stepped back, "This looks like one of the exploding puck-shaped drones you pitched to General Rouse last year, except it is five hundred times bigger." Sims stepped over, looked in and then looked at Jess, "You've been holding out on me." Jess just smiled, "You don't have the proper clearance, Mr. Sims."

Trish pried open the right side revealing the flight console and guidance packages, "Oh shit this thing flies? Please Lord let me try it out."

The new drone was perfectly circular, four feet in diameter and fifteen inches tall. It had oval intakes or exhaust holes all around and a harness rig extending from the bottom. The drone was made to silently attack and destroy structures and personnel.

It was equipped with Mesh Battery Storage; meaning it could run for a long time and recharge itself as it was operating. Jess had done some testing with the drone and knew what it could do now. She also knew after another fourteen months of work, this drone could be three times more proficient then it was now.

The basic strategy was to move silently into the enemy's space, launch video drones to record thermal imaging, regular video, and mapping of the surrounding area. Once received, the data would be assessed and a plan of attack decided.

Either the pilot/sniper would find his attack point, land and destroy those targeted or he would destroy the targets with the attack drones. Never seen, never heard, never there.

At 3:15 am, Sims drank his last beer and crashed on the couch. Sims missed Molly stealing the good end of the couch when he stayed over.

Chapter Twenty

4:20 am
Military Impound
Johnson City, TN

Master Sergeant George Hollis and Private First-Class Stone were tasked with transporting the evidence from the warehouse on Jackson Street to the Military Impound in Johnson City. Stone, a Virginia born, Appalachian raised boy had vomited multiple times while loading the truck. Hollis, from Buffalo, NY was forty years old and crusty; he had gone very quiet; neither of them had ever seen anything as fucked up as what they had in the back of their truck.

As Stone drove toward Johnson City, they had a forward and rear escort supplied by Sheriff Barlow. There was no real threat, but the protocol was protocol. Johnson City was a strange shaped city, almost an oval with a transformer type head on it.

The key point was that the main blvd. went all around the perimeter of the city. They had to get from the west entry of town to the northeast side of town; there were numerous lights along the way. Every stop was an opportunity for them to be messed with.

They entered from the west, and the four-way interchange was backed up a bit for 4:45 in the morning. The problem was all the lights were blinking red. It took an extra eight minutes to get back on their way to the military impound.

As Hollis and Stone badmouthed the lights, trying to forget what was in the back, they were startled by a flash of darkness; like a shadow that removed all light for a blink of time.

Hollis looked at Stone who had leaned forward, looking up through the windshield trying to get a look at what flew by, "What are you doing?" Stone looked at Hollis a bit confused, "Trying to see where it went." Hollis shaking his head no, "You saw nothing, it was nothing." Hollis now shaking his head yes. Stone caught on, "Right, no idea what that was." Hollis shook his head no again, Stone shaking his head yes, "Right, never saw anything; nothing at all. Don't want to be here all night." Hollis smiled shaking his head yes.

Once they were halfway around the city, the lights were further apart and allowed for some actual drive time. After several lights, there came a loud boom on the front wall of the truck right behind Hollis' head, "Jesus, what was that?" Stone replied, "He might be the only one that would know." Hollis bug-eyed, "Who are you talking about." Stone freaked, "Jesus."

Something hit the truck twice more. Private Stone in a hushed and panicked voice, "Holy shit, the only thing back there is her. What if she's trying to get out? What if she was reanimated by some kind of devil shit like at the crime scene?"

Completely at a loss, Hollis looked at Stone, "Really? What the hell is wrong with you?" Whatever it was, slammed the truck even louder this time, he picked up the radio, "We have an intruder, stop. I repeat we have an intruder, stop. Draw your weapons and stop, stop, stop." Stone mumbled, "Damn right we got an intruder, dat bitch is comin' out."

When Hollis exited the truck and walked around the vehicle, he made sure all the officers were following the protocols laid out by General Rouse.

Hollis took out his cell phone and called the General. It rang three times then, "This Corwin O' Caheil, Captain of United Nations Special Operations. General Rouse has forwarded your call to me. What have you got?" Hollis was about to respond when Stone, with his eyes bugging out, was slinking toward him, "She is screaming to get out." Hollis giving him a stern look, "Back off and do your job Stone."

Corwin was half-awake and not in the mood, "I repeat what have you got and make it quick." Hollis pulled his eyes away from Stone, "This is Sergeant Hollis, I am overseeing the transfer of the evidence from Jackson Street to the Military Impound at Johnson City. We have an intruder on the inside of our sealed payload."

Corwin was staring at the ceiling now, "Hollis, how did you guys let this shit happen?" Hollis defensively, "We didn't Sir the evidence seal remains unbroken." Corwin sarcastically, "Well Hollis, who packed this guy in with the evidence?" Hollis more defiant, "No one Sir, General Rouse sealed the evidence himself."

Corwin was having a hard time figuring out if, Hollis was incompetent or just a confident squared away soldier doing his job. He decided to clean this up himself, "Hollis explain the General's protocols for your trip." As Hollis went through every scenario, Corwin got his answer and realized that if this was not a mass hallucination they had a real problem.

As a favor, Sheriff Barlow picked up Corwin and went full sirens all the way to the scene. Hollis walked Corwin through the entire thing again.

Corwin noticed Stone pacing around near the back of the truck, "What is his deal?" Hollis lowered his head, "He thinks the victim has been reanimated by the devil and is trying to get out." Corwin looked Hollis in the eye, "Well, that would not be the weirdest thing we have going on with this case." Hollis' mouth dropped open. He looked over at Barlow who just shrugged his shoulders."

Corwin had no choice, he had to move the truck and everyone involved to the Impound, he had to find out what was going on. Hollis had to order Stone to get back in the truck.

Once they had everyone and everything in their proper places, with the proper protections, Corwin cut the seal and stepped back, "Open it up; let's see who is making all the racket."

When the doors were finally pulled back, the only thing they found was a night orderly who could not explain why or how he came to be in the truck. In addition, he was pissed he missed his shift at the Johnson City Veterinary Hospital.

All the evidence was gone, no Kat, no nothing. Hollis turned to Stone, "We have got to tell them what we saw or we will be arrested." Stone looked at the ground, "We are gonna be arrested no matter what. I will tell them what I saw, you just fill in what you need to." Hollis nodded and motioned to Corwin.

At 6:10 am, all those who had participated in the evidence transfer were arrested and put in Barlow's jail. As Barlow's thoughts turned toward sleep, he received an urgent call. He had to run back over to Johnson City; something had happened at the Veterinary Hospital. He wondered if he would ever sleep again.

Chapter Twenty-One

4:00 am
Johnson City Veterinary Hospital
Johnson City, TN

If Molly was going to live, she would have to make it through the night. At 9:00 pm, the resident vet checked Molly's vitals and gave her pain and sedative injections. He finished his rounds then locked up for the evening. Dr. Peters, Molly's critical care vet, would arrive around noon.

What no one knew was that the night orderly was not going to come to work; he had been detained. That meant that Molly and the other animals would not get their early morning medications.

Molly became aware of herself slowly. Under the massive swelling of her face, her eyes were darting in all directions trying to find Kat. She tried to open them to no avail. She heard a massive, heavy and loud bark.

Using her nose as a guide, she could make out many different smells, dog and otherwise. One of them would have to be extremely large for such a bark. As Molly wondered about getting help, she allowed her eyes to stop and slipped away.

At 4:00 am, Molly was awakened by pain; pain everywhere; the injections were wearing off. She had to access her injuries, what could she do? What worked? What didn't work was almost everything.

The worst was her inability to swallow and breathe freely. She could not move anything, and she could not communicate with her hips or rear legs. Her front paws twitched on and off and she could make her right one move.

As the pain increased, she needed to breathe deeper and more rapidly than she could, she was beginning to worry; her eyes began looking for help but there was no way to know if there was anyone around for her.

Molly was beginning to gasp for air when she heard the loud bark again, then again. She could feel that the dog barking was alerting the others; trying to warn anyone who could hear.

Coinciding with the barking, came creaking and cracking noises from the front of the building; the giant Mastiff barked louder and more aggressively. The cracking sound gave way to a sudden shattering explosive burst that was followed by the sound of debris from the front door and wall hitting the floor.

Molly was now in trouble; her heart rate was exceeding her ability to bring in enough oxygen. The needed expansion of the rib cage and diaphragm increased her pain beyond her threshold. She had become fully engaged in a battle for her life when things took an evil turn; she could smell them.

Fear gave way to terror; it was the smell of death and rotting flesh. Molly had barely escaped, and John was killed the last time she smelled them. The Mastiff was silent.

Molly could not breathe; she believed her heart was going to explode. She felt cold surround her, she thought of John. The cold began to intensify, she was shivering, but her heart rate began to slow, the pain in her chest was reduced and the cold air was now flowing into her lungs. As it got colder, all her pain was neutralized but she still had no movement. She felt as if she was floating somewhere, she took a deep breath, and all was dark again.

At 6:30 am, from where Sheriff Barlow was standing it looked like Johnson City Veterinary Hospital had been hit by a missile strike. As the Sheriff walked through the debris, he was struck by how cold the area was and that it smelled like dead things.

Barlow stood in the middle of the mess and thought back to what he had heard about the siege at the compound. There had been creatures that had killed Marko and John, but somehow John came back to life.

Barlow remembered that they would envelop, squeeze and freeze their victims while feeding on their fear, and they smelled like death.

He immediately went to check on Molly. She was gone, but her pen was still locked. The entire pen area was cold and wet as if it had just thawed out. All the other animals were hiding in the back corners of their cages; something very wrong had happened here.

When Barlow confirmed their night orderly had not come to work this morning, he contacted General Rouse and told him Molly had been abducted.

Chapter Twenty-Two

7:05 am EST
6:05 am CST
Somewhere in Colorado

Barlow went into his office, fired up his computer, got on Amazon and bought a blue striped winkie cozy. He paid for it with the card Glenn had sent him for such purchases. Now he had to wait.

Glenn and Nick were hard at work updating all the information they were receiving from Hoss, Corwin and now someone had purchased a winkie cozy.

Glenn went to his online winkie cozy store and verified the means of purchase and shipping mode. The winkie cozy had been selected for Prime, next day shipping, and the buyer was Sheriff Barlow. This was an urgent message.

Glenn switched to his secure SAT phone and dialed Barlow's cell phone and encrypted his end as he answered, "Glenn we have a problem I didn't think you wanted me talking to John about."

Nick motioned to Glenn who put the call on speaker, now their voices would be heard throughout the workstation, "Sheriff this is Nick, what's happened?" Barlow a bit hesitant, "I... Kat and all of the evidence from the crime scene on Jackson Street has been stolen and Molly was abducted from the Veterinary Hospital in Johnson City."

Glenn stunned, "What the hell happened?" Barlow told the entire story including the flash of darkness Private Stone and Hollis had seen and the conditions and smells at the vets.

Nick hurt and pissed, "These sons of bitches aren't trying to hurt John they are trying to kill him. First, they kill his wife and dog, then the rob him of saying goodbye at a funeral. We may never find any sign of Makayla." Nick looked up to see Glenn staring at him, "Wife?" Nick nodded, "The day they were kidnapped."

Barlow with authority, "I agree, but I believe that the evidence was stolen by something, not someone. Compare the events at the compound two years ago to the weird shit that is happening now.

"The evidence seal on the truck was never tampered with, but when we opened it the evidence was gone. Molly was gone from her pen, but the pen was still locked. The front of the building was caved in and the entire front of the hospital was cold and wet as if it had just thawed out; it smelled like rotting flesh. This is something different."

Nick let out a sigh, "We have others that mentioned a flash of darkness, exact words. Also, strange things that ought not to be are aplenty in the woods around the compound."

We just finished updating the info from Jonesborough and all the activity related to these darkness pieces of shit." Jeff, I will call John. We really appreciate your discretion and actions on John's behalf at Jackson Street.

Please continue your efforts with the State Police to find Makayla. Barlow said he would and ended the call. Nick looked at the clock, it was 7:40 am, he wondered if John was awake or still past out.

Chapter Twenty-Three

8:06 am
Hart Compound
Sims' house
Jonesborough, TN

John rarely dreamed these days, but the last thirty-six hours had crushed his mind. He leaped up off Sims' couch trying to shake an image from his head. It was of Kat hanging from the roof at Jackson Street. In the background were two huge eyes filled with blood, and black pupils reflecting John's face back at him; he was being watched.

John staggered into the bathroom, he vomited while in the throes of crying spasms. He choked, coughed and spit his way out of the bathroom to Sims' refrigerator. He grabbed a beer twisted off the cap and drank it all at once. He threw the bottle against the wall at the back of the kitchen then collapsed back into the couch.

John found himself looking for Molly. She had always been there when he crashed; she had always saved him from himself. Now she was gonna die in that damned hospital and he would not be there for her. John forced his face deeper into the cushions of the couch and screamed.

As he started to sit up again, his cell phone began to ring. He could hear it, but it was not in his pocket. It sounded buried somewhere in the kitchen. John screamed, "What the hell is going on, leave me alone. Leave me alone."

He stood up and followed the noise; the phone was in the refrigerator next to the beer. He picked it up, "What? What the hell do you want?" Nick calmly, "John, did you get any sleep?" John feeling mean, "I was having a wonderful dream experience until you called. I was watching my wife hang from the roof with some assholes eyes burning into me; so yes, really good sleep."

Nick now trying not to cry, "John someone stole Kat's body and took Molly from the vet; we have no idea who it was." John was now sitting with his back against the refrigerator, "Shit, someone really hates my ass. This is great, how many more people are going to die because I exist?"

Nick became the big brother, "Quit being a selfish prick. We all worked very hard to destroy those crazy bastards. They are just starting with you. They wanted that gate open, tuff shit for them, we slammed the door. Now they want to get even.

"I want them dead, but we can't get that done without you, John. It is time to fight back; someone just stole your wife's body, so we need to put them in the dirt. You get that?"

After a couple of minutes, John wanted everyone back and working from the compound right away. Nick covered the phone for a minute then "We can be there in four hours. Dom will bring us back home. Trish, Jess, and Sims are at your house right now. You already know that Hoss and the gang are waiting for you in the main house."

John was quiet for a second then, "Nick thanks for getting me up. Molly wasn't here and…" the phone went dead, John had hung up.

John went to the basement of Sims' house and drove a golf cart through the lower level tunnel to Lab 1. He keyed his way in, went to the far-left corner of the lab, reached between the two glass cabinets and pulled what looked like a fire alarm. The glass cabinets retracted, revealing a stairway leading down below the lab.

This was John's personal space, his lair. He could retreat here on the bad days and remind himself how lucky he had been. Here he would visit and confront all the demons from his past. This is where he would battle them, the infamous they; those who tried to hold him back or destroy him.

He went to a niche near the light switches. He activated his sound system and selected loop number one. He listened to this song when he lacked courage when he was overwhelmed; when THEY were winning.

The metal music pounded him as he moved to the table in the middle of the lab and opened the far-right hand drawer. He took out his nine-millimeter Sig and the phone he had used the day he blew up the compound and slammed the door on Abaddon.

He was staring at the phone. John was thinking it through, had he been careless blowing up the compound? Was it a mistake? He thought about it repeatedly for the last two years. Was all of this his fault, had he just killed his wife?

John turned to face the source of the music, "Bullshit I blew up the whole compound to save everyone, we stopped it all, we saved everyone. We ended Zhang and screwed the Russians as a bonus. John was sure he had taken every precaution.

He reached into the left-hand drawer and took out a large black permanent marker. He walked to the whiteboard and wrote in huge letters, "Fuck Them".

He turned back to the table and his old phone was blinking. His eyes started burning. His brain caught fire, he whispered, "Semjaza?"

Semjaza was the leader of the cult that attacked the Hart Compound. In Glenn's zeal to build the compound, he had outbid a group of individuals for a specific house in Maine made from a rare type of wood.

This group had been trying to buy the house for over two hundred years. To them, it was the portal or gate, which would unleash demons from hell in the last days. Their major problem being, they felt the last days were in two days.

During the siege, John had been killed by one of Semjaza's creatures. Only to be revived when Semjaza looked into his mind and saw his dreams.

John was terrified; now mumbling to himself, "He said we were done. He said he couldn't harm me even if he wanted to. No, he can't come after me. No, but Kat? Could he harm Kat? Why would he come after Kat? Son of a bitch!"

John stood staring at the phone; he was still shaking his head no. He didn't want to touch it. While John was locked in indecision, the phone answered itself and went to speaker, "John we don't really need a phone to have a conversation but since you insist I will project my thoughts using the speaker."

John did not recognize the voice, "Who are you and how did you get through to this phone?" The caller chuckled, "John you blew my poor host to atoms. My current vehicle sounds different of course but it is still me on the line. John, kill all the power to your phone and you will have your answer." John punched in the codes and the phone went off their network. There wasn't a way to kill the power to the phone you could only make it deaf and dumb.

John no sooner finished the shut down when the caller's voice filled the entire room, "Well see we don't need a phone now, do we? Can we get to the reason for my call?"

John was about to point out how the caller was beating the system, when he found himself outside, on the front lawn, halfway to Sims house.

The caller a little put off, "Damn, you are stubborn, now can we have a little chat. I am miles away, sitting in a chair, thinking about you, and saying what I need to say. You are now on the lawn devoid of devices doing the same. I will explain all of this someday but today we have much to discuss.

"John you need to listen to me carefully. I in no way harmed your wife or her sister. The events of the past thirty-eight hours have led you to believe various things that are not as they seem. We need to meet so I can bring you up to speed on what is really happening."

John was stuck on a word, "Wife, you said my wife, how would you know that?" Semjaza more serious, "John if you know it, I know it, all I have to do is look into your mind, and find what is important. So, no, I did not harm your wife or her sister. I think I can help you understand what has actually happened these past hours. I can only do that if you meet me at my place.

"I do not wish you harm, and you know that if I wanted you dead I would have left you that way the other day." John interrupted, "The other day, it was almost two years ago."

"John, as I said back then the life of a human, is but a blink of time to my kind, so let's get together so we don't waste any more blinks shall we."

John was too tired to think, "How do we make this happen?" "I will wake Sheriff Barlow and he will pick you up and bring you to me." John shut his eyes trying to imagine the trouble he could get into; when he opened them, he was back in his lab.

John looking around, "Ok, wow. Sheriff Barlow and you go way back, do you?" Semjaza smiling, "Never met the man, but he stood by you when everyone was treating her like a thing. He did not see her as evidence."

Semjaza closing, "John, it is 8:40 am your time, so expect the Sheriff in about an hour. See you soon."

Chapter Twenty-Four

7:25 am
The Corner Cup
Jonesborough, TN

Corwin O' Caheil was rereading the brief he was about to upload to Glenn. He was looking for a better way to explain the theft of the evidence and could not find a way to explain how it happened.

He pushed the laptop away from him, picked up his coffee and leaned back in his chair; he had to think. He didn't know John but he had been told of his many good traits. General Rouse had pointed out a few questionable decisions, which had led to questionable outcomes, but for the most part, he felt he would like the guy.

Corwin let a half-smile slip onto his lips when he thought about all John had been through in a very short time, *Talk about a bad day, someone is trying to destroy him.* Corwin was running down the list of all that had transpired when the fact that he called Kat his wife started him thinking.

Corwin was told she was his girlfriend; now within a day, she is the wife. As Corwin kicked around the possibilities, he felt there might have been an engagement the night before the murders. He decided he would talk to Nick privately when he called in his report.

Corwin went back over the scene as he had discovered it that morning. He called Sergeant Mitchell. As they were catching up he asked, "Mitch, who do I talk to for a list of the victim's personal possessions." Mitch was quiet for a couple of seconds, "What are you looking for?"

Corwin hesitated, "I had a case in Wales years ago that was similar to what happened at Jackson Street. I want to check to see if maybe something strange came up on that list." Sergeant Mitchell said just a minute then, "I have access to all the documents filed with the General as do you. I cannot divulge them to you but you can look for yourself from your computer."

Mitchell spent a minute with Corwin showing him where to look and then ended the call. Corwin went into the operations file, put in the case number Mitch had given him and found the evidence document he was looking for.

After several minutes of checking all the documents, he did not find an engagement ring. Corwin began checking off the boxes as he thought to himself, *why remove the face? With no face, no one could know who it was without testing. You leave the purse to show who it was because you were not sure yourself. You didn't know about the ring or you took it. The Druid never took anything. So no face, no ring, not Kat; it was Makayla. To cover it up, you steal the evidence so John will never know. That is why we can't find her – we already had her. Who has Kat? Shit, the Druid doesn't know that either!*

Corwin grabbed the phone and dialed the number he used to update Glenn. Nick picked up the phone sounding sad, "We have everything put in except your brief related to the theft. We need to run the tags as soon as we can. What have you got for us?"

Corwin changed the subject, "Nick, I need to talk to you about something that may be extremely important." Nick seemed a bit put off, "Ok, what are you thinking?" Corwin just went straight to the point, "Did John give Kat an engagement ring the night before the murder?"

Nick seemed a little angry, "Why the hell would you want to know that?" Corwin stayed on edge, "Because there was no ring found at the scene, I just looked at the logs it is not there." Nick was quiet, "I went with him to buy it last month; it was over the top beautiful and cost plenty. Anyone who took Kat would have noticed it and taken it."

Corwin said, "This is between you and me, but Rouse and I have seen this method of murder before. It has not been done again since we took care of that situation. Now the exact M.O. is used in this situation, it's gotta be the same guy. He never took anything."

Nick wasn't sold, "Kat could have packed it in her gear, we haven't checked there." Corwin interrupted, "I have looked at all of the logs from the abduction and the theft this morning; it is not there. She would have worn it to show her sister."

Nick now pissed, "Is there a point to all of this O' Caheil?" Corwin upped the agitation in his voice, "Clear your head and listen up. No face, why? Staged the purse so we would know it was Kat, why? No ring, why?"

Corwin with a raised voice, "I will tell you why he didn't know which girl he had because he lost one of them; probably had both purses. He cut off her face so nobody would know if it was Makayla or Kat. He left Kat's purse because he wanted John to believe it was Kat.

The theft of the evidence seals the deal. He could not allow any testing after he had to improvise at the time of the murder; he wanted John to feel this. Lastly, no ring tells me that Makayla was the one slaughtered and Kat is somewhere he can't reach her; because if he had her, all of the other shit would be unnecessary."

Nick was stunned and sat down on the couch looking out the big picture window somewhere in Colorado; struggling with the new info, "Shit that is a real probability. Did you work this out with General Rouse?" "No, but I wouldn't be surprised if Barlow hasn't figured it out by now. Rouse probably worked this out a while ago and is withholding it from you. I don't like that."

Nick now more controlled, "Kat must be with someone who has double-crossed the murderer; probably waiting it out to sell her back to John." Corwin calm, "So how do you want to handle this Boss Man?"

Nick surprised, "You want to work with us?" Corwin laughed, "Ask Glenn, I been working for him for the past three months. I want these pricks out of the picture. I think the ones we arrested from the van the afternoon of the murder, are the cutter's helpers. I would give them to Phu and let him do his magic."

Nick surprised again, "You know Phu?" "I know his work; he still outsources now and then. Put them with him he will get what they have. Save us a bunch of time.

"The cutter is a sadistic pig; they called him the Druid. He is no joke. If he is here, we are all in danger, so buckle up boys, this could be just the start of our mess."

Nick felt a little better about things, "Ok we will put in your briefing, start plotting the moves of each tag and see where we are right now. Let's see it is 9:10 am, so I will call Sergeant Cartwright and have him sick Phu on those van guys. We should have something from all of this a little after noon."

Corwin felt that the next forty-eight hours were going to be a very dangerous time. He wondered what the General was doing. He had gone silent, probably sleeping.

Corwin thought that was a great idea. In less than an hour, he was back home, face down on his couch, with his forty-five semi-auto sidearm under the cushion.

Chapter Twenty-Five

10:40 am CST
11:40 am EST
Somewhere in Colorado

Nick and Glenn were hard at work analyzing the people they had tagged in the Jonesborough area. Glenn had isolated eight active tags that he could say were definitely working together. Included in that group were Rocky and Bull Winkle, and the boys in the van.

There were two anomalies, the leather goods merchant's tag disappeared when he was drugged, and that tag never reappeared. One of the guys at Jakes disappeared as well. With six of the eight accounted for, Nick was anxiously awaiting results from Phu's meeting with the mutts in the Van.

Glenn was having a numbers problem. He couldn't get enough tags in the right places to cover the activity that had happened. He had eliminated many of the forest people based on intel from the people running the compound. He tagged them anyway just in case there was an error. He had accounted for everyone.

Glenn leaned back to Nick, "I can't put everyone in their place. I am missing the leather guy and a guy from Jake's, they disappeared from the grid. There were no tags involved in the evidence heist. We picked up four in the van that we can place at the scene of the van shooting but can't place them in the warehouse on Jackson Street.

Nick put his feet up the coffee table, "So every guy we ever tagged in Tennessee, but those two, are still here and on the board?" Glenn looked at him funny, "Why would I do that, many of these tags were one time and were shown as leaving the area." Nick yawned, "Did you run those to see where they are now or if they were ever seen again?

Glenn was a little flustered, "What do we have to gain by doing that; besides this is a focused area we don't need to worry about people somewhere else killing us here." Nick smiled, "I would like to know the location of everyone who had evil thoughts about me, wouldn't you?" Glenn bushing it off, "I would need a much bigger area and don't have that here." Nick not kidding now, "Then get one."

Glenn rolled his eyes, "I will just snap my fingers and easy-peezy-chili-beanie poof it will appear." Nick very sharply, "How 'bout you put all these assholes on your cancer tracker and find out where they are right now. You can delete them later."

Glenn sat silent for at least a minute, "That's a great idea. It will take a little time, but we should be able to see where they went and where they are now." Glenn got busy on it.

At 11:30 am, Hoss called from the compound. Glenn picked it up and put it on speaker, "Hoss what have you got for us?" Hoss sounded tired, "Phu milked those guys and got everything they had.

"Most of it we already knew, but they were adamant that there are three more players and the Master. They said they only come in for major operations and they handle it quietly and on their own.

"They use some of the others for surveillance like they did with Rocky and Bull Winkle. The last they knew the big boys were hiding out on the backside of Johnson City and they have back up in Knoxville.

"They said these guys are all suit and tie like CIA type guys. They run Cadillac sedans; black and rolling hard.

"Phu said that all these boys feel the Master is the devil himself. They told some pretty far out tails. One said The Master ripped a guy's arm off with a wave of his hand and he can read everyone's thoughts. So, good luck with this.

"John was in his lower lab for a while and then took off with Barlow somewhere. That was around 9:30 am. Give us something so we can end this bullshit." Hoss was gone, and Nick and Glenn were staring at one another.

Nick broke the silence, "How much you wanna bet one of the big boys is NSA?" Glenn smiled, "Now Nick, don't go getting all crazy on us now; I know how you feel about these guys." Glenn turned just in time to see Nick flip him the bird and, "We got to get this done. Dom will be waiting for us at the airport, we gotta be there by 1:00 pm.

Glenn a bit frantic, "I have added all of the Jonesborough tags in with the rest of the cancer tags. I have put in priority and identity algorithms, so we can tell who is who..." Nick cut in, "You have a way of knowing if one of our players goes both ways?"

Glenn stopped, he was staring at Nick. Nick shrugged and raised his arms, "Yes or no?" Glenn smiled, "Why would that happen?" Nick smiled, "You started working this with General Rouse to find who was killing the cancer doctors?" Glenn a little pissed, "No."

Nick came over and stood next to Glenn then continued, "I think Rouse was setting you up because he felt someone in the NSA was leaking the vendor sites. If he believed what you said about the NSA he knew you tagged at least one of their employees and he could follow along. What would look like random actions for this guy to you, could tell General Rouse another story altogether."

Glenn eyes glazed over; he was going down the rabbit hole. Nick knew he would put it together. Glenn stood up and went to the big picture window.

Glenn talking very slowly and quietly now, "None of this shit is about payback from the darkness freaks. Someone wants to get close to our technology as a classified vendor. If they can take John out of the picture, and use their NSA traitor to get in the door, they would get very close to the original specs." Nick leaned over and patted him on the back, "Welcome to the game son."

Nick walked to the couch, "Now does this change how we feel about General Rouse; is he being pressured to send reports to these people as well? They have been ahead of us the whole way.

"The report we are preparing from the cancer tracker is the whole deal, we should be able to see everyone and where they have been. How long will it take to spit out something that makes sense?"

Glenn thought it through for a bit then, "We should head for the airport. I will launch it now; it can work while we are flying. When we land, at 1:40 pm and get to the compound say 2:15 pm we should have our first look. We may have to mess with our parameters and run another pass; we will know when we get to the compound.

As they were leaving, Glenn phoned Hoss and told him to clear the turrets on the four corners of the house and lock down all access to shooting stations one through three. He was going to use all seven-satellite dishes and all the computer power from all nine stations.

Altogether, Glenn put together enough power to follow every tag's actions for the last year.

Chapter Twenty-Six

10:15 AM
Martin Creek Road
Erwin, TN

John and the Sheriff had been on Martin Creek Road for about 10 minutes. It wound through dense forest, and after a while, John wondered if there was indeed a creek or any other thing in this part of the world.

John, still in a foul mood, was now enclosed by trees; he felt isolated from the rest of civilization. He guessed that was the point of living in such an area. Barlow looked at John, "So, I am supposed to know where this guy lives?"

John was cursing Semjaza for his vague methods and secret crap, "Yes, you will know it when you see it." Barlow grinning, "How did you like the town of Erwin?" John's head went back, "The gas station and convenience mart were a town?"

Barlow knew he had John now, "They are more famous for their elephant." John scoffed, "So they have a one animal circus?" Barlow laughing, "No, back during the depression, a circus came into to Erwin and when they left they didn't take their elephant."

John sat up straighter as the Sheriff turned off Martin Creek road on to a small service road, "Cool, that's when they started their one animal circus?" Barlow turned onto another side road, "Well no, they thought the elephant would leave, but it didn't. It stomped on and ate their crops and when still hungry, it would crash into their barns and cabins looking for food."

John looked at Barlow, "Time to shoot that bitch." Barlow frowning, "That is what they tried to do, but every time they shot him, the elephant went crazy. It would chase after them and bash down the town's buildings."

John was getting tired of the story, he looked at his watch it was 11:26 am, "So they called in the military and PETA threw fake elephant blood on them; the end." Barlow determined to keep John's mind distracted continued, "No. They decided to start a fire that would force the animal off a cliff and down a ravine to its death.

"What happened was not what they expected. The elephant went over the edge but got caught upside down in a tree along the shear wall of the ravine."

John actually grinned, "Let me guess there was no way for them to reach the elephant, so they had to listen to it die, and then suffer the smell for the next year." Barlow nodded, "That is exactly what happened.

"Many of the residents left during the months that followed; Erwin has never recovered." Barlow turned left off the narrow road into a driveway, he and looked at John, "Here we are, see you knew how to get here all along; excellent directions." John thought of Semjaza.

The final left-hand turn led to a right hand curved circular drive-way. It revealed a beautiful Southern Colonial right out of Gone with the

Wind. It was fronted with large green lawns, with walkways bordered with colorful flowers. They were greeted by a footman who escorted them to the front door.

John used the large doorknocker, which echoed throughout the house. He turned to smile at the footman; he was gone as was the sheriff's patrol car. John reached for the knocker for another try when the door swung open on its own; he thought, *of course, he is not here.*

Barlow not hesitating entered looking in all directions taking the amazing appointments within the house. There was a large staircase on the right. The footman, now dressed as a butler, motioned for them to take the stairs and they did. The stairs led to a top landing with hallways left and right.

John looked left and saw nothing. He looked right and shook violently then dropped to his knees; Molly walked slowly to him and nuzzled into his arms for a long-awaited hug. Her tail was working a mile a minute. John heard gasping from behind him, Barlow had tears in his eyes and a smile worth a million bucks, "Molly girl, you look so much better."

Molly whined an excited whine and spun around a couple of times then headed down the hall and sat by a door grinning from ear to ear. John looked at Barlow whose eyes were welling with expectations, "Go, John, let's go."

John grasped the doorknob and gave it a slight turn; it was open. He turned it all the way and slowly opened the door, Molly bolted inside. Across the room, sitting on the side of a twin bed was Kat. It seemed like she had just woken up, "Molly was that…oh my God John."

Barlow held Molly by the collar for a minute while John and Kat embraced. As John hugged Kat, he turned and looked at Barlow with a look that said, *how do I tell her about Makayla?*

As things settled, John and Kat had time for questions. It turned out that Kat couldn't remember anything after she fell asleep in John's arms the night before she left for training. Kat thought she was waking up to head out to training.
John felt that Semjaza might have had something to do with that.

During all of this, Barlow noted that she was still wearing her engagement ring. For Kat's sake, John looked all over the room for her purse; of course, it was not there. Kat made references that it was in her go-bag at the front door of the house.

It wasn't until 12:40 pm when they started to leave Semjaza's house, that Kat realized how strange things were. Now very perplexed, and disorientated, she got into the back of the patrol car with John; Molly looked at John then wiggled her way unto Kat's lap just as she asked, "How did I get here…Where is Makayla?"

Once on the road Sheriff, Barlow called Hoss at the compound. Barlow spent several minutes conveying John's instructions.

Chapter Twenty-Seven

11:30 am
Lil' Pine Cabin
The Town with No Name, TN

Sims began to stir around 10:30 am. When he realized what time it was he was shocked and a little embarrassed. No one had called him during the early morning hours; he felt it could be a good sign.

He was thinking of making a big breakfast until he opened the refrigerator and found Kat had cleaned it out expecting to be gone for the week. Then he thought of Sammy's Diner.

It was a brilliant idea. They could get the best grub around and catch up on what had gone down during the night.

He called Sammy and found he was slamming out full service round the clock; John's tab. Sims rousted the ladies so they could set off for the diner.

It was 12:30 pm when they finally got to Sammy's Diner. Sims was afflicted, as most men are, by the underestimation of women's needs related to their preparation before stepping foot into the real world.

They got lucky, Jacob, from Confidante in Knoxville, was just pulling out. He had been summoned by Hoss to be Glenn until Glenn arrived; then he would be Glenn Junior.

Jacob had played a major role in the incident at the compound. He had created a 3 D camera array that gave Glenn and John the most important elements they needed. It allowed John to see the streak of light screaming from space for the compound; that told him Abaddon was about to join the fray.

As they were seated, all eyes were on them. Most of those present had worked the entire night on surveillance or retrieving assholes tied to trees. They were wondering what was really going on, and they knew Sims, Jess and Trish would have those answers.

Bev came out from the side room usually reserved for weekend overflow, saw Sims and turned back into the side room. The next person who came out was Adam; he motioned them to join him. When they did so, they found Phu and Lil' Joe in there as well.

By the time they had finished their first cups of coffee, they had learned of all the action in the forest. The heard about the Master, his eyes, and that all his men believed he was the devil.

Lil' Joe started talking about the new guy, Corwin O' Caheil, and his assault on the van. Sims finished the legend by telling them about how he saved John from hearing Kat's body splat on the concrete in the warehouse.

After the stories settled down, Phu asked Sims, "So John was out of his mind pissed and he couldn't lay a glove on this Cackel dude?" Sims was raising his coffee cup to drink, "He set John down on the ground like a dad setting down his child." Phu just shook his head.

Adam jumped in, "Hoss showed us the video of him taking down the van. Son of a bitch ran almost full speed five hundred yards uphill firing single shots that kept the bad guys from getting out of the van.

One man got out, stood up, and within a second a bullet went through his knee. Sergeant Mitchell saw it from the air; said it freaked him out." Trish asked about Sergeant Mitchell and seemed pleased he was in the area again.

Jess asked how John was holding up. Adam said, "Hoss told me that he and Barlow were going out past Erwin to check out a lead. I don't know what that meant but John has not been John." They all nodded.

When asked what they had been doing, Sims stood up and excused himself to the restroom. Jess had the floor, knowing that everyone around her could be trusted; she started telling about her latest toys. Trish kept adding that she was going to pilot the first mission. Phu said, "Sims isn't going to like that, he is the mission dude." Jess looked at Trish and winked, "Sims is too fat for this mission."

Phu, Adam and Lil' Joe were laughing when they saw Sims approaching. Phu, always the instigator, "Sims is too fat? What are you talking about?" Sims leaned over and whispered in Jess' ear, "What are you talking about?" Trish quick to respond, "The weight limitations of the attack drone. You are a just a bit over the edge honey." Sims truly embarrassed, responded with a bad Arnold Schwarzenegger impression, "It's a girly machine."

Trish leaned back, "We are doing trial runs today; just waiting for Hoss to give us a mission."

Chapter Twenty-Eight

12:10 pm
Corwin O' Caheil's quarters
Jonesborough, TN

Corwin's fourth hour of sleep began with his phone ringing; it was General Rouse. Corwin, somewhat awake, and trying hard to listen like a good soldier. Rouse was going on about the Greenbrier Hotel in Sulphur Springs, West Virginia.

When the General had hung up, Corwin realized that he was going for a chopper ride to The Greenbrier. He was to meet with the General and a few others at 3:30 pm; the topic was classified. Corwin hoped it was Sergeant Mitchell doing the flying.

At precisely 2:30 pm, Corwin stepped out of his cottage. As he locked the front door, a silver SUV pulled up. All the windows were tinted so he could not see the driver.

Corwin walked behind the car and opened the passenger side door, "Well Master Sergeant Sims, good to see you...I think." Sims somewhat reserved, "Yes Captain, I want to thank you for saving John from that horrible sound; I wish now you could have taken me out as well."

Corwin looking down was slowly nodding. Sims realized right then Corwin O' Caheil heard that sound in his head quite often. Sims pressing a bit, "How did you know what was going to happen?"

Corwin trying to avoiding the truth, "I was the one who found her that morning. I cleared the scene and secured the area until the teams arrived." Sims smiled, "So you're not going to tell me? We all operate under the same classified mandate; that includes you now that you are part of the team."

Corwin locked eyes with Sims and understood the seriousness of what he had just heard. He was part of all that was going on and was trusted to do his part.

Corwin sat a little taller, "Thank you, um I have seen this murderer's work before; as has General Rouse. We tracked him into the solid rock caves of Wales; cold, wet and nasty. I thought I had killed him; I even cut off his head, but here he is again.

Rouse checked with the NSA yesterday, no one has reported a murder like this since then; now this. I had been the hasty one back then, the one to cut the victim down; I live with that sound; no one deserves that."

Sims shook off the whole thing, "Ok, so tell me why we are going to the Greenbrier?" Corwin smiled, "Typical Rouse, I have no idea he said a car would come for me. So, we will find out when we get there. Where are we meeting the chopper?"

Sims turned to check for a reaction, "At Hoss' wheat farm?" Corwin looked back at Sims, "Ah yes, Sergeant Hoss Cartwright's International Airport."

On the way to Hoss' access road, Sims and Corwin exchanged stories related to meeting and working with General Rouse. Corwin had spent a great deal of time with Rouse and Sims avoided the man. When Corwin wondered why Sims avoided him, he shrugged and told Corwin most of his operations were unsanctioned by the General, but necessary to maintain the John Hart Group.

When they arrived, they were glad to see Sergeant Mitchell and Mitch was surprised to see Sims, "The General said it would be O' Caheil and someone else, but two heavy hitters on the same mission…must be going after a whale."

Wanting to change the subject Sims smiled and turned to Mitch, "Trish Baltran seemed pleased that you would be in the area for a while; what's up with that?" Mitch a bit shy, "Maybe she wants to show me her scar." Sims just nodded.

Corwin kept looking back and forth waiting for either of them to fill him in, but they just ignored him. He finally asked, "Her scar? Where is it?" Mitch looked at Sims, and then Sims grinned at Corwin, "You woulda had ta been there." Both men turned and walked toward the chopper.

Halfway through the fifty-minute flight, Mitch told Corwin about the gunfight on Boone's Creek Road, just outside the town of Boone's Creek. Corwin laughed and shook his head throughout the tale.

Trish Baltran, call sign Tbal, had taken on four gunmen who worked for Zhang Jei. He was a Chinese operative that specialized in stealing American secrets and technology. He was after Jess and her continuous power tech.

At the peak of the battle, Tbal had already killed two of her attackers, and she was pinned down by the other two. She timed her last volley to assure that both men would be exposed while firing at her.

Tbal killed one attacker and was dispatching the second when she was hit in the right chest and went down. Her attacker went down as well. Mitch had fired a missile that hit the shooter's SUV the exact second Tbal was hit.

Once the chopper landed, Hoss went to the SUV and Mitch tended to Tbal. She was lucky because the bullet hit the vest but had made its way through the vest and into Trish.

When Mitch checked to see how badly she had been hurt, he found the bullet barely penetrated her leaving a quarter of an inch of it exposed. Mitch took a pair of pliers, distracted Trish for a second and then quickly ripped it out; she punched him between the eyes, followed by a thank you.

Corwin was impressed, "So you want to get a look at that scar." Mitch being Mitch, "Well every professional wants to make sure that they have indeed done their best work, so yes I think a quick check to see how it healed would be in order."

They finally landed at a private chopper pad away from the Greenbrier proper; an SUV was waiting. They loaded into the white Tahoe and found themselves deeper and deeper into the hills and dense forests of Virginia.

When they had reached a point where no one could be living, the SUV pulled on to a tiny pathway that expanded into a two-lane circular driveway; it led to a log cabin mansion.

The driver turned to his passengers, "We must wait for our escort." The huge front doors of the house opened, four MP's emerged and stood by each door. When they were sure all was safe, they opened the doors and had all four of them inside the home in a matter of seconds. No one could have made out who was entering the cabin.

Once inside they were taken to an elevator that seemed to go down forever. When the doors opened, they entered a war room right out of Dr. Strangelove (YouTube). It was a vast circular room with large computer monitors as walls, all displaying world maps and various forms of information.

At precisely 3:30 pm, General Rouse and two other men came out of a hallway on the right side of the room. As Rouse got closer, Sims began to smile, Sergeant Mitchell and Captain O' Caheil snapped to attention.

Sims still grinning, "My, my gentlemen, it appears that someone is gonna get a mighty ass whoppin'. This is murderer's row." Sims now shaking hands, "Good to see you again General Jackson Dunn, Brigadier General Benjamin Creps; Wow, I gotta know, who are we hunting?"

Chapter Twenty-Nine

12:30 pm
Hart Compound
Jonesborough, TN

Sergeant Hoss Cartwright was having a busy day. General Rouse had left instructions that Sims was to join him at the Greenbrier Resort. Sims was to pick-up Corwin O' Caheil on his way to meet a chopper at Hoss' farm.

Hoss had no sooner hung up from the General than Sheriff Barlow called on his way back from a strange house deep in the trees south of Erwin. John wanted Hoss to prepare the little pine cabin to receive a top-secret guest.

He wanted the area totally secure but without showing their presence. Hoss was to scan the area and remove any surveillance or trespassers; burn them if he had to.

Hoss finally interrupted, he felt John was listening, "Sheriff I can't do a good job if I don't understand what I am dealing with; I need to know who we are hiding." Barlow looked at John in his rearview mirror, John nodded Barlow resumed, "Hoss, we found Kat, she is unharmed as much as we can tell.

"She and John are dealing with the Makayla issue. No one can know she is alive, or they will come for her again. We need the murderers to believe they have succeeded so we can track them.

"We need you to send someone to meet us just south of Erwin on Martin Creek Road, so I can go back to the station without them and they can slip back into the little house.

"Oh, remarkably, we have Molly with us." Hoss stunned, "How is that even possible?" Barlow looking at Molly in the rearview and then at John, "I think John is the only one who might have an idea; if you know what I mean?" Hoss quiet for a second, "Roger that, I am on it. When will we see Wonder Dog and friends?" Barlow responded, "About 30 min after the exchange."

Hoss more positive, "I will send a crew over to the little cabin now. Jess and Trish can scan the area. Sims is with General Rouse at an undisclosed location, so just Jess and Trish will be there which is perfect for Kat.

"In addition, I am sending Dr. Peters to the house. He came here from the Hospital looking to find out what was up with Molly." Barlow looked at John; he nodded his approval. Hoss ended the call.

Barlow surveyed the scene in his rearview mirror, John was all the way right on the passenger side, Kat had her head on his chest, while Molly had her chin on Kat's thigh. Barlow was saddened thinking many more horrors might come their way.

Hoss called Phu and told him to quietly clear and seal the area around John's house. He would inform the occupants of their presence. Whatever they needed would be provided.

Chapter Thirty

1:15 pm
Hart Compound
Jonesborough, TN

Hoss had sent one of their silver SUVs to fetch Nick, Dom, and Glenn, and drop them off at Sims' House. As they entered, they came across John's mess from earlier.

Nick started cleaning up the wall and the glass from the beer bottle, "The ol' toss a beer stress relief trick." Glenn opening the refrigerator, "As opposed to the ol' whiskey glass through the wall trick?" Nick dropped the mess in the trash bin, "Beer, whiskey they all get the job done."

Dom was shaking his head, "I kinda expected the ol' bullet holes all over the place. I can't imagine how pissed I would be if my wife was whacked by some sick son of a bitch."

Nick sighed and looked at Glenn; Glenn nodded, "Better to not have married then to expose yourself." Nick looked at Dom, "You know firsthand that it isn't limited to the wives, its anyone you care for…Marco?" Dom turned away from Nick walking to the front windows, "If John hadn't blown all those smelly ass creatures and their ringleader to hell, I would still be totally out of my mind. I was lucky you people got it done. We gotta get it done for John."

Glenn looked at his watch, "We gotta get to lab 3, so we can check out the results of the tracking update. I have to be ready to relay the information to General Rouse before 4:00 pm today.

Nick turned to Glenn, "You have to what? Why are we worried about his ass right now, we got to track this ourselves?" Glenn lowered his head in frustration, "Nick this is a daily thing, this is how we do it. He gets his info, we get ours and I get mine. Remember he is the satellite. Besides if this goes global, we will need Jack to get this done."

They drove the golf cart on the gravel path from Sims' side yard all the way to the west side of the house at the front porch. As they came in the front door, the people they passed nodded and continued on their way; Hoss met them at the door and escorted them to Lab 1.

Hoss filled them in on what activity was going on. He included the beefed-up security at the little house in the woods, sighting the new toys Jess and Trish were testing. Hoss told them that a full lunch was waiting for them in lab 3, along with beers and cots.

Nick excused himself to use the restroom, and Dom and Glenn headed for the food. Glenn dove into bringing up the updated tracking program; he did so with a half a sandwich held in his teeth. Dom walked by placing a beer on his left, "You will need something to wash that down with." Glenn mumbled something through the sandwich and kept on working.

Nick worked his way up to the widow's suite at the top of the house. So much had gone on here that last day when the siege of the compound came to its end. The room was larger than the ten by ten-foot original. This was where the serious shit had gone down.

He looked down at Sims' house then turned and looked the opposite direction at the gun range and shooting station 3. Glenn and John had waged the war against Semjaza and Zhang Jei simultaneously from inside station 3. Nick, Jacob and Gavin Tanner worked from Confidante to support them. Nick was impressed that John and Glenn had made the compound even better.

Now that he was alone, he decided to call John to check on him and Sheriff Barlow. He needed some good news; this negative shit had to stop.

Chapter Thirty-One

1:35 pm
Lil' Pine Cabin
Jonesborough, TN

Jess Williams and Trish were working on the back patio when they heard noise coming from the front of the house. Trish turned to see what it was when they heard the sound of Molly's claws clicking on the tile.

As they entered the kitchen looking across to the front door, they saw Molly coming their way. They were confused, then Kat came through the front door and they shuddered from the shock of seeing her with John walking in behind her.

Jess burst into tears, "Kat my God is that you? How..." Trish was acting as if she had seen a ghost; her head turning side to side, shaking, her hands over her mouth. Kat started crying and with a hoarse voice, "It was Makayla. I am so sorry, it was Makayla." Molly was whining trying to comfort everyone.

John got Molly under control and they settled in the living room. He let the ladies work through the shock of seeing Kat and Molly again. He was starting to explain how he had found them when his phone began to ring. He started to move out onto the patio when there was a knock at the door. It was Dr. Peters for Molly. John watched as Peters and Molly went out the front door into the yard.

John picked up after the third ring, "Nick, you at the compound now?" Nick could sense a positive note in John's voice, "Yup, how are you doing? I had to clean up a little mess in Sims' kitchen; that had me a little worried."

John ignored the comment, "Where are you calling from?" Nick's hunch about privacy had paid off, "I am in the widow's suite by myself, what's up?" John a bit hushed, "Barlow and I found Kat in a house supposedly owned by Semjaza."

Nick was glad he was sitting down, "What are you telling me right now?" John again, "We have Kat and Molly." Nick's brain was not picking this up, "John please make sense, what the hell happened? Semjaza? How did that asshole have Kat? Are you telling me Makayla was in the warehouse?"

John slowed down, "I was in my private lab deciding how I was going to handle this mess when my phone rang. I ignored it, but that didn't matter, the speaker came on and Semjaza was on the other end.

"It took some time, but he convinced me he was on our side on this one, and we needed to talk. When I got to the place he said to meet, he was gone but Kat and Molly were there and in perfect health. Barlow and I almost had heart attacks, but there they were. Kat doesn't remember anything after she left for Jake's and Molly looks like she has been working out at the gym."

Nick was quiet trying to work it all out in his mind when John said, "Nick, don't try to reason this out; that won't work right now. You need to help me keep them safe and not let anyone know where she is." Nick lost, "Where is she? Where are you?"

John realized Nick was overloaded, "Look we cannot let anyone know she is alive. We have the advantage if they think she is dead. We can't help Makayla, but we can avenge her for damn sure."

Nick was catching up, "One more time, where are you guys?" John caught himself, "Sorry, we are at our little house, we have Phu and the crew handling the security but they don't know for whom yet. We arrived without anyone seeing Kat; she is talking with Jess and Trish about Makayla now."

Nick managed a smile, and a tear, as the news broke through his analytic mind to his heart; "This is good news. Who have you told besides me?" John more businesslike now, "Barlow had to tell Hoss to get the house ready; now you." Nick, "Is Jeff still with you?" "No, he is heading home to sleep."

Nick was thinking, "John you have to tell a few more people to make this work. I hope you know that." John still in business mode, "I ain't telling anyone, I am gonna leave that up to you and Hoss."

Nick on to business, "Ok, but the biggest thing we got going right now is the update of Glenn's tracking software, it could give us the data we need to go after these guys. All the interrogations we've done gave us a good feel for the players, but we need to find them."

John relaxed, "Look, I know I have to get to the compound soon but I am going to make sure this place is set. I took a quick look at the new drone Jess has built and it can turn this situation around for us. I want to see it work for myself; I have plans for it."

Nick laughed, "I think I should make a big deal about telling Glenn; you remember what we did to him last time." John, "Good idea, last time was fun but he needs to be the frontman on this…agreed?" Nick nodding, "I will defer to him often as we do anyway."

John said, "Do me a favor and ask Gavin how fast he could produce one hundred and fifty dragonfly drones?" Nick confused, "What?" John held up his hand, "Humor me, just do it. I will try to get there at some point tonight or early in the morning."

Gavin Tanner was the owner of Confidante, John's cover business. Confidante was a niche company making high-end burner phones for the rich and famous.

These phones were better than the best regular phones offered by the mainstream cell phone companies but were a fraction of the cost. Owners would fall in love with their phones and sign up for a subscription, which opened up a completely new world of secure communications.

Nick recruited Gavin to take the company to its full potential while running the lower three floors where John and Jess created their toys for the military.

John was thinking about his call with Nick when he saw Dr. Peters and Molly coming back inside.

John joined them and they went out the front door and stood facing the woods.

Molly was leaning into Dr. Peters leg as he was scratching her ears, "She is perfect. There is no sign of trauma. I looked at the photos they took when she was evaluated and I am at a loss to explain why she is alive or why she is now twice as strong as she has ever been."

John smiled and looked him in the eye, "Doc, let me tell ya, we have had a bunch of miracles happen in the past twenty-four hours but they would take hours to put into context. I will buy you dinner when I come to L.A. later next month. Cool?" Peters just nodded and shook John's hand then Molly's paw.

Chapter Thirty-Two

2:35 pm
Hart Compound to Greenbrier Resort
Jonesborough, TN
Sulfur Springs, VA

Glenn loved the improvements the software changes had made to the tracking update. Nick and Dom were waiting as Glenn finally got General Rouse on the phone. To his surprise, Glenn was now the key presenter of a classified meeting regarding the unearthing of a traitor within the NSA. Glenn turned to his friends and mouthed, "Be quiet."

General Rouse introduced the two Generals Dunn and Creps, both were former Judge Advocate Generals or TJAGS. Now retired, they were valued consultants for both John Hart and General Rouse. Jackson Dunn was John Hart's lawyer when he was awarded the sixty-three million dollar settlement from the State of California. Also, in the meeting were Chris Sims, a former Army Master Sergeant and United Nations Special Operations Captain Corwin O' Caheil.

Glenn did a quick overview of the information now available. He also gave an example showing how they could select a time in the past and track all the movements of any tag from that point forward. He reviewed how they could create reports from the data as well.

Glenn was about to start with his findings when General Rouse jumped the line, "Glenn, do you have any glaring anomalies that you can't make sense of?" Glenn caught off guard, "Have you already accessed the information General?" Rouse impatient, "No I just have some hunches I want to check out, I don't have much time."

Glenn had a couple of abnormalities that really bugged him so he went with the weirdest one, "Let's start with this, I have twenty-seven instances where individuals have flown from one place to another and have disappeared leaving an inactive tag; never returning to their point of origin.

Each individual had been tagged because they had been in the company of those who were suspected of murdering one of my friendlies or where with one of our tags in Jonesborough."

Rouse was quiet, and then Glenn heard murmuring in the background. Rouse asked, "Will this thing play go fetch?" Glenn stuck his chest out, "Sure if you are willing to wait for the response." Rouse confused, "Aren't you maxed out for this meeting?" Glenn sarcastically, "Yes Sir, you will have NSA wait time; are you good with that?"

Glenn heard more murmurs then, "Glenn this is Jackson Dunn good to be working with you again. Now, go fetch a sampling of the twenty-seven individuals that went inactive and check local sources for reported deaths of these people or missing persons filed for them in their place of origin. Can that dog hunt?"

Glenn responded in the positive and went to work. He gave them status as he worked then said, "Go fetch" as he launched the search. Nick was intrigued by Dunn's question; he was suggesting these people could have been murdered after they served their purpose.

Glenn excited, "Jackson, I sampled eight tags and three were murdered and another four died suspicious deaths; all have missing person reports filed." Dunn was surprised, "What do we think of that Glenn?" Well, Sir, I feel I should look to see if these people crossed paths with my solid five tags that appeared at all of the doctor murder scenes." Dunn said, "Go fetch."

Glenn knew that the missing tags had been with or around the murder scenes but he had never had the opportunity to get this precise. When the report came back, Glenn was anxious, "Jackson, everyone in the sample had spent time with our five top suspects and flew to the sight of their demise from the same airports and same times as our five; only their final destinations were different."

Brigadier General Creps' voice came on the line, "Glenn I know you may already know this, but I want to know how many of the prime suspects have been in Tennessee lately and also check to see if they have been in the company of any tags you may have of NSA personnel."

Glenn started to deny he was tracking any NSA people when Rouse cut in, "Glenn we don't care about the law right now, do your job please." Glenn thought of how he would put together his go fetch questions when he added a wrinkle of his own, "Ok, it is fetching."

When the results hit the screen in Lab 3 Nick jumped out of his chair, "Holy shit!" Jackson Dunn smiling, "Nick you hiding in there with Glenn?" Nick now busted, "Yes Sir, but you got to hear this."

Glenn started reporting hoping he could control the narrative, "Gentlemen, I have an NSA tag traveling with seven of the eight sampled individuals who disappeared. Each time he flew into Greece and deplaned with Andreas Seraph Stavros. Stavros is one of the largest military contractors in the world and one of the three people who control Big Pharma."

While Rouse, Dunn and the others were contemplating the results Creps' voice rang out, "Glenn, are you going to answer my question? Of all this shit we are jumping up and down about, how much of it is related to the murder on Jackson Street?"

Glenn meekly, "Sorry Sir, let me run the rest of the question." Glenn was trying to make sense of what he was seeing in the report, "General Creps Sir, I will need another minute or two to make clear what I am seeing."

After another minute Glenn took a deep breath, "Of my top five, only two came to Tennessee, but four others from the top ten came as well. We had one tag disappear in the forest and we tagged a new individual the next day.

"That tag flew to Alaska late last night and we have no activity after that, but I have a video of those boarding a flight to London with a connection to Greece. Facial recognition picked up Stavros boarding under a different name. On top of that, we have a confirmed booking on the same connecting flight from London to Greece for Stavros.

"Now for the icing on the cake, our NSA tag was in Jonesborough the night of the murder, then took a room in Johnson City and left for London that morning. He also has a booking on the same connecting flight to Greece as Stavros."

Sims had been sitting quietly the entire time; he looked at Corwin then asked, "Glenn, is there any shipments or private charters we can tie to the activities of Stavros? Let me give you an example, say a tag disappeared did anyone ship anything to Stavros or his companies locally or is there another person that always flies to the same locations in question...does that make sense?"

Glenn didn't respond right away, he had to figure a way to let Sims know he understood the riddle, "So you are thinking of a guy like the leather goods dude from Johnson City?" Sims smiled, "Exactly." Sims turned to Rouse and the others looking like the cat that ate the canary.

After what seemed like forever, Glenn was heard in the background, "Son of a bitch" it was quiet again then, "I am working on that, I am searching alternate ways of getting people moved around the world incognito." Sims smiled again, "Glenn, are you thinking Gun Closet?" Glenn laughing, "Wish you hadn't said that out loud, but yes, you know me too well. It would have to go where he would be staying or a place close by."

Sims added, "It might not even be him unless it was the last leg of the trip; you following me?" Glenn excited, "What a fucking scam, this is some Semjaza type shit." Rouse's head snapped around and looked at Sims, "What are you guys getting at?" "Nothing yet Jack, but you won't believe it even if it plays out."

All of the hustle and bustle on Glenn's side of the phone call went dead quiet, and then they heard Nick and Glenn whispering back and forth. Finally, Dom said you guys are full of shit."

It was quite a while longer, then Rouse pissed off, "You guys are really testing my patience what the hell are you doing?" Glenn's voice was next, "Sims, we are at one hundred percent." Sims shifted in his chair, "Ok Glenn, tell them what we are thinking." Glenn responded, "Oh no, you can let them think you're crazy."

Sims was squirming around in his chair, "Glenn put the shipping and travel records on the monitors, so we can see what was sent and how." Glenn relieved, "Good idea, give me a second."

Directly across the table from General Rouse, on the wall above Corwin's head images began to appear. There was the face on a passport that looked exactly like Stavros. The name of the passport was William Clairmore of Kent in Great Britain. He had white hair, stern features, with olive skin; seemingly, Mediterranean. The passport said five foot ten.

When the stamps on the passport were shown, Glenn had highlighted twenty-one different places that related to all the activity they had discussed so far in the meeting.

Jackson Dunn chimed in, "So he uses a different name so as to not attract attention." As he was finishing his sentence, Stavros' passport came up on the screen showing most of the same destinations but with completely different flights and charters. Jackson was shaking his head.

Next, on the screen came the names and passports of those who were missing, murdered or died mysteriously. They all matched William Clairmor's activity except Clairmore always arrived the day before. Two records showed shipping containers that were delivered to parking lots of Hotels followed by a murder and Clairmore's passport showing booking connections to Greece. Creps sat back in his chair, "What is this shit? My God, what are you saying?"

Sims sat up and leaned in, "I want you to think back to the attack on the compound and our debriefing; we saw some weird things we could not explain.

"Now that we are all back there, let me explain. Taking into account all the testimony we have from the weird-ass people around the compound, and what we have seen and heard today, I have to believe this Stavros person is a master of transference; he uses or inhabits people's bodies to do his bidding and get around undetected.

Dunn and Creps started to react. Sims held up his hands, "Remember John vaporized Semjaza when he blew up the compound; Semjaza left him a phone message that night. During the standoff, Semjaza spoke of needing different bodies for different occasions. We all thought that was bull, but now we are looking right at it."

Corwin looked right at General Rouse, "I cut the Druid's head completely off, yet he shows up again on Jackson Street. I probably killed some farmer as he watched from the ceiling. That is how he does it. I think this Semjaza and Stavros are the same types of thing and one of them is the Druid. Either way, it has been playing this game for a long, long time."

Chapter Thirty-Three

2:45 pm
Lil' Pine Cabin
Jonesborough, TN

John finished his call with Nick, went through the kitchen, and on to the back patio. He walked around the drone while carefully reading the operations spec Trish had been studying. He was impressed with how lethal it could be in the hands of a ruthless operator. He smiled; Trish Baltran was the perfect pilot.

John called Hoss and asked what frequency he was using to speak with Phu and wrote it down. He told Hoss he was going to have Trish find them during the scan and invite them in for a drink. Hoss laughed and said he would call and tell them not to shoot her ass out of the sky.

John turned to see Molly leading all three women out to the patio, they all had beers; Kat had two. They all sat on the sectional that curved right to left on the left side of the patio. There was an Adirondack style lounging chair off to the right at the beginning of the sectional. Jess motioned to the chair; he too thought it was time.

He moved the chair closer to Kat. Molly had squeezed in between Jess and Kat. Kat handed him a beer. He raised his bottle, "To Makayla." They raised their bottles and repeated his toast and all were quiet. Jess leaned forward, "John, where are we? What do you know?"

John took another drink, then set his elbows on his knees and began, "Right now Sims, that O'Caheil guy, Rouse, Dunn, and Creps are somewhere under the mountains at the Greenbrier Resort. They are talking with Glenn and Nick trying to sort out who is responsible.

"It turns out that regardless of what else they find, they have found a spy within the NSA. This spy has been feeding information about our operation to one of the richest men on the planet.

"What Glenn is really doing is tracking everyone who was involved in the murder; he has it down to about six or seven individuals. I…I mean we are waiting for a location for those who have stayed behind. We have to eliminate or capture them before they take the next step against us. Kat almost in a whisper, "Don't you mean against you."

John now very self-conscious, "That is what everyone believes, but I think there is more to it. I feel, as does Nick, that they know if they killed me, in the ensuing chaos the NSA guy could award them contracts that would make them our vendors; another step closer to finding Jess' work. This rich guy will have a name by the end of the day and we will know the extent of his reach."

Trish sitting back relaxed, "If we start our scans and sniper hunt now, we can be ready for what the night brings. This will give us the best opportunity to work in all stages of light and see how the visuals perform. We should be done about an hour after it gets dark."

Jess was not done, "John how do you explain what went down with Kat and Makayla; what went on last night?" John was quiet, they could see him looking inside of himself wondering how to say it, "I was a mess when I got to Sims'. I had some beers and passed out for a few hours. Later I was down in my private lab when I got a call from Semjaza."

Kat's eyes were filled with fear and Jess and Trish were now sitting on the edge of the sectional. John looked up at the patio cover, "I had thought it was him when I heard about Kat. His voice was different, so I didn't believe it was him, then he reminded me I blew him up and he had to find a new body." Trish said something in Spanish and Jess felt the same fear she had during the shootout on Boones Creek Road.

John started again, "He convinced me that he was on our side of this new threat and wanted to discuss what he knew; but I would have to go to his place. When Barlow and I got there Semjaza was not there, but we were led to Molly and Kat.

"I still haven't sat down with Semjaza, but seeing Kat and Molly stopped everything for me. Hoss has given me some information but I need to know a lot more.

"The trial runs you guys are going to do now are extremely important. I have started some planning based on what I think is going on, but all I know is that this rich guy is not a normal person. I really believe Semjaza is going to tell me that this guy is like him; whatever in hell that is."

Jess really freaked now, "John you can't tell us this little bit and leave it at that. If Trish, Kat and I go after these guys tonight, we have to know what you are thinking. Anything weird or special we don't recognize could get Trish killed."

John stood up and walked back to the drone, then pulled out the battle suit and put it over a chair. He started shaking his head, "You are going to think I am crazy." Trish cut in, "Too late, crazy was creatures, tornadoes, millions of screaming whatevers, and beasts blasted all over the compound. Crazy is the new normal. Let's have it"

John was stunned, and then he started smiling, "Shit, since you put it that way." He walked into the kitchen and came back with another round of beers and chew stick for Molly.

Sitting back down, "I do believe that Semjaza and this new bad boy are somehow related to one another in some historic way. I believe that they both can do things none of us can grasp."

John scooted his chair so he was right in the middle of the ladies, "I figure that at Jakes, Semjaza, or one of his men, had taken over one of the kidnappers, grabbed Kat and moved her to safety. He put the two purses together in the car that had Makayla to cause confusion. I don't think Semjaza knew this asshole was hell-bent on murder.

"I am guessing that Semjaza figured the investigation would prove it wasn't Kat and news of that would cause these guys to come after us some other way. He stole all the evidence leading them to believe their plan was working. That would buy us valuable time to respond, and that is what we are doing.

"I think when Glenn and the boys are done we will have a plan to snatch the NSA guy and he will give us the location of the devil boys who were left to monitor us.

Kat looked at Molly, "So why did he take Molly?" John teared up, "A show of good faith. She was going to die or maybe she had died. He did for her what he did for me; he brought her back to life. He has now saved me, my wife and Molly." Trish and Jess turned and looked at Kat, "Wife?"

Kat smiled, "Let's get the drone and suit ready for Trish, and I will fill you in. John does not like me telling the story of his proposal.

Chapter Thirty-Four

3:23 pm
Hart Compound to Greenbrier Resort
Jonesborough, TN
Sulfur Springs, VA

Jack Rouse had locked eyes with Sims and was searching for the right words, "This is really out there Sims. This Stavros is using Clairmore's body for his Stavros business, and then hijacks some innocent person to use for his murders. On top of that, he has a logistic team that makes sure his Clairmore's body is ready and waiting for him when he dumps the hijacked body. This is what you are selling?"

Sims didn't blink but turned his gaze to Jackson Dunn, then back to Rouse, "That is what is happening. I am guessing Clairmore is well paid or a prisoner. Now think back to your debriefing after the events at the compound. The most used phrase concerning the creatures or materials in question was, "Not from around here", was it not?

Rouse sat back and looked at the monitors, "Corwin, what do you think?" Corwin leaned forward and took a second to look at each of them, "I say we snatch up this NSA traitor and have a chat. We must do it so absolutely no one will know where we have taken him.

"I am betting that this guy can tell us what we need to know." Glenn chimed in from the compound, "Jack should I tell Sims and Corwin who he is?" Rouse looked at Creps and Dunn; they nodded, "Ok Glenn let him have it," Sims, "The tag is one of the Deputy Directors of the D.C. NSA; the honorable George Browning."

Sims winked at Corwin, "Honorable my ass. Let us take him somewhere and introduce him to Lieutenant Phu Nguyen. We will need a copy of the evidence Glenn has put on the monitors so he understands we understand."

Sims looked at Rouse, "Glenn where is that bastard right now?" Rouse was huddling with Creps and Dunn discussing how much of a sling their asses would be in if this operation went sideways.

Glenn with a bit of fear and urgency in his voice, "He just checked into the Holiday Inn in Johnson City. That is not a good sign." Corwin laughed, "Bullshit, the fish just jumped into the boat."

Rouse stood up, "Glenn, find me Stavros and Clairmore right now." Glenn sounded a bit panicked, "What, why…oh shit, what if?" Rouse cut him off, "Now Glenn, now."

Everything went quiet. Creps had not been in action with the group before and he was focused on the monitors. Then he leaned forward and calmly, "Glenn, it is important that we know where every tag in Tennessee is quick."

Glenn gathering himself, "Ok, I am starting over to include all the info in one report." Nick was heard in the background, "Hope they all are hanging out listening to Ozzie while chomping deep-fried pigeon heads." Creps cut in, "I heard that Ozzie found Jesus." Glenn coughed, "Yup, and I am Tiger Woods." Got it!"

Glenn was struggling with where to start, "Ok, here is how the info came out. Clairmore is on a flight from Greece to New York, with a connecting flight into Knoxville. Stavros' private jet is in New York on a layover. He has submitted a flight plan to Chicago, and onto Tri-Cities airport in Blountville.

"We know that Director Browning checked into the Holiday Inn and is not moving; probably in his room. Finally, as Nick had hoped, there are five tags in what I am guessing is a cabin off Bill Bennett Road, just northeast of Johnson City.

Sims to Glenn, "Can you put that up on a map for us and put a tracking alarm on the five tags to alert us if they start moving?"
Glenn, "Yup, I can get that done; here is your map." Nick in the background, "I wonder if it will sound off if they move, or will one of them have to buy a winky cozy?"

Sims lowered his head trying to control his laughter. He looked up to see the rest of his group looking at him. Sims a bit red-faced, "I swear you do not want to know."

Rouse with a knowing smile, "Gentlemen we have five bad guys playing swap the cozy, and a spy in a hotel room right in our back yard. We know Stavros has already picked up his new body because Clairmore is in the air. Anyone have a plan to take down these guys without alerting Stavros and rest of his underworld?"

Nick cut in, "Jess Williams and John are creating a plan for just this type of thing. She has some new toys she brought with her from Canada. Let's get them on the line and see where they are."

Chapter Thirty-Five

4:00 pm
Lil' Pine Cabin
Jonesborough, TN

John watched the ladies huddle together as they walked toward the pile of technology on the far side of the patio. He saw Kat mimic her elbow punch followed by a hand snatch. Then she pulled her ring out of her pants pocket and put it on. They all turned and looked in his direction. He shrugged his shoulders as they laughed at his expense, and then gave him two thumbs up on the ring.

John took that as his cue to take Molly outside for a walk. As he watched Molly sprint around in the front, sniffing all the small trees, his phone went off.

He found a chair on the porch where he could watch Molly then answered, "General Rouse how can I help you." Rouse quite grumpy, "There is so much weird shit happening all over your neighborhood I am going act as if it's normal.

"We have found five of the sons of satan hold up in a cabin below Johnson City. We have identified our NSA traitor, who is now relaxing at the Holiday Inn in Johnson City. Also of note, their fearless leader, one Andreas Stavros, is flying into Tri-Cities airport tonight. I hear you are working on a plan for just this occurrence."

John leaned into the chair looking back toward where Jess was working, "We have some new equipment we are testing. It should allow us to get right on top of these guys. We will be able to take them out without making any noise."

Sims chimed in, "Is the suit going for the ride?" John cleared his throat, "Yes, we want to deal with them up close." Rouse said, "We have their location, we are sending it to you now, what do you have in mind?"

John was quiet for a short time, "What is the rest of the situation?" Rouse and Sims told John about Stavros and that they expected him to land around 9:00 pm at Tri-Cities. John whistled and Molly returned from the front gate area, "So do we want to wait for Stavros or do we want to leave him waiting at the airport with no one left to pick him up?"

Rouse responded, "Leave him waiting, tag him again and follow him. Do we think he would recognize Barlow?" Corwin interrupted, "Look Barlow is the Sheriff, not an operative. If we put Hoss' boys on him, they could track him anywhere and watch their own back at the same time."

Sims summing up, "So I think this is what we are thinking, Jess' team takes out the boys in Johnson City as soon as they can. Corwin and I will have Mitchell bring us back to Jonesborough; we are Team 2. We capture Browning and take him to a safe place. That leaves Hoss' team three to follow Stavros…problems?"

Corwin leaned in, "Glenn do you have a way to isolate Stavros when he shows up as someone else?" Glenn nodding, "Well, let me work on an idea and I will get back in a few minutes. Go on with the others."

Creps was shaking his head, "How do we take Browning without hurting civilians?" Sims looked at Corwin, Corwin nodded, "We will knock or pick the lock, depending on our exposure, then drug him with a dart, and walk him into the van. If we catch him in the open, we snatch him then disappear. Glenn, is his room on the ground level?" Glenn sounding distracted, "Yup, I mean yes, he is on the ground floor. I have a way to identify Stavros."

Nick talking to Glenn, "That is pretty cool I must say." Glenn said, "Look at your middle screen; you will see a green circle tagging the person. This is number two of my top ten on the murder squad. I have never seen his face or even got a shot at facial recognition; I use gate tracking within the software to identify this guy."

Jackson Dunn smiled, "You got that from the NSA didn't you?" Glenn a bit sheepish, "Yes, but their version won't hold up in a court of law, not that I would ever release my version."

General Rouse, "Are you talking about the way the guy walks?" Glenn replied, "Yes, we all have different patterns to the way we walk, from our footfalls, the pace, to various other indicators; it's as good as fingerprints."

Rouse shaking his head, "So what took you so long to figure out if we could use this on Stavros?" They could feel Glenn grinning, "Well, we just found out about Stavros, or should I say Clairmore;

they won't have the same exact gate unless Stavros is using Clairmore. On top of that, I was able to match Stavros' gate to our sample. I had video of three of those who disappeared, or were murdered; they all walked just like Stavros. We can find his ass as long as we know where he is going.

Creps doubtful, "First of all, how can all of those people have the same gate? They are different heights and their stride will vary." Glenn pointed out, "That is why we use their gate, not their stride length. Gate is mental, sub-conscious. It is built into us over the years; it's a biorhythm. The canter is what makes the gate."

Rouse back on track, "John what do you need?" John hesitantly, "I could use Adam as a backup for Trish. When she goes in after these guys, he would be on the ground trailing her. He will cover anything unexpected that might come in to cut her off once she hits the ground."

Rouse agreed, "Good idea, I will have Hoss join Lil' Joe on surveillance. They can run a two-vehicle tail." Sims looking at Rouse, "Then we know what we have to do. John and I will coordinate our team's actions so that Browning cannot contact any of the tags.

"Hoss' team will be paced by Stavros' actions once he is on the ground. Glenn, make sure you can pick him up on the airport cameras." Glenn, "Will do boss."

"Sims added, "Also, make sure we have all three teams in real-time on our monitors, and we can all talk; coms for everyone."

John's voice, "I will contact Phu and the boys and get them on board. I will want them to clear the property once more and take time for some food."

Sergeant Mitchell arrived, gathered up Sims and Corwin, and was airborne heading back to Jonesborough a few minutes later.

Chapter Thirty-Six

5:30 pm
Team 1
Lil' Pine Cabin
Jonesborough, TN

John and Molly were in the front yard greeting Phu and the boys. They were in full gear having just returned from clearing the property. While John was filling them in on the new operations, he kept glancing up and behind the boys.

Adam noticed Molly was sitting at attention looking up as well. Adam finally turned and looked. A hundred feet above them was a large drone. Beneath it was a robotic looking figure sitting in a harness. The pilot reached above their head and seemed to push some buttons. Adam jumped back while looking at his chest, and then pointed to the others, they all had been Lazar tagged.

John looked up, "Now Trish, let's not make our guest uncomfortable." Trish brought the drone down to ten feet, flew around the group twice, and then shot straight up. She was above the trees and out of sight in a matter of seconds. Molly attempted to chase the drone, but could only bark her approval as Trish disappeared.

Phu looked at John, "Wow, that thing is scary quiet." John smiled, "She watched you guys sweep the site from five hundred feet." Adam, "She saw us do that from up there?" John shook his head, "She said she couldn't see you at all, but infra-red never lies."

John invited the boys into the house to eat and to finish going over the plans for the cabin by Johnson City. He intentionally decided not to tell them about finding Kat. He wanted their reaction to be natural. Sammy's diner had delivered a spread and when they came into the kitchen, Kat was placing the beers into the ice chest on the counter.

Lil' Joe was the first to enter, he froze in mid-step and the others stacked up behind him. Kat looked up and began to cry. Phu pushed through, set down his weapon and put his arm around her, "God, it's great to see you. I can't imagine, so sorry for your loss." The others looked at John; he nodded toward Kat, "Now you know why we needed you guys here."

Kat composed herself, "Thank you guys for working so hard to help find us. I just learned what had happened a few hours ago, but I am ready to work. We have to get the bastards who took Makayla from us. Trish and I will be testing the drone and battle suit until we get enough data and Trish gets up to speed on the drone. John will fill you in on the rest. I have to go help Jess, as you know Trish is airborne."

As Kat left, John told the guys to make a plate, grab a beer or two and join him downstairs. They all looked at each other puzzled. They all had been to John's house several times after John and Kat moved in, but he had never mentioned a lower floor.

They piled food on plates and balanced drinks. Lil' Joe made sure each of them had brought extra for Molly. It was a strange sight to see three Special Forces legends following Molly. She led them to the guestroom, which was her room. Molly went into the back closet, sat in front of the black panel, placed her paw on the glass and the doors opened inward; she headed down the steps.

Chapter Thirty-Seven

6:05 pm
Team 2
Hart Compound
Jonesborough, TN

Hoss was waiting when Sims and Corwin arrived at the compound. Rouse had already briefed Hoss and his crew would act as the backup for all three operations.

Hoss had them gather in John's private lab beneath lab 1. Corwin had never been to the Hart Compound before. He was impressed by its amenities.

As they began to work, Hoss put up the maps and all the logistical info for the Holiday Inn on the monitors. Nick, Glenn, and Dom were napping.

Sims and Corwin focused on Browning's room location, escape routes and possible hides. Hoss pointed to the alley behind the Inn. It had three entry points.

There was an entry at each side of the Inn, and lastly, an alley from the strip mall behind the Holiday Inn. The strip mall and the inn were back to back, the alley created a T-intersection.

Sims groaned, "Wow, you thinking we should cover each of those angles?" Hoss replied, "It's the only way to be sure you aren't cut off from them or blindsided." Corwin nodding, "We should have some people there now to scout and set up firing lines to defend each egress. When it is fully dark, and lights come on around the area, it will all change"

Hoss looked at Sims. Sims nodded, "Set it up." Sims noticed that Hoss had one of the groups special phones, "Hoss, you know how to use that thing?" Hoss self-conscious, "John gave me lessons at the Coffee Hole, and I practice with Phu and the boys."

Sims laughed, "Shit, I am surprised Molly doesn't have one. Hoss grinning, "John is working on voice recognition commands for Molly so she can open doors. He doesn't want her to get trapped like last time." Corwin shook his head, "A lot of trouble to go through for a dog." Hoss more serious, "That dog is a weapon and family." Corwin raised his hands in surrender.

Hoss contacted Lieutenant Colonel Jimmy Gantry. He talked to him for a few minutes setting up manpower and the rules of engagement. Jimmy looked at the images of the Holiday Inn and knew what must be done. Hoss finished the call and turned back to Sims and Corwin.

Sims looked at Hoss, "How many ex-military are there here?" Hoss making motions like he was counting in his mind, "Let's see... just about all of them. They all work for Rouse, in other words, they all work for me.

"That said, we need to keep this from John as long as we can; the whole town was created to monitor and protect you guys and the compound."

Sims smiling, "Well shit, I thought that everybody really liked me. They are just doing their jobs? That is kind of a bummer." Hoss shaking his head, "Some people really like you. However, most of them haven't spent that much time around you, so that could change. Speaking of which, you and Kill-heel need to get dressed for work."

Glenn, barely awake, appeared on one of the monitors, "Browning just ordered take out, the delivery guy will be to his room in forty minutes. What do you think, a great time to hit him? We could redirect the delivery guy and take him when he opens up to take his food."

Sims and Corwin looked at all the information. Sims turned and looked at Glenn, "You look like shit. We know the restaurant and how long it takes to get there; so you know the route?" Glenn yawning, "Yes we researched that through the desk at the Holiday Inn."

Corwin was thinking, "Hey, could we get Sheriff Barlow to pull the delivery guy over just after he leaves?" That wouldn't alert anyone who might be watching Browning." Glenn responded, "Barlow is awake. I had to give him an idea of what was going down tonight. I didn't want him or his deputies rolling up on trouble they couldn't deal with."

Sims stood thinking for a second or two, "All right, let's go with this. I need the armored SUV by lab 1, add Taser holsters to go with the tranquilizer gun. I want him to drop like a rock."

Corwin turned to Hoss, "Cover our asses, big guy. This could get nuts if he has security laying back." Hoss moved closer to Corwin, "Let Sims take him, you cover his backside and then carry Browning if necessary. Kill-heel may have to show up big time."

Sims was leaving the lab, "Glenn get everyone online. Call John first, have his team help you watch the traffic cams, and get Dom up ready to fly if need be."

He and Corwin came out of the lab and stepped into the silver SUV. Sims drove out of the tunnel, past the back gate at the end of the gun range and headed for Johnson City.

Corwin took out his phone and punched in about fifteen numbers, after a few seconds he was on the line with General Rouse. Corwin put it on speaker, "Jack, you there?" Rouse came back, "Got you Kill-heel, we are up to date, what can we do for you?" Corwin said, "I was hoping you could warn the authorities in Johnson City about the operation. I don't want untrained police trying to do the right thing if Stavros has Browning under surveillance."

Rouse was contemplating, "I can tell them to stay out of the area, say one-mile radius." Sims asked, "Jack, is there time to get Mitchell up high, in case Stavros succeeds at grabbing him and running?"

Rouse snickered, "I have put Mitchell in a baby Bell Copter in a Local News' flight pattern. He is packing a single missile and a good camera pack."

Corwin continued with Rouse, "We are twenty minutes out. Browning is expecting his food in twenty-five minutes. Hoss' team should be set up to cover the alleys in about seventeen minutes. Hope we don't draw the wrong kind of attention. Thanks, Jack, keep an eye out for something weird; you know who this guy works for."

Chapter Thirty-Eight

6:15 pm
Team One
Lil' Pine Cabin
Jonesborough, TN

As Phu, Adam and Lil' Joe reached the bottom of the steps they stopped and allowed their eyes to adjust. The room looked like a larger version of the shooting stations from the gun range. Computers and wall monitors were the only sources of light.

They noticed that Jess and Kat were using the right-hand side of a large curved control console, which dominated the front of the room. There were couches, small tables, and chairs near the entry, and there was floor to ceiling cabinets on both sides of the room.

Phu set down his food as Molly sat right in front of him, using her most polite posture. Phu tossed her some roast beef and she made sure it didn't hit the carpet. She decided to seek further gifts from Adam and Lil' Joe.

Phu looked over at Jess and Kat. They were watching the live feed from Trish's POV and the drones other cameras. He placed a beer in one hand, a sandwich in his mouth, and a bowl of chips in his other hand as he worked his way to where the girls were working. He set down the chips as if to say, *have some* when Jess turned and smiled, "Not on the console cave boy." Phu tried to match her gaze as if to say, *who you calling cave boy*, but thought better of it and retreated. He set his plate on a chair further back.

Kat had set up a series of targets in various locations, so Trish could test her ability to engage several targets while maneuvering at high speed. Phu watched as Trish began her run.

Phu noticed that three targets were lit at the same time. It appeared that the drone was programmed to take them out. It was eerie to watch the night vision images.

The drone was deadly accurate and moved like a water bug in midair; pretty scary stuff. Phu turned to tell Adam and Lil' Joe to check it out, but they were already standing behind him with their mouths hanging open. Adam whispered, "So glad they are working for us." Both Phu and Adam were nodding.

Trish's voice came over the com, "Holy shit that was like bronco riding, but once I relaxed and just let it work, I was fine. I am going to run it again free stick; see what I can do."

Kat responded, "Ok fly girl, you have to beat 36 seconds, and not miss a damn thing." Trish started laughing, "Yes, my lady of the ring." John choked on his coffee.

Trish activated the harness' handlebars above her head. She switched to the manual controls, which were in the handle grips; like a motorcycle.

Trish lined up the drone and started her run. She matched up to the speed of the first run and took out the first target. Her transition to the second target was a little ragged but she nailed the target.

Trish deviated from the original run path and laid herself out at 90 degrees as she tightened the turn into target number three. She fired as the drone righted itself.

The target exploded and the drone went through the wash that followed. Trish felt the impact of the wave and had to fight like hell to keep the drone from diving into the trees.

Jess swallowed hard, "Trish, this is the only one of these on the planet. So, you know…how about not destroying it? Trish shouting, "What was my time…oh, sorry, Jess. Kat, what was my time?" Kat being sarcastic, "Don't get so excited. You only beat the machine by three seconds." Trish sounding contrite, "Sorry My Lady."

John and the rest of the boys were nodding and shaking their heads. Molly used the distraction to clean out all the roast beef in the room.

Glenn's face appeared on all of the monitors, "Team two is approaching the Holiday Inn to take down Browning. Sorry, we didn't loop you in earlier, but we were monitoring your test. Browning ordered take out and we are using this as our in.

Barlow will divert the delivery guy. Sims and Corwin will knock and take him when he answers. Glenn put all the video feeds up on John's screens. Because it was nighttime all of the surveillance looked like an episode of COPS.

John looking at all of the feeds, "Are we coming in from the alley or from the street?" Glenn, "We will be using the main driveway and will continue straight to Browning's room, which I will flag now. A pale green glow lit up room number 112.

Glenn intense, "Here we go people."

Chapter Thirty-Nine

6:55 pm
Team Two
Holiday Inn
Jonesborough, TN

Sims had driven by the Inn to scan the area. He wanted to enter from the east so the front of the SUV would be facing Browning's room. As Sims was turning around, "Jimmy, how does it look back there?" Jimmy came back, "Too dark. Can we check satellite files to see how this place normally looks at this time?" John's voice, "We will take that Glenn, you stay on the SUV."

Hoss asked, "Jimmy, have you thought about how we can keep the SUV out of a crossfire if they come that way?" Jimmy, "They would have to have shooters on the rooftops; they are only ten feet up. The bad guys would have to drive through our lines of fire to block the two entrances. So, they would be dead in their cars blocking the road. I don't see any problems unless they come from above." John's voice, "Jimmy, you are looking at normal."

Sims turned into the driveway and proceeded slowly toward room 112. Corwin reached down and picked up his Israeli prototype machine gun. It was compact, spit out rounds in a hurry and could be used with a scope; deadly within seven hundred yards. They were approaching room 112's parking spaces.

Corwin looked at Sims. Sims looked at the weapon, "Sure that's not too much gun for you?"

Corwin's eyes lit up, "It's been way too much gun for several people this week, but I'm cool with it."

Sims parked two spaces to the right of the room, creating a bad sightline from the room's windows. Sims left the SUV running, "Glenn how do we look far and wide?" Glenn answered, "We have the delivery guy, and I see nothing all around." Corwin looking around, "Jimmy what have you got?" Jimmy looking up, "We got empty roofs and no movement."

Sims got out of the SUV, opened the rear side door and retrieved a cardboard box filled with lunch bags; it looked like a take-out order. Sims was wearing a pair of jeans and a sweatshirt. He had his Taser in the small of his back with the sweatshirt pulled down. Corwin would leave the car and trail Sims. He was wearing a dark gray suit to hide his weapon.

Sims casually walked up and knocked on the door. Corwin exited the SUV. Browning opened the door. Sims led with a head butt, to Browning's nose. He rammed his way in and followed with the Taser.

Stavros sat straight up, his red eyes flashing with anger. He could see Sims' face in his mind. He saw Browning on the ground. He stood up in a rage pushing his head against the ceiling of his private Jet. He yelled to the pilot, "Land in Knoxville instead of Tri-Cities." He would send Rameel.

Corwin was inside at the window watching the street and parking lot. Corwin looked at Browning. Sims was just letting off the Taser. Sims found the proper lunch bag, pulled out a funny looking air gun. He shot Browning in the leg with a tranquilizer dart.

Corwin still looking outside, "Glenn, talk to me. Jimmy, what have you got?" Both answered all clear. They got Browning up and on the bed. Corwin took hold of Browning while Sims brought the SUV parallel to room 112.

Corwin thought this was when he would attack. Kill the kidnappers and Browning; win the lotto. Corwin opened to door, rushed Browning onto the rear seat and then jumped on top of him; Sims was moving.

Sims was about to pull on to the main street when he heard Jimmy in his ear, "Bogey, bogey come to the back now, repeat now." Glenn was late to the party, "Late model Black Cadillac SUV coming at you, turn right, right, right."

Sims almost overshot the alley. He just missed the brick sidewall, and then accelerated down the alley. As he came around to the back of the Inn, he saw Jimmy waving for him to turn into the midway alley and back out to the street via the strip mall. Sims just caught that turn as well.

Corwin was up and looking out the back, he saw Jimmy pull his weapon and level it at the oncoming SUV. He heard several rounds fired from multiple directions, then quiet.

Sims hit a dip going about 55mph and that brought Corwin back to looking toward the front, "There is no longer an SUV bothering us. Jimmy and the boys took care of that."

Sims was looking back, "Well then, that just leaves us and Sergeant Mitchell." Mitchell's voice came online, "Nice driving Sims, did you learn those moves playing bumper cars?" Sims smiling, "Ah Mister Mitch, heard you had to requalify to fly that dreidel you're in."

Mitch laughed aloud, "Yeah, I know. I pulled the string on this thing as hard as I could, but I don't how long I can keep up. Sims, "I am just hearing from Rouse, that the SUV Jimmy stopped in the alley was NSA. They had assigned a detail to keep an eye on Browning. Jimmy and the boys shot out their tires and then made them explain their actions.

Sergeant Mitchell followed the SUV around the outskirts of Johnson City then back west toward Jonesborough. The SUV went under an overpass that paralleled raised train tracks. Mitch lost sight of them. He climbed higher and circled but they never reappeared.

Mitchell was confused and worried, "Glenn, the SUV didn't come out of the underpass. I have circled twice. I have lost them." Glenn let out a long sigh, "I guess that was part of Corwin's plan. He didn't want anyone but he and Sims to know where they were going."

Chapter Forty

Day Three
7:15 pm
Team One
Lil' Pine Cabin
Jonesborough, TN

Everyone except Adam was huddled around John; Molly was in the middle. Trish was suited up and ready. They were talking through their operation step-by-step. On the Team Two monitor, Sims and Corwin had just cleared the alley and were heading east, working their way back to Jonesborough.

Jess looked at the big map on the Team One monitor. It showed a blinking red dot where the cabin was located. Circles indicating distances were radiating out from the location. She looked at Trish, "Call signs only once we start."

She turned to John, "We should scout it first, then figure the best way go about eliminating them without a ripple. John, looked at Trish, "Program the route via the Spring Street transition, to Mill Springs Road and on to Johnson City. Then we pick up Bill Bennet Road, and creep straight line east until we are within a mile of the cabin." Trish left and sat next to Kat while they updated the drone's navigation system.

Adam rejoined the group. Everyone turned to look at him, he was wearing Jess' new sniper-surveillance suit. It looked like the battle suit but sleeker and lighter.

Adam modeling the suit, turned around and did a runway pose, "Like my new suit? It is a JessSay." Jess walked around Adam looking at every detail.

Jess lifted up Adams left wrist, "Get familiar with your control panel. You want to be on stealth mode which will make sure you stay at ambient temperature so thermal imaging won't pick you up. In addition, it will deflect or absorb all Forward-Looking Infra-Red (FLIR) or Doppler radar.

"The suit will stop cutting weapons and most bullets. If you are shot, you are going down and you will need help."

John looked at Jess, "It is 7:15 pm, it's all you now Jess." John looked at Kat, "Time to put things right. Like Jess said, remember slow and easy is how we go without causing even a ripple." As John was leaving, Jess took him aside and handed him what looked like a two-inch by two-inch monitor on a stick, "What is this?" John said, holding it up in front of his face.

Jess took it by the stick and unfolded the device. As she did, it began to look like the right-hand side of a pair of granny glasses, "This is your monocle. Just put it on and press this, and you are on the network; powerful and wireless." John put it in his jacket pocket and headed out.

John and Adam climbed into John's Polaris and they headed for Jonesborough. Trish was airborne and trailed them from three hundred feet. Jess was cruising at thirty-five miles an hour. The estimated time to Bill Bennett Road was fifteen minutes.

There was no moon, so Trish, call sign Tbal, felt safe in the darkness. She could see all the beacons lighting up the high wires and towers that protruded into the night. She could see several aircraft in the pattern coming from Knoxville to Tri-Cities.

Trish was coming over Jonesborough and she had to find Spring Street before the drone turned in that direction. As she found it, the drone started the turn to follow Spring Street and onto Mill Springs Road. She smiled, "Tbal to Croft, just lined up with marker one." "This is Croft, copy." She felt she would learn faster if she competed with the drone.

She increased her speed to forty mph and aligned the drone with John and Adam, "Elrond, this is Tbal, at your twelve o'clock." "Tbal, this is Elrond, copy. Sync at forty."

Adam turned to John, "Are we all going to be checked out on the drone. John looked over at him, "Jealous?" Adam nodding, "Oh yeah."

John grinned at Adam, "You know Hoss ain't going anywhere near that thing. Could you imagine him in the suit? Adam's eyes got wide with surprise then started laughing uncontrollably. John continued, "He is six foot six two hundred and ninety pounds, it would take a flying saucer to get his ass in the air." Adam started choking he was laughing so hard. He managed a deep breath, "Oh my God, please shut up."

As Trish was approaching the south end of Johnson City, the drone started its descent. She projected the night vision as far as she could. Finally, she saw the tree line where Bill Bennett Road would be. She was thinking now the drone should swing way south and come around to get a straight-line approach to the cabin. It was a mile and a half west of the road. The drone started to respond.

Trish was right again. She started to smile when everything went black, not dark, but black. She couldn't even see the instruments. She was turning her head left to right when the drone was hit by a wave of air that slammed it back left and down. Trish reached one hand up and could feel the controls. She was about to switch to manual when everything went back to normal.

Trish started yelling, "Croft this is Tbal, did you see that?" "Tbal this is Croft, there was a skip in transmission but we didn't lose you."

Trish trying to think, "Croft, I was just hit by a huge gust. Maybe I flew through something. Everything went black, and I mean black. I could not see the drone or my own hands. Then I felt a blast of air, like a jet wash that knocked the drone down and to the left." "Tbal, this is Croft, we do see and zigzag in your track. We show no traffic near you at all."

Adam's voice broke in, "Tbal, this is Eve, look at the horizon where you think it was going. Is there anything that interrupts the stars, a hole or block covering a section?" John looking at Adam, "Not this shit again." Adam shook his head, "No, this is different shit."

Trish was confused but did what she was told. She was scanning when the drone came into alignment with the cabin. On the horizon, she saw what looked like a blanket covering a portion of the stars on the horizon. It seemed to be two miles out.

It twisted and moved in a rhythm. The fabric went up and then dove below the horizon where the cabin was and didn't come back up. Trish freaked out, "Holy shit, Eve. I saw it. It was like a flying blanket of absolute black. I think it landed at the cabin."

Jess had her head in her hands looking down at the carpet, "Eve this is Croft, is this what you couldn't explain about your encounter in the forest?" "Croft, this is Eve, roger that."

Jess looked up at the screen, "Elrond, proceed to Eve's drop off. Tbal, join Elrond and Eve. Elrond, think about this. Keep in mind the story you told us on the patio. Come back to me with a plan." "Croft this Elrond…copy."

Chapter Forty-One

8:09 pm
Hart Compound to Greenbrier Resort
Jonesborough, TN
Sulfur Springs, VA

General Rouse was not happy with what he was hearing. They had started with a clear operational plan and now things were starting to slip away.

Corwin and Sims had told Rouse he would be the only one they would tell where the safe house was; they lied. Sergeant Mitchell was still in the air looking for anything that would give them a lead. He, Creps and Dunn needed to question Browning.

Now Team One was stalled because some spooky shit had just happened. He started in on Glenn, "Glenn what the hell is with the flying hole in the stars shit? What are you guys thinking?"

Jess was listening in. She wondered how much Glenn knew of what John had told them earlier. Glenn kept it simple, "General, nobody knows what Semjaza or Stavros is when they are not in someone's body. We need to know if what just happened with Tbal and the drone was caused by Stavros arriving at the cabin. Does he already know somehow that we have Browning? The final part of this goes to the point of what happened with Semjaza at the compound."

Rouse and the others were confused, "What the hell are you talking about Glenn?" Dunn yelled. Jess broke in on their conversation, "John blew the shit out of him at the compound. He was standing at the front door when it blew. John has spoken to Semjaza two times this week."

From the back of lab 3, Nick yelled, "Jess that is far enough. Stay on track." Jess was frustrated, they needed to know that Semjaza had saved Kat and probably had Makayla's remains.

She couldn't let it go, "Nick damn it, enough is enough. It is too dangerous to move on without having all the information. John told me he left it up to you; now step up. John, Adam and Trish might come face to face with…" Jess stopped and almost growled in frustration.

General Rouse stood up leaned into the conference phone and yelled, "I am done playing games with you people. You started all this shit and I am here to help you figure it out. However, I am telling you right now, if someone doesn't start talking I am going to take the whole thing out of your hands, and take my wrecking ball to the whole damn thing. Am I clear?"

There was an uncomfortable silence. Nick moved next to Glenn, they looked at each other and then Glenn said, "We got to finish this before we lose the advantage of moving fast."

Nick was pissed off, "Semjaza has been helping us with our efforts to find Kat and Makayla. He somehow knew that Stavros' men were trying to kill or destroy John and he intervened. He was able to steal Kat away, but he couldn't get Makayla. He made sure Stavros got both purses.

"Later that night he stole Makayla's remains, took Molly from the vet and put the night shift intern in the truck to keep him from seeing what was going down with Molly.

"Once Semjaza knew Stavros had left the area, he had Sheriff Barlow bring John to his house over by Erwin. They were supposed to meet, instead, they were led to Kat and Molly. Kat is alive and working with Team Two."

General Rouse had returned to his seat but was still lost, "I am glad Kat is alive, but what does that have to do with what is happening?"

Jess interrupted, "General, Semjaza, and Stavros may be enemies from way back in the day. John believes they can move about unfettered without using bodies, and we cannot see them unless they want us to.

Semjaza controlled Barlow the whole time he was driving John to his house. Barlow thought he was hearing the directions from John. So think about it General, if stringing up Makayla the way Stavros did was his idea of a good time, what do you think he might be able to do to our team if we surprise him at the cabin?

Rouse looked at Creps and Dunn, they were both wide-eyed and shaking their heads. Creps leaned forward, "Jack, we don't know shit about Stavros. If he is outside of a body, we have no idea how dangerous he could be. Shit, we can't even kill him.

General Rouse hesitated, he was thinking. He focused on his and Corwin's time hunting the Druid. Gruesome images of how the victims were staged ripped through his mind.

Corwin had contended the whole time that there was more than one killer. He felt no one man was strong enough to put the victims where and how they were displayed. Rouse looked back at Creps, "You're right. It makes sense now, these things fly, they are big and strong. Jess, this is your team. We will follow along in case you need help.

Chapter Forty-Two

8:19 pm
Eve's Drop Off
Bill Bennett Rd
Johnson City, TN

Trish hovered above John and Adam, she was scanning everything around them using all the forms or surveillance the drone had. When she was convinced it was clear, she brought the drone down to eye level and engaged the standby mode then stepped off the drone and joined the boys.

Adam rushed to her, "How big do you think it was? How fast was it going and what the hell was it?" Trish held up her hands deferring to John.

John was leaning against the Polaris, "Jess just filled me in on how General Rouse feels about this. He is upset but seems to understand our dilemma. Trish, "Dilemma? No shit, that thing was alive; it was flying." She turned to Adam, "I think it was about the size of Dom's plane."

Adam got into the back seat of the Polaris leaving the door open, "We need to creep up to the cabin and let the dragonflies do their jobs. Trish moved to the drone, worked on the keypad a bit then turned back, "We are a mile and a half from the cabin as the drone flies.

John used his phone to contact Jess off-line, "Jess, I need a refresher. What is the range of the dragonflies for sending high-resolution video back to the drone?" Jess thought a minute, "If the drone is above the trees and has a good angle in relation to the dragonflies you can get two miles. So, poor resolution out there would require higher and closer, thus improving your image."

Trish stood up and headed for the drone, "I will program the dragonflies then set them loose. We have six; I suggest we use three so we can combine the images to give us 3D telemetry if needed." Adam nodded, "That will give you the ability to target lock and shoot your smaller missiles right thru the windows."

John walked up and put his hands on each of their shoulders, "I think that would cause a few ripples people. Let's see if we can approach without losing our asses, ok. Trish, get up there so we can have a look."

John opened up the network com, "Croft this is Elrond, we have Tbal airborne launching dragonflies; images in a minute."

Trish let the dragonflies go the second she cleared the trees. She triangulated the drone with the cabin to find her best altitude and settled in to track their progress.

She turned on the tracking monitor and could see the dragonfly's point of view. They were working just above the trees, on their way to the cabin.

The dragonflies were smaller drones that looked and flew just like dragonflies. Their micro-technology combined with the mesh, self-charging power system, allowed it to be a powerful weapon.

The drone had imaging via night vision, thermal and chemical analysis. The weapons targeting and missile guidance for the onboard smart weapons used cruise missile type 3D software. Now, if it all worked that would be nice.

Trish was getting impatient; she directed one of the drones to climb well above the trees so she could find the cabin sooner. She flipped on the thermal image option and located the cabin's heat signature. She decided to do the same with the other two dragonflies. Trish heard John in her ear, "Much better Tbal." Trish responded, "Tbal copy."

Trish increased her speed and adjusted the drones to match. As she progressed, Trish slowly climbed to her optimum altitude. When she reached the spot, she settled in and hovered while watching the drones do their job.

Trish could see the cabin clearly without the cameras; she was one hundred and ten yards from the front of the cabin. She moved the dragonflies to three hundred feet above the cabin, and then programmed them to circle so she could get a good look at it.

The first look was with thermal imaging, "Tbal to Elrond, ready for thermal broadcast sending now." Trish activated all three of the little drones and had them hover and slowly rotate around the cabin.

Trish could see five active heat signatures within the cabin. Two were sitting at what looked like a table, two on a couch and one standing facing the front entrance to the cabin.

John smiled, "Croft this is Elrond, it appears the Wizard's (Glenn) tagging system works; we have all five tags in the cabin. Glenn responded, "Elrond, this is Wizard, you are on the network, great job team one."

Trish switched to night vision and brought the dragonflies down to the level of the windows but not near the windows yet. She used the search mode to have them survey the area around the cabin. The area was well kept. General Rouse commented that it looked like brush had recently been cleared.

Following the search protocol, the drones mapped the outside of the cabin and noted all windows, doors, vents and electrical and gas connections. Apparently, there was a butane tank somewhere near the house.

Trish searched again using a chemical vs organic material mode and found a chunk of metal thirty yards from the back of the house. In addition, she found a satellite dish in the front west corner of the clearing. They were online.

John, "Tbal this is Elrond, lets peak in the windows, so we can have the Wizard make us a 3D rendering of the cabin and a set of floor plans. "Elrond this is Tbal, copy." Trish had to be careful to avoid the lighted areas around the windows.

Trish decided to have them hover at a distance and she would zoom in to see best she could. As the drones moved back and forth and up and down everyone could see flashes of the layout and the people inside.

Glenn's voice, "Tbal this is Wizard we have enough; the floor plan is up on the team one's screen. Now let's have a look at these guys one at a time." "Wizard this is Tbal, copy, setting up overwatch now."

Trish sent one of the drones up to one hundred and fifty feet above the cabin in thermal mode. That drone would watch the occupants continuously. "Wizard this is Tbal you should see all." "Tbal, roger that, let's look in the window directly across from the guys on the couch." "Wizard, we are moving now."

It was a scary thing for Trish having to move a dragonfly closer to the window. She kept looking at the thermal image of the two on the couch while she worked the drone into a position so it wouldn't be in their right peripheral vision. When she did so, the images that she got where mostly that one side of their faces; she hoped it would be enough for Glenn's facial recognition software."

Glenn kept urging Trish to get closer and move right to get a better look. General Rouse broke it, "Damn it, Wizard, run the software and see what you get." Glenn not happy went quiet for a few seconds. "Shit, great design Croft, we got them both; on the couch, we have tag six sitting next to tag three on the murder squad list. These two have been in town since the beginning. Let's get a look at the others."

John nudged Adam, "Start your approach, see if you can find a spot to cover the open area and the cabin." Adam nodded and picked up his headgear and started walking toward the cabin on Bill Bennet Road. He stopped turned back to John, "We're still gonna kill'em right?" John smiled, "Before the night is through."

Trish worked the little dragonflies carefully taking her time until they had tag nine and five identified. They were having trouble getting a straight shot of the last guy sitting at the head of the table. He was blocked by furniture, the angle and tag four's head. Finally, tag five turned to talk to one of the guys on the couch, and Trish got a second of video of him face on.

It was completely silent for what seemed like forever. John wanted Adam, "Eve this is Elrond, are you seeing this? What do you think?" Adam slow to speak, "This one is not like the others. Just like the leather goods boy in the forest. If you can filter the camera and run it through the sniper scope settings, on one of them, his eyes should turn red. If they don't, then he is legit; if they turn red we should back up a bit and think about who we are about to deal with. If they are red, then this is the boy that jet washed Trish."

John was flashing back to the siege of the compound. Sims could only see the aberrations when he switched the scope's setting, "Try switching to the starlight setting."

Trish went into the imaging settings and selected filters. She was looking for starlight but was having trouble, then she saw scope settings and found starlight. Trish serious, "I have it selected now I just need to get another look at this guy."

While Trish was working the drone into position, Glenn started talking, "I found this guy in the facial recognition; he is the owner of the Corner Cup, a coffee joint in Jonesborough. Dunn came on, "So we are thinking he is not a devil dude, and right now he is under the control of whomever."

Adam came back, "When we confronted this thing last time it bolted. "Lil' Joe jumped in, "Eve, remember those guys that Phu questioned said that guy was the boss. The boss should bolt. But, what if the boss sent this in his place? This thing may be here to fight?"

Glenn broke into the conversation, "I think Lil' Joe has a point. Stavros' plane was diverted to Knoxville, and Stavros was on board. We can reallocate Team 3.

Trish hurried, "Ok, I got his face squared up and I am switching to starlight, nothing…now whispering, "Oh my God, this guy's eyeballs are black as coal, floating in a sea of blood. Holy shit, he is looking right at me. I got my finger on a missile let me light him up."

Jess and Kat were transfixed by the images they were seeing. Jess was worried about Trish and the drone, something was inside this guy and she had no idea what to do.

Kat needed to turn away from the monitor. As she turned, she caught a glimpse of Molly at the back of the room. Molly had backed into the corner, her ears were down, her tail was between her legs and she was trembling.

Kat looked closer to see Molly had urinated on the floor below her; her eyes were frozen on the images on the screen. Kat elbowed Jess and nodded her head at Molly.

Jess took one look and knew what was going on, "Elrond we have a situation you should take note of. Molly was looking at the monitor. It is causing her to back herself into the rear wall. She is trembling and has peed all over the floor. I think she knows what's up."

John responded, "Croft, thanks, no doubt about that. Tbal, back off, recall two drones, leave the overwatch and you sink back."

John was pacing, "Nick you there?" "I'm here, what are you thinking?" John stood still and looked up into the night, "This is the guy I was dreaming about this morning when you called.

"In the dream, he came from behind an image of Makayla hanging from the roof. He came closer and closer until his eyes were all I could see. There was fire flickering in his pupils; I think this thing is here for me."

Jess looking at Molly, "Elrond, then Molly knows this thing is not from around here." John nodding, "So true, she and I have been here before."

Adam had been listening while he was carrying out his last order. He had found the perfect little place for his sniper's hide. He had a clear line of sight to everyone in the cabin.

He was monitoring the overwatch images and found that all five of the devil boys were now sitting or standing at the table. They seemed to be listening to what Black Eyes were saying. Just like in the forest, the weird eye guy was in charge.

Adam called John on his phone so they could talk offline. John picked up and said, "Give me a second." John walked over to his car after he left the conversation on the network, "Adam what's up?" Adam whispering, "I found my spot. Look at the overwatch image. They are all around the table listening to your dream boy. I could take down all of them in a second or two; save the last shot for him. Either way, we get to see him bolt without a body and on the record. Whadda ya say, Johnny?"

John paused, "Let me talk to Trish, I will conference when I get her." Trish answered, "What the hell are we doing sitting around here, time is going by." John all business, "Tbal listen up. I want to know if you can shoot him down if he goes airborne." Trish thinking, "Yes along as he stays in range so I would have to jump right on him."

John was thinking, "Adam, reverse the order of fire. That will cause the devil boys to stand still, as they gawk at the hole in Black Eye's head."

Adam excited, "So we are going to do it?" John was still thinking, "Tbal are you wearing the full suit with all the toys?" "Yes, why would you want to know that?" John, "Cuz if you tickle this beast with a missile he may want to return the favor up close and personal." John looked at the time, 9:50 pm, "Ok, sit tight, I'm gonna tell everyone we're going."

Chapter Forty-Three

8:21 pm
The Coffee Hole
The Town with No Name
West of Jonesborough, TN

Corwin and Sims' had switched cars four different times, driven miles out of their way, and taken back roads before they arrived behind the Coffee Hole. Anyone in town would be at Sammy's Diner. Sims drove the last two hundred yards without the lights on.

Browning was still drugged and babbling while semi-conscious. He was in the back seat of the Honda Fit. Corwin looked at Sims, "Time to call Phu." "Sims smiled, "Torture by doughnut; poor bastard."

Phu was just leaving the compound when his phone alerted him, "This is Xanadu, what can I do for you, Kill-heel?" Corwin now on speaker, "I need your services and entry to your dugout. We have someone you need to talk to." Phu feeling wanted, "Is this the guy that pulled a dine and dash at the Holiday Inn?"

Sims leaned overlooking at the phone, "We are tired and jacked up, as you probably are, after these last forty-five hours. We would like to crash until team three is done." Phu laughed, "Gentlemen, there is no team three, we have been relieved. Stavros has rerouted to Knoxville and apparently sent another of his kind to fill in for him at the cabin."

Corwin smiled, "So how soon will you be home?" Phu said, "In about twenty minutes. I am going to make sure Glenn is sending me the network feeds on team one. They are about to take the cabin. It seems to have a special guest drop into their fifth friend at the cabin has delayed the party a bit."

Corwin perked up, "I knew he had at least one friend. No one man could have killed those women and displayed them by themselves."

Phu sounding matter of fact, "Well consensus is that these things are not human. Oh, and Stavros' buddy almost crashed into Trish and the drone as he flew by her just outside of Jonesborough. Trish says it was about the size of Dom's plane." Sims mumbled, "Marco's plane." Phu immediately, "Yes, sorry."

Phu about to enter the lab and talk to Glenn, "Are you thinking of letting Rouse in on the interview, or are you just going to report?" Corwin looked at Sims, Sims replied, "His eyes only." Phu nodded, "Ok then, I will need to talk to Mr. Black." Corwin confused, "Who is Mr. Black?" Phu replied, "He is the only person on the planet who can get around Glenn. We need a secure feed without Glenn looking in."

Sims was concerned about this Mr. Black thing. "Does Glenn know about this guy?" Phu laughed, "Well, you would have to ask Glenn to tell you that story, but Mr. Black is the only reason Glenn didn't spend his first ten years after high school in jail." "So they are good friends?" Phu smiled, "They both shared the same income sources back in the day, and they went to school together; Black was older. No more questions or you can set this up with Glenn."

Sims and Corwin were getting impatient waiting for Phu. They were watching the front of the store when they both jumped at the knock on the window. Phu was still in his work clothes and came through the woods unseen. Corwin and Sims retrieved Browning from the back seat and walked through the back door of the Coffee Hole.

Once inside Sims said, "I have never been back here, just out front." Phu laughed, "Good thing too, can't have you learning all my secrets." On the west wall was a walk-in freezer; Phu led them to it. It had four racks of various doughnuts exposed and frozen solid. Phu moved one of the racks and key coded his way through the back wall and down a switchback of steps. The lights came on as they went down the steps; they led to the middle of the space.

The initial area was eighteen by eighteen square, with a narrow hallway on the east wall. It led to three rooms. In the far right of the main room was a mattress lying on the floor. Phu nodded and Sims and Corwin dropped Browning on it and looked around Phu's dugout.

Phu told them to make sure Browning was out so they could all get some sleep. Corwin suggested an alarm for three hours. They all agreed. Sims went to give Browning another dose when he noticed Browning was looking at him with somewhat clear eyes, he was holding out his phone, "I had no choice, please look at this...please." Browning's eyes went somewhere else and he faded away again.

Corwin took the phone from Sims and looked at Phu, "Do you have what we need here?" Phu took the phone, headed for the hallway and went to the first door on the left. Opening it, he waved the others into the room, "After you, I hope I have what you are looking for." Sims and Corwin were silenced by what they saw." Phu proudly, "I have only seen one other like it, and that was today at John's cabin in the woods." Sims smiled, "I know where another just like it is. Jess has one in her London, Canada office. This is her design. She had Glenn signed off on it after the debacle at the compound. Shit, let's dive into this phone. Who needs sleep?" Phu and Corwin raised their hands.

Sims had the phone so he looked at recent calls and texts. He turned to Phu, "There is nothing suspicious that I can see." Phu rolled his eyes then looked at Corwin to help him make fun of Sims, but Corwin just shrugged his shoulders as if to say don't look at me.

Phu realized he was it, in this game of tag. He told them to go to bed; he would see what he could get from the phone.

Corwin and Sims went across the hall where there was a dorm-type setup. They checked the room next door, which turned out to be Phu's living quarters. They went back to the dorm and passed out.

Phu found the phone's files. After an hour of digging, he found that certain files were actually set up as separate phones. They held their own files, apps, etc. Only one file in the phone was password protected.

Phu struggled with trying to guess the password, and then realized that one way or another he could get it from Browning. He went to the mattress and shook him, but he just moaned.

Phu was tired and had lost his patience, with this whole deal. Phu grabbed him by the front of his shirt, jerked him up into a standing position and growled in his ear, "What is the fucking password to the last file." Browning rolled his head around until he was looking at Phu, "Stavros." Then he passed out again.

Phu went back and entered the password and a video cued up. The image that was frozen with the start arrow was of Browning. He and a woman were naked on a bed, in what was clearly a seedy motel.

Phu pressed play and the scene progress slowly, so he hit fast forward until he went by something he hoped he had not seen. He rewound it.

Browning seemingly possessed, grabbed the woman and threw her across the room. She slammed into the entry door. He came back into the frame with a large knife in his hand and brutally murdered the woman.

Phu paused the video, stood up and started pacing. He had learned two things. First, a third party was recording the scene, and secondly,

Browning lost his mind in a rage that was more animal than human. He realized he was pacing, which he knew was because he had anger that needed to be exercised somewhere. Phu left the control room and headed for Browning.

Phu grabbed Browning again. This time he slammed him into the wall, put his left forearm under Browning's chin, and used his right hand to squeeze Browning's adam's apple.

Browning's eyes popped open when the pain and lack of oxygen became a real problem. Phu had his attention, "You sick bastard. You wanted me to watch that so you could enjoy my reaction. Well, this is my reaction; enjoy it as you die asshole."

Browning was thrashing about, and trying to talk while fighting for air. Phu saw something in his eyes and let go of his throat, "What could you have to say?" Browning gasping, "You have to watch it all, wait for the ending, you will see…" Phu clutched his throat again, "If it is the same shit again, I will be bringing my knife."

Phu turned and was startled to see Corwin standing behind watching, "Geeze Kill-Heel you scared the shit out of me." Corwin still half-asleep, "Well, I am a pretty scary dude." Phu motioned let's go with his head and went back into the control room. Corwin shuffled behind him, "What did you find?"

Phu realized he would have to show them to explain what he found. He turned to Corwin, "Go get Sims, we need to see this together and there could be some part of the file I have not seen."

Corwin nodded and went to get Sims. Phu walked to the far left side of the room and started the large coffee maker. The room filled with the smell of coffee.

When Sims and Corwin came into the control room, there was no Phu, so they went for the coffee. As they filled their cups, they heard Phu coming down the steps; he had a box of day-old doughnuts and some napkins.

He poured himself some coffee then sat down holding out the box. Corwin and Sims picked the ones they wanted, and Phu took another bite of the one he had started while coming down the steps.

We are going to enjoy these before I show you what I found; you will thank me afterward for being such a gracious host. They mumbled back and forth talking with mouths full of doughnut.

Phu went to the coffee maker and returned with the pot. He topped off everyone's cup, then sat down in front of the monitor. Browning's phone was plugged into a black box that led into the console. There was a blurred and paused image on the monitor. Phu put the cursor on the progress bar on the bottom of the video and dragged it back to the beginning.

Sims still chewing, "Bad dog Mr. Browning, that is not your wife." Phu clicked on the start arrow in the middle of the image. Just as before, once the action had been identified he fast-forwarded then resumed at the point when Browning lost his mind.

Corwin moved in closer to the screen, he shuddered as a chill flashed down his spine, "Jesus, he went nuts, like an animal ripping her up; what the hell was that?' Sims turned to Phu, "You are a gracious host, thank you."

Phu paused the video file, "This is as far as I got. I was really pissed, I think I might have killed him, but he kept trying to say something. He said we have to watch to the end of the file."

Corwin left his chair and looked at the entry wall of the room as if he were seeing Browning thru the wall, "He wants us to see how he poses the body, the smug bastard."

Phu motioned for Corwin to sit back down, "Remember he said this would show us he is not a traitor." Phu clicked on the start arrow. During what appeared to be the last moments of the murder, Browning looked at the cameraperson and told them to clean up his mess.

The image went black, but the progress bar kept moving to the right. They watched the bar for another fifteen seconds. The image jerked around, then settled into a stable picture. They were looking at Browning addressing the camera, "Well George, this should freak you out. I am you and I just killed a woman in a motel room. I have videoed it for the entire world to see.

"Now, you are not going to remember any of this. You see, I can take over your mind and body, do whatever I want and you won't remember it. Nevertheless, all the actions will have been taken by you…your DNA etc. So, watch the video, acquaint yourself with your crimes, and then think what would happen to you if this video came out.

I own you now Georgie boy, so you are going to help me crack the code on John Hart's technology. If you don't, I will release the video. However, as a bonus, I will visit your house, as you, and sample your wife's home cooking, if you follow me. So, let's get cracking Georgie.

Corwin was looking at the monitor. His eyes were filled with hate, "That's how he did it; Stavros is the Druid…no doubt. It's almost 11:00 pm, General Rouse needs to know what we've found."

Chapter Forty-Four

10:05 pm
Eve's Drop Off
Bill Bennett Rd
Johnson City, TN

John was explaining their plan with the rest of the network when Jackson Dunn cut in, "Whoa John, we are going to kill the owner of the Corner Cup as if he is the thing, not just being violated by the thing?"

John thought for a second, "Ok, we will shoot the four devil boys, then see what the thing does. If that is to hunt us down and tear us to shreds, then we can still rest easy knowing that people can still get their morning brew at the Corner Cup." Dunn laughing, "Excellent, justice wins out over expedience."

John contacted Adam and Trish, "Eve and Tbal, any thoughts?" Trish responded, "I have seen that thing fly, I would feel better on the ground if it goes up. I could program the drone to haul ass back home and see if it will play fetch." Jess jumped in, "Scratch that, put you and the drone on the ground or in the trees."

Adam deflecting, "Look, that thing is going to attack the line of the fire. He will be looking for me, but I will be harder to find cuz of the suit." John replied, "That makes sense, but that's what worries me, not one thing normal has happened in the last two days.

"Ok, Eve, we will wait and go on your action. Tbal put your suit in full defensive mode. Get the best video you can, and then react to the beast. Eve, it's on you."

Adam reset the sequence in his mind, visualized it; then relaxed. His start point was to look at the owner of the Corner Cup, and then start left shooting his way around the table in less than two seconds.

Adam came back to his mark and was ready to move left when the owner looked up. He looked right down the scope into Adam's mind and smiled; his eyes flashed black then back to normal. Adam continued left and completed headshots on the other four guys and went immediately back to his mark; he was gone.

Adam worried, "Tbal, did you get that?" Tbal whispering, "Great shooting Eve but the Corner Cup dude, a.k.a. Ol' Black Eyes, is now standing on the front steps of the cabin, looking right at me. He can't see me, but he knows."

John made his decision, "Eve, line him up again and tell me what you see." Adam looked at the front of the cabin, Black Eyes was looking off to his left, toward Trish.

Adam brought his silenced weapon to bear with crosshairs right on the bridge of his nose. Black Eyes slowly turned his head, again he was looking into Adam's scope, he smiled just as he had before. Adam pulled the trigger then followed up with two additional rounds.

Trish was making sure she kept Black Eyes in the middle of the frame, so the action could be seen with the most detail. Black Eyes' head jerked back violently, staring straight up at the stars, then it came slamming back down as his chin went to his chest.

The body fell in Trish's direction. She could see that he had been shot between the eyes with a double-tap to the heart. He went down in a heap and then rolled off the steps to his left.

She heard John yelling, "Eve, what did you do, damn it. Eve, what went wrong?" Adam breathing hard, "He locked onto me. He was looking right at me, and then his eyes flashed black. I shot his ass before he could get into my head."

John was pissed; they had just murdered the owner of the Corner Cup. He started to yell at Adam, then stopped, "Tbal, switch to starlight and see if you can find Black Eyes. Trish made the switch while looking at her monitor. What she saw could not be explained; she put the image on the network feed.

Glenn's voice, "What in God's name is that?" John still sitting in the Polaris watching his monitor, "Tbal, look at the front stairs of the cabin, what do you see?" Trish leaned out from under the drone and looked at the cabin. There was nothing for her to see except the Corner Cup guy's body by the steps. "Elrond, with the naked eye I see nothing, but on starlight, we can see it standing on the steps."

John was silent as were the others. On the steps stood what looked like a dark gray hologram of a sixteen-foot-tall man with long black hair. He was lean and powerfully built, with what looked like giant bird wings growing out of his back. The secondary hinge, or wrist of the wings, was two feet above its head with the wings folding down toward the ground ending at his ankles.

It was naked from head to toe. The forehead looked a little Neanderthal as did the jaw and pushed out mouth and lips. Its gaze was in line with Trish's position.

John whispered, "Tbal, get your headgear on and do it quietly." Trish sat stunned looking at the beast on the steps. John's voice snapped her back. She then realized they had no idea what this thing was going to do. It seemed to be looking in her direction.

Trish starting with the headgear, "Elrond this thing looks like a very pissed off and evil angel; if those two words can go together." John still quiet, "Get your gear on and start backing away very slowly. Put the two drones in an orbit around the overwatch and get the 3D imaging up and running."

John needed Jess, "Croft can we get power and movement potentials from your software? You know how fast, strong and flight speed kinda deal." Jess rolled her eyes, "Well, we can project fast and strong but the flight speed of a man with a thirty-foot wingspan is not in my database."

John staring at the beast, "Let me guess General, you've never seen anything like this." General Rouse sarcastically, "John, I had never met anyone like you before either. Every day we wake up to a new world. Are we going to see how long this freak can stand on the steps or are we hoping he flies away." Adam back on, "I am all for the just fly away shit, that sounds good right now." Trish came on, "I have got the drones aligned and it seems our friend didn't notice."

Lil' Joe had watched Adam's work and he was bothered by what he said about the thing getting into his head, "Eve, this is Snake, I want you to sight in on him again. Can we have this beast in a close up when Adam tags him?"

Rouse butted in, "Snake what are you trying to do?" Lil' Joe replied, "I'm thinking he senses threats and keeps track of them. He may be able to see differently than we do. Like maybe he has been keeping track of the drone, feeling he has no reason to watch Eve."

Rouse buying the concept, "Eve you ready, we got everyone on board?" John hesitating, "Eve what is your plan if he bolts in your direction." Adam uncertain, "Not be here for starters." John to Trish, "Tbal get in as tight as you can on this guy's eyes. Adam, wait for Tbal to get set up then go ahead, and don't shoot him please."

Trish relocated the drones so that one was directly between Adam and the beast. She aligned another drone between it and her, leaving the overwatch in place. Trish updated the monitors, "Elrond we are set."

Everyone on the network was glued to a monitor somewhere. They were watching to see how dangerous this thing was. Adam moved the crosshairs to between its eyes. The beast blinked then slowly turned so his eyes were looking straight down Adam's scope again.

This time he didn't get a smile, he got a snarled up face, full of teeth, angry black eyes filled with fire, followed by a roar that John could hear back at the car; it was pissed.

The beast stepped off the steps and took a stance like a sumo-wrestler, with his wings half-unfurled. It took in a deep breath as if he was going to howl again when Adam shot it three times in the face.

Adam immediately realized that he had just fired three rounds into the front door. He saw the beast turn toward Trish when two small missiles passed through his wings and exploded in the woods.

The beast started walking toward where Adam had been. John yelled, "Trish and Adam, get the hell out of there now."

The creature moved like a blur to where Adam was. Adam was suddenly staring into the snarled face and black eyes of his enemy. Adam whispered, "This son of a bitch is right in my face trying to decide what to do with me. I could use a little help." John started the Polaris and began rolling toward Adam.

Hoss, Lil' Joe, Dom, and Nick were heading out the door. General Rouse reached for the phone. Adam tried to move so he could put a tree or two between him and the beast; it was too fast. Trish moved to the area where Adam had been and started the cameras. The network reloaded with the image of Adam getting choked to death by the beast.

Just as Adam made the decision to move, it grabbed him by the throat. Even with his headgear and suit on, the creature's hand was large enough to encircle his entire neck. Adam yelled, "He's got me by the throat, but the suit is holding. He has me by the headgear connector ring."

Jess had an idea, "Eve did you attach your grounding wires as you put on the suit?" "Yeah, so what? Oh, shit! I think the connector ring is starting to bend. This thing is too strong."

Jess put the suit on remote and took over control, "Adam this may hurt a bit but you will be fine."

Adam was about to respond when Jess redirected all the electricity in the suit to form a single charge. She sent it all through the connector ring.

Adam felt every hair on his body stand on end; he heard a loud snap, and then he passed out. The beast let go and then looked at its hand. More pissed now it reached for Adam again.

John pulled up to the scene. Just off the road, he saw Adam being thrown down on the ground and then seemingly strangled by something unseen. John in a hurry, "Croft don't do that again; it just made him mad."

John remembered the monocle. He reached into his jacket, pulled it out, pushed the thing, then put it on. A blinking green light gave way to a full view of a monitor.

The beast stopped pummeling Adam long enough to notice John approaching. The monocle made figuring the scale and perception difficult; a small image of a giant coming toward you was not ideal. John still moving forward, "Croft this is a mess, I need real dimensional sight. The beast is now looking at me; looks harmless on the monitor, but is massive in reality." Jess quickly back, "Push the thing like a double click on the mouse and you should see a change."

Slowly, John felt his way to the thing with his right forefinger and then performed the double click. When the green light stopped blinking this time, it was as if he stepped inside the monitor with the beast. It was like he was seeing with both eyes in 3DHD. The beast was about thirty feet away, dragging Adam with him.

John didn't think backing away would send the right message so he stood his ground, "Eve can you hear me?" Adam sounding weak, "Yes, this is Adam, call sign Raggedy Ann. Thank God for this suit; I should be in pieces. I think I may have some internal bleeding going on though."

John shook his head as the beast was slowly but deliberately moving toward him, "I am going to ask him nicely to let you go. If he refuses I am going to kick his ass." Adam coughing a laugh, "That should do it."

John called Trish, "Tbal are you getting this?" Trish answered, "Yes, are you going for a viral You Tube death?" "No, I want you to come down and show this thing the external monitor."

The beast dropped Adam and then seemed to be deciding what to do about John. Trish swooped in behind John. She was now hovering. It began to stare at its ugly mug on the external monitor.

John pointed to his monocle, to it, and then to the monitor while nodding his head yes. John needed him to know he had the power to see him.

Everyone on the network was screaming in John's ear to get the hell out of there. They were begging him not to be stupid. Then came Nick's voice, "John, I know what you are doing. You only have a coin toss's chance in hell this will work; good luck."

Glenn calmly, "John, you need to factor in that Stavros landed in Knoxville twenty minutes ago. This thing is not acting alone, Stavros could be in control." Everything went dead silent.

John remembered the reaction the creatures in the compound had when they killed him. He was hoping that this thing would react the same way. John stepped forward and extended his hand while motioning the beast to take it. The beast stepped back.

John let out a long sigh; he felt he had bought some time, a kind of standoff. He had another thought; he could pretend this thing was Semjaza and try to talk to it. John looked it into its black eyes and said, "I am John Hart. I was killed by Semjaza yet I am alive. I need you to go now. You and I know you cannot kill me without permission, if you do, Semjaza will come for you."

Stavros had just entered his hotel room at the Springhill Suites by Marriott when he staggered grabbing his head. In his mind, he saw John Hart's face. He realized that Rameel was seconds from crushing him. Stavros was stunned by what Hart had said. He could never figure out how Semjaza had failed to welcome Abbadon at the Hart Compound.

What Semjaza had told the Messenger was true. He had killed John Hart not knowing he had Angel's blood running in his veins. Semjaza was a Grigori, a Watcher; he should have known.

Now that Stavros knew, he could feel it was true. Hart was protected by Semjaza under the watchful eyes of the Messenger. He could sense Hart's blood rushing through his veins. It was stronger than any he had felt amongst the humans.

Stavros, known amongst his peers as Azazel the Unrighteous, could not risk drawing the ire of the Messenger. He quickly explained what he knew about Hart and the pending dangers of Rameel. Stavros redirected Rameel to The Coffee Hole. His orders were to kill NSA Deputy Director George Browning.

Azazel wondered if the Messenger knew that Semjaza had revealed himself. Did Semjaza shield Hart using one of his incantations? Maybe Hart had found out about Semjaza, but had not yet seen him? His greatest fear was crossing paths with Semjaza.

He had to think. Would the Messenger give Semjaza permission to lock him away or even kill him? Azazel felt vulnerable for the first time in eons.

John was about to lose his nerve when he tried one more thing. In the final hours of the siege of the compound, he had commanded some of Semjaza's creatures to leave and they did. John stepped forward, "There is nothing for you here, it is time for you to go." John yelled, "Leave my man and get the hell out of here."

Mr. Black Eyes snarled at John, and then he snapped his head around and looked toward Knoxville. Its eyes were moving from Knoxville back to John. It slowly turned again, this time looking in the direction of Jonesborough; it was sniffing the air.

In a blink, the beast's face was so close John could feel its breath on his own face. It growled in a low, guttural and vicious manner; then vanished.

At first, John did not realize he was shaking uncontrollably. He looked at his hands, and then gasped for air; he had not breathed in a while.

Everyone on the network heard him say, "Holy shit. I...I need a beer." Adam replied, "Roger that beast whisperer. Now get me out of this suit and to a hospital. We'll grab beers on the way."

Trish was in shock, at the end she was within ten feet of the action, she chimed in, "I got shotgun." Jess said, "Tbal go ahead and drive those two fools to the clinic in Johnson City, I will bring the drone back by remote."

Trish took John by the arm and together they finally got Adam out of the suit, which they threw in the bed of the Polaris. John looked at the time, "It is coming up on midnight we should go to the

ER at the hospital in Jonesborough instead. Trish nodded, "But first we are gonna hit the liquor store at the Spring Street junction." John handed her the keys, "You're in charge. I will be in the back checking on Adam."

Chapter Forty-Five

> 11:05 pm
> The Coffee Hole
> The Town with No Name
> West of Jonesborough, TN

They had been arguing about checking the network to see what was going on with team 3. If they logged on, Glenn would know immediately where they were. If they went through Mr. Black they would be delayed, and that didn't fly with Phu or Sims.

Sims decided he would call Nick and tell him to hand the phone to Glenn. That would slow Glenn down enough to keep him from starting a trace before Sims could get a word in first. Corwin and Phu hemmed and hawed then nodded for Sims to try it.

Nick answered Sims' call, "This better be good we are in the shit right now and don't have time for drama." Sims pissed, "That's fine, hand your phone to Glenn." Nick started to object and Sims cut him off, "Give the fucking phone to Glenn right now!"

Glenn was distracted, he had just told John that Stavros had landed in Knoxville, "Who is this?" Sims speaking fast, "Shut up and listen. Don't touch anything just listen."

Glenn was irritated, "Sims what the hell, we are working here." Sims, "We are going to log on the network, but we don't want anybody to know where we are except you. If you won't do this for us, we will have Mr. Black get us online and you won't know shit."

Glenn went blank when he heard Sims mention Mr. Black. Glenn was confused, "I don't understand why you don't trust me." Sims shaking his head, "Look we lied to all of you to get the level of security we have now, so deal with it. We need to see what is going on so we can deal with General Rouse as we conduct our interview with Browning."

Glenn was too busy and conflicted to care, "Fine, do your thing." The line went dead. Phu logged in and the monitors lit up. Sims and Corwin brought Browning in. Corwin set up a table in the corner with food and water. Browning busied himself with both.

As Corwin looked up from dealing with Browning, he became enthralled by the images he was seeing on the screen. He didn't know John Hart well, but he was learning fast that the man had no fear when it came to protecting his people.

Corwin joined the others at the console as they watched John distract the beast away from killing Adam, and then put his own face nose to nose with a sixteen-foot winged monster from God knows where. He told the thing to get the hell out, and it did.

Corwin looked at Phu, "What the hell?" Phu shook his head, "He does this shit all the time. When John gets pissed, something comes out of him that causes these things to do what he says." They went back through the record of the evening and were able to see the Corner Cup owner go from black eyes to the beast.

As they finished, Glenn's voice came across the network. He told everyone that Trish was taking John and Adam to the hospital. General Rouse wanted everyone that was rushing to John's defense to continue to the scene, get it controlled and ready to be investigated.

He also told Sergeant Mitchell to bring a fire crew in to keep the forest from burning down from Trish's missile strike. Hoss was to bring the bodies to the compound so Sheriff Barlow could process them.

Sims was full of adrenaline knowing John was still alive after pulling another stupid stunt. He looked over at Browning who was wide-eyed and pale; the man was scared.

Sims snapped his fingers, made eye contact with Phu, and winked. Sims went to the table and sat across from Browning. He made sure he blocked Browning's view of the monitors, "You look like you've seen a ghost." Browning became more composed, "What do you guys make of that thing?"

Corwin sat near Browning on his right, "Well, that thing, is an employee of your boss Stavros. Truth be told, your boss and that thing are the same kinds of creatures. That is what they look like when they are not in your body or some other body.

Sims stood up, as Phu rolled an interview cart over to the table; he aimed all the equipment in the right directions and turned them all on record.

Sims sat back down across from Browning, and Phu sat behind the cart. Corwin, now to Sim's left, asked again, "Director Browning are you saying you didn't know this creature was part of Andres Stavros' team?"

Browning's eyes were darting all over the room and then they stopped. He lowered his head then looked up at Sims', "How could you have possibly put me together with Stavros?"

Sims nodded to Corwin and Corwin said, "The General and Glenn Berquist, one of John Hart's men, have been collecting evidence for three years. They just didn't imagine that it would lead to all of this. Nevertheless, what they have put together is staggering.

"It started when Glenn Berquist told General Rouse about his new software program. It could find individuals that had been tagged, no matter where they were on the planet.

"The actual tagging in all is very technical, but Glenn was able to identify and track most of Stavros' murder squad. You know the one created to kill anyone who had found, or was about to find, a cure for cancer.

"These murders were designed to keep Big Pharma in business and to remind politicians who is in charge. Oh, I forgot to tell you, this Glenn fella, well his mother died of cancer because you killed the man who was treating her. So, as you might guess, he is highly motivated.

"Now imagine what we thought when members of the murder squad, showed up here in Jonesborough. They mingled with the ever-growing crowd of devil worshipers and then they started killing our friends.

"The prize in the Cracker Jacks box was you, Director. You were tagged early when you began covering Stavros and his merry band of murders. After finding you and the others, we were able to figure this entire thing out.

"Having that information is the only reason we believed you are telling us the truth about the video. Now if you would please answer the question, why were you surprised to see that thing working for Stavros?

Browning seemed to be moving back into director mode, "Look, I had no idea how Stavros and his guys operated, but from looking at this stuff tonight it seems that all of his guys could be these things. Your technology is what made it possible to see them. How the hell would I know?"

Sims knew that Corwin was about to lose his temper after that statement, "Wait a minute we have you in Jonesborough the night of the murders on Jackson Street. Are you saying that some guy carried her up there and puzzle her together? It would take a team."

Corwin could not take it, "Listen, Director, you are coming close to losing all your options with us and the General. You tell us exactly what happened or we are going to publicly arrest you and put you in front of the media. Then when Stavros knows right where you are, we will leave the door open a crack so one of his beasts can feed on your brain."

Browning still resistant, "Not only do I have my rights, but no one at the NSA will buy this crap. It will be my word against General Rouse; who is known for bending the rules."

Phu started laughing, "Really Director, you really need to get a grip on where you are and who you are dealing with." Phu moved over to his laptop, "Ah let me see…yes, here it is." On all the monitors came images from the remote cameras recording in the bunker at the Greenbrier.

When Director Browning saw TJAG Creps and TJAG Dunn working next to General Rouse, his chin went to his chest. Phu turned back to Browning, "Those boys have been watching and directing us since before these boys pulled you out of the Holiday Inn.

They understand how you were tagged. They have verified all of your movements' right down to traffic and airport camera footage. In addition, you will be tried in a military court; so you are pretty much screwed."

Sims shaking his head with a big smile, "Jeez Georgie, you can't catch a break. First Stavros sticks you with a murder, and now we got you cold on treason, espionage, and domestic terrorism. Damn, that really sucks. What are you going to do?"

Chapter Forty-Six

11:55 pm
Spring Street Junction
Jonesborough, TN

Trish, Adam, and John were parked in the soft yellow light behind Jonesborough Wine and Spirits. Adam was half sitting up in the backseat of the Polaris and John and Trish had turned their seats so they were facing him.

The first six-pack evaporated in the face of the evening's adrenaline, and now they were sipping their beer with much slower heart rates. John looked at Adam, "Raggedy Ann, are you feeling cold anywhere?" Adam pointed at the hand holding his beer, "Just here." Trish smirked, "You should be dead. That thing threw your shit all over the forest." Adam started to laugh but his ribs reminded him it was not a good idea.

John nodded, "You guys did great out there, but why did you keep shooting the Corner Cup guy?" Adam waving hand as to dismiss the comment, "It was the voodoo. That thing was trying to get inside my head like he did the with leather goods guy. I had to stop him somehow."

Trish turned and looked at John, "What about you psyco boss man. Calling that thing over like it was Molly. What in the hell did you think was gonna happen. When that thing jumped back into your face I thought he was gonna bite right through to the back of your skull."

John drank the last sip of his third beer, "I didn't think he was gonna kill me. I think he isn't allowed to. He needs permission to kill me." As John said the last two words, he realized he had said too much. Adam had not been on the patio earlier that day, "Oh yeah, he was supposed to raise his wing and ask, *Ah sir can I kill you now?* Trish responded, "No, that Stavros dude probably wants John alive for some reason."

At hearing that John sat straight up in his chair, "No, No, No…I blew it. That thing was looking at Jonesborough, west of Jonesborough. Shit, shit." He grabbed his phone and dialed Phu's special number; a number you were sworn to answer no matter what. Phu picked it up on the third ring, "John?"

John was yelling into the phone, "I am not sure where you are but I am telling you that Stavros has a way of finding Browning. I don't know if you know about…" Phu cut him off, "We were watching." John back, "Well then you will understand this. That big mother is heading your way. When I was dealing with him, it acted as if he got a call. At one point, he looked in the direction of our little town."

Phu covered the phone then, "Ok we are on the move." John intense, "It will find you if you are in the open or anywhere near the location he was sent to. If you can go underground, that would be best." Phu let out a sigh, "That's great cuz we are going deep." John added as an afterthought, "Tell Sims to use starlight to see him; good luck."

Chapter Forty-Seven

12:00 am
The Coffee Hole
The Town with No Name
West of Jonesborough, TN

Phu set down the phone, "Let's get ready to roll." Sims and Corwin had cuffed Browning and cleaned the dorm in the time it took for John to finish his warning.

Phu told Corwin to roll the interview cart back to its place. He turned to Sims, "Take Browning to the blue X on the floor in the control room and pull the fire alarm on the near wall. I will be right back."

Phu headed back up the steps to the kitchen behind the counter. He fired up the doughnut fryers and turned the exhaust fans on recycle. He set the fry time for six minutes and headed back downstairs.

Sims found the X on the floor, un-cuffed him and told Browning to stand still. Sims moved to the fire alarm and pulled it. Browning was engulfed in the light of an electric scanner. It circled him several times then turned off. The monitor next to the fire alarm came alive. It showed a 3D electronic rendition of Browning with a blinking light below his right ear.

Corwin and Phu were standing behind Sims looking at the monitor; Phu let out a long sigh, "That is location and sound. Stavros has heard every one of his conversations; including tonight."

Without saying anything, Phu went over to the workbench and came back with what looked like a security wand. He walked behind Browning, then quickly put the wand under his ear, and pushed a button. Browning flipped up into the air and landed flat on his back.

Phu pointed to the fire alarm, Corwin pushed it. The machine scanned Browning again, and Sims said, "All clear, the device is dead. Now we have to carry this asshole around the rest of the night." Phu said, "Not so Mr. Sims." Phu took an ammonia stick from his pocket, snapped it in two and put one part up each of Browning's nostrils.

Browning jolted up clawing at his nose, "What are you assholes doing?" Corwin picked him up, "Stavros put a bug in your head; we just killed it. Now we got to go." Browning looked at Phu, "Why are you making doughnuts now?" Phu on the run, "So this place doesn't smell like us, or more specifically you."

Sims started leading Browning toward the steps leading back up to the diner; Phu waved him back as he picked up his laptop, "Not that way, follow me." Phu shut down the network console, hit the emergency data dump and then worked his way into his living quarters.

Once inside his quarters, he made sure everyone was inside of the bathroom; he pulled the antique flushing cord for the toilet and the bathroom moved downward like an elevator. Sims looked at Corwin and they began laughing.

When the elevator stopped, they were facing in the direction of Sammy's diner but were looking into a tunnel-like the ones below the compound. Corwin was confused, "Did John designed this too?" Sims was looking at Phu for an answer, "Well, what the hell?" Phu smiled, "This is all Sammy's baby. He was an engineer with the Seabees. He secretly worked with General Rouse so Glenn wouldn't know that the compound was going to be a black site."

As they walked under the street toward Sammy's, Sims was getting pissed, "I don't think John would agree to that." Phu nodded, "Rouse never put it to him. The compound is John's, but the Joint Chiefs have classified it as critical to national security, and all your asses are protected by everyone in this town. That is why we don't have a name or a post office.

"So now, you know the best-kept secret in town. We cannot believe you people haven't figured it out. Bev, Sammy's wife, told Kat right after the incident at the compound." Sims smiled nodding his head while Corwin wondered what they were talking about.

Just as they reached the elevator that went up to Sammy's, they were rocked by the impact of Rameel's assault on The Coffee Hole. Phu stopped and looked back, "We should wait and decide where we should go based on what that thing does. Son of bitch better not ruin my shop."

Chapter Forty-Eight

12:35 am
Springhill Suites at Turkey Creek
Knoxville, TN

Stavros, or Azazel, was lying on his hotel bed with his eyes closed; he was watching the assault on the Coffee Hole through Rameel's eyes and ears. He had lost the signal from Browning's device only minutes earlier. Even if Browning were dead, the bug should have remained active.

Rameel circled Browning's location several times. It smelled of burning fat and he could not feel any life below.

His ability to sense the human spirit was acute; he had felt John Hart's blood, smelled his fear and hesitated when faced with his courage. He felt nothing, smelled doughnuts and was confused. He decided to crash through the front of the building and kill whatever moved.

The Coffee Hole was no match for the power of the supernatural. He stood to his full height and shook off the debris from the façade and roof. Stavros spoke into Rameel's mind, "Show me everything. Look for hidden pathways, rooms and destroy the electronics."

Rameel moved around the doughnut shop tossing tables and chairs out of his way until he reached the shop's counter. He looked down the aisle to his left which led to the restrooms, then he leaned over the counter and looked into the back where Phu did all of his cooking. He pulled the counter out of his way and threw it on the pile of rubble behind him.

He heard Stavros, "Look for a way to get under the floor you are on. Show me." Rameel shuffled around the small space looking at everything and then, "There, the chrome door, the walk-in freezer; look inside."

The giant moved slowly crushing and breaking his way down the narrow path to the freezer. He bumped into a fryer and some of the hot oil splashed on him; he growled at it and moved on. He looked at the levered handle, pulled it back, and the door swung outward; the lights came alive.

Remeel was not a dumb beast; he was second in command of Stavros' small army. He was a tactician, one who led Stavros' humans. He was not a beast or creature, but one of an evil remnant of fallen immortals from the heavens above.

He, like Azazel and Semjaza, had been banished to outer darkness for seventy generations until they were released. That was more than two thousand years ago. He led many of those who hated their captors and their love for humans.

Rameel ducked into the freezer, he scanned the area so Stavros could see. Stavros had him look closer at the thermostat at the rear of the walk-in. Stavros studied it for a few seconds, "Pull it off of the wall." Remeel removed it and showed the back of it to Stavros.

Stavros had Remeel turn and look at the cooling unit above the entry door.

Stavros had an idea but needed to be sure, "Remeel, pull the cooling unit off of the wall and move it to the middle of the room." Remeel looked at the wiring on the back of the unit so Stavros could see.

Stavros was quiet and Remeel asked, "Are you thinking four wires at the thermostat and two wires at the cooling unit, what are the other two wires doing?" Stavros pondering, "Yes, but I believe one of the walls has a door or the wall is the door. Let's find out which one it is."

Remeel nodded, dropped the cooling unit on the floor worked his way back to the wall with the thermostat. He had to figure out how to leverage himself in such a tight space, then he smiled, "Azazel give me a moment." He quickly stood to full height, fully reaching upward with his arms and expanding his wings to their fullest, thus ripping open the ceiling, exposing the attic, and punching a large hole in the roof.

Rameel studied what was left around him, and then ripped away everything attached to the wall with the thermostat. He scanned for Stavros again, showing him the workings of a hidden door.

On Stavros' command, he reached down, ripped the door out of the wall and threw it into the street in front of the building. He then followed the stairwell, tearing his way into the lower floor revealing the control center.

Chapter Forty-Nine

12:55 am
Underneath The Town with No Name
West of Jonesborough, TN

Sims and the boys had been listening to Phu's doughnut shop being destroyed. On several occasions, the ground had shaken from the force of Rameel's pounding.

Phu was getting pissed, he started messing with his phone, "Damn it he is in the control room; I can't see him, but things are getting airborne; he is destroying everything. We need to call in an airstrike; Stavros is getting the bill for this shit."

Corwin looked over Phu's shoulder, "Is there any real information they can get from down there?" Phu reached into his pocket and came up with a three-inch by three-inch leather hard case, "Nope, I got it all right here, and I loaded everything into the network for Glenn?

They are probably going bat shit trying to contact us. We need to get into Sammy's freezer and work from there." Sims put his hand on Phu's shoulder, "You said we had to decide what to do based on what this thing was doing. Does that mean we have options?"

Phu looked at Corwin and Browning then to Sims, "Yeah, we can actually work our way to John's cabin, Jimmy's gas station, or we can go the other way to a bunker about a half-mile out, just west of the entrance road into town."

Sims was thinking, "You said when John called, that Stavros had a way to find Browning right?" Phu shrugged, "We killed the device, so?" Corwin shook his head yes, "Sims, you think this thing can sense people right?"

Sims was still hesitant; he was replaying the video he had watched of John and the beast face to face in his head. He turned and faced the others, "That thing is just like Stavros, so he is smart as hell; he knew John and was probably listening to Stavros while he was looking John in the eye. I think this beast is a big-time tracker; Stavros' hunting dog, he can sense where we are."

Phu was one of the best trackers that ever wore a uniform. Sims statement made complete sense to him, "The only reason he hasn't found us is because of the way the tunnels were made. We need to lead him away from John's house and town."

Corwin caught a glimpse of Browning moving his head up and down in the affirmative, "So he is right, aye Georgie boy; you have had conversations with him, haven't you? You better not be betting on him, his only mission right now is to kill you. That became obvious when he didn't kill John." Browning looked Sims in the eye, "He is Stavros' number two and he can find anyone."

Sims looked at Corwin and asked, "Edge of town?" Corwin turned to Phu, "How do we get there?" Phu winked at Sims, "We have to go back to the junction by my bathroom." Browning's eyes widened, "You mean we have to go back to the doughnut shop?" Phu started to smile when he noticed Corwin's eyes were a tad wide as well.

Phu started walking toward the doughnut shop, "Trust the tunnels, they can't be seen by any technology and they are airtight; let's go." Corwin put Browning in front of them and told him to lead the way.

Phu ended up in the middle with Sims on his right. Sims found himself reaching for his weapon, "No good pulling a gun I guess." Corwin pulling out his Glock, "Nope no reason." By the time they approached the junction, they each had their weapons out and ready to go.

Phu tapped Browning on the shoulder and whispered for him to fall back. Phu moved forward to the door to enter his code. Corwin came up on his right side, "When was the last time anyone opened that door?" Phu smiled, "During the last inspection." He finished punching in the code and grinned at Corwin, "Two years ago." and hit the enter key.

There was a short air fart then the door pulled back quietly. Corwin entered the tunnel as the lights came on. Sims was slipping by Phu after pushing Browning ahead of him, "You are a frickin' nut." Phu whispered, "Thank you, Master Sergeant."

Phu followed, then turned, pushed the close button, and watched the door start to close. He was about to turn away when the door screeched to a stop with six inches left to go. Phu's heart jumped into his throat, and then the door loudly slammed shut; all the noise above them stopped.

Chapter Fifty

12:43 am
Hart Compound, Lab 3
West of Jonesborough, TN

At 12:11 am, Glenn was getting desperate to find where Sims was. He had heard from him at around 11:15 pm wanting access to the network without being traced. He didn't have time to play Sims' game and just let them do what they wanted. Later he had found they had accessed the network from Phu's bunker.

Glenn spent much of his time putting together what he could from the cameras in Phu's shop. As he was about to run the video timeline, John called from the Wine and Spirit's parking lot.

John agreed, they were in The Town with No Name and were heading for cover. Glenn told John about the network dump and control room shut down, and now he had lost contact with them. Glenn had tried each of the bunker sites in town including the one by the entry road, and nothing.

John asked Glenn to bring everyone back to the compound and send Team 3 into the tunnels to find them. He told Glenn to send any interview records or visuals of Browning to General Rouse to keep him busy.

Glenn hesitated, "John I was just about to run the snippets of video I sequenced from the network cameras. Maybe you could sync your phones with the network and watch them with me." John turned to Trish and Adam, "Get your phones on the network; Glenn has some footage for us. Glenn, go ahead."

Glenn had started with Browning's murder video, including the threatening ending. The next snippet showed Sims and Phu killing the bug in Browning's head followed by his interrogation.

John was pondering aloud, "Wow, how could you beat that? Before today, we would have fried him or sent him to the funny farm." Adam looked at John, "What?" John ignored him, "This Stavros is really twisted; it would be nice if we could neutralize him but…"

Glenn fast played the video from John's call to Phu closing up shop, and all of them going into the bathroom. Glenn said, "Now we have to use our imaginations. The image started with what looked like the middle of an explosion.

Glenn paused it, "The cameras in the front of the shop are motion activated. What we are seeing is not an explosion but the result of some invisible force that crashed into the front of the Coffee Hole; my guess is our friend from the cabin. These cameras are too old to adjust for starlight mode; we won't see him."

John was about to pass out from the beer and fatigue, Adam was nodding, weak from his wounds. Trish read his mind; she turned her seat to the front, and started the Polaris and headed for the hospital.

John continued to watch the destruction of the control room. John and Glenn said nothing for a few seconds, then John now weak, "Tell Team 3 to hit the bunker at town entrance first, that's where they will be; they would never lead that thing toward any of us."

John asked Glenn to see if Barlow and Nick could head over to the cabin. He wanted them to support Kat, Molly, and Jess. Glenn sighed, "Think we are heading into a ground war?" John distant, "If we could kill the enemy, we would do well, now...Get them going Glenn and have Nick call me after the cabin is secured." John hung up.

Glenn ever the optimist was thinking, *Well between Corwin and Adam we are way ahead.* Then he remembered Makayla, and thought about what Kat and Molly had suffered; he realized they were way behind.

Chapter Fifty-One

1:16 am
Team 3 Entrance road to Town
West of Jonesborough, TN

Hoss, Lil' Joe, and Dom quietly exited Hoss' big truck. Hoss and Lil' Joe were in Ranger gear and Dom looked like a SWAT leader.

Lil' Joe took the lead holding a small remote locator in his hand, "Ok we are locked on the entrance to the bunker, Stay spread out and stay small." Hoss was carrying his sniper rifle, which was exactly like Sims'. He set the scope on starlight and scanned the night sky, and then looked ahead and as far as he could see, "All clear on starlight."

Hoss felt something was wrong, "Let's take a minute; you two on me." Lil' Joe and Dom closed on Hoss and they all took a knee. Lil' Joe clipping the remote on his belt, "You feel it too?" Hoss nodded, "Dom, you were the tunnel rat what are ya thinking."

Dom said, "I agree. I am feeling something is up here and I am worried we won't get down there fast enough; does that make sense?" Hoss took in a long breath, "Lil' Joe, go with Dom, I will stay up here and be overwatch." He paused, "Give me a second."

Hoss activated his network com, "Glenn, is our boy still ruff housing in town?" Glenn tentative, "Everything just stopped about a minute ago; it is like it is listening for something. On top of that, our boys switched to radio silent. So I am not making a sound."

Hoss was thinking, "Where are Sammy and Bev?" Glenn hesitated, "Ah, they are bunked here in the rec room, breakfast for all at sun up." "Did Jimmy go home?" Lil' Joe asked. Glenn perked up, "Yes, he is working in his control room putting the entire town's video together for the network." Hoss smiled, "Put me through to Jimmy."

Hoss put Jimmy on speaker, "Hoss what are you guys doing?" Lil' Joe jumped in, "We are trying to get Team 2 out of the tunnels without spooking the thing that is tearing the shit out of the Coffee Hole."

Jimmy on task, "Well, I got the boys in the tunnel between Phu's place and the bunker at the edge of town. They appear to be on the right side of the door, so I doubt they are in much trouble." Hoss held up his hand, "Can you still see or was this a while ago?" "No I can't, it's been a good three minutes since I lost everything." Hoss thinking, "Ok stand by."

Hoss turned and looked toward town, "Glenn, "Is it still listening." Glenn wavering, "It seems to be circling around the area above the door where the boys went in; not good."

Dom looked at his watch, "It's been another three minutes, it is 1:17 am we got to get them out of there, or we will all have to hunker down in this bunker." Hoss told Lil' Joe to get to the tunnel opening and plug into the external access port and status the bunker; Lil' Joe sprinted off.

Hoss turned to Dom, "When Lil' Joe establishes it is safe, you get in there and head down the tunnel. You find those guys, bring'em into the bunker and we will get the hell out of here." Dom grinned, "Will do."

Hoss had a plan of his own to assist his crew. He dialed General Rouse's high priority number. The General picked up, "Hoss what do you need?" Hoss relieved, "I assume you have been following along?" Rouse, "Of course Master Sergeant, how you going to get them out of the bunker with that thing wandering around?"

Hoss laid it out, "Well my plan is to have Jimmy wake the town up via Operation Mardi Gras, and I was hoping Sergeant Mitchell could supply the fireworks. General Rouse laughed, "So you plan is to make a whole lot of noise and confusion." Hoss proudly, "Yes Sir. He will be looking everywhere but where we are.

"It will take us about ten minutes for us to secure them into the bunker. The hard part will be driving them out of the area without alerting the death from above."

General Rouse paused, "This could be risky for Mitchell." Hoss agreed, "I thought he could fire from afar; maybe a double dose of Hellfire missiles. That would save Phu from having to demo his basement; save a lot of taxpayer dollars." General Rouse, "I have always been a sucker for a bargain; let's dig a hole."

Hoss scanned the skies again and then joined Lil' Joe and Dom at bunker's hatch. Lil' Joe had the laptop up and he was evaluating the bunker's readiness, "I have the bunker up and sent the status up to the network. All of the doors and protection systems are at one hundred percent."

Hoss looked at Dom, "Get in there, clear it and set up at the tunnel door." Dom looked at Lil' Joe, "Open it." Lil' Joe hit enter and the round hatch slid horizontally out of site, the lights flickered on revealing the steps, and Dom went down the steps, his MK18 out in front.

Chapter Fifty-Two

1:24 am
Team 2
Tunnel heading out of town
West of Jonesborough, TN

Phu and the others reacted to the sound of the door closing as if someone had clawed a chalkboard. Phu was hopping up and down whispering, "Shit, damn it that was loud." Corwin looked at him, "Not so funny now aye?" Phu smiled, "If we get out of this, you know we're gonna laugh our asses off when we talk about it." Corwin managed not to smile.

Sims had them all go radio silent and turn off all their equipment, everything. Browning finally said something without being asked, "Kinda like being in a submarine waiting for the enemy to drop depth charges on your ass."

Phu smiled and pointed at him, "See you were one of us, weren't you. Browning frowned, "I am one of you; I just had to protect my family. I worked in Afghanistan, Syria, and Turkey; I am one of the few operators that have made it to Deputy Director." Browning was still whispering, "No one was getting hurt. Stavros was just corrupting deal after deal using my influence. Then when I saw what he did to that woman in the warehouse, I lost it and I panicked. All I could think of was finding someone who would believe my side of the story.

Sims walked over and put his face in Browning's, "You know what he really is and how he appears to be a human right?" Browning nodded and Sims continued, "What do you think he did with all of the people he invaded?"

Browning's whole countenance changed, "What people? I have only seen him as Stavros. He never showed me his other side. I had not seen the real Rameel before today. I know he took me over but that is it. I don't even know when the video was made."

Sims was about to get really pissed until he realized that Glenn only showed Browning meeting with Stavros right before he went to business deals or back to his place in Greece. He put his hand on Browning's chest, "I will worry about all of this when we debrief with General Rouse."

Phu looked at his watch; it was 1:19 am. They had been silent for five minutes and still no noise from above. Phu raising his eyebrows, "We've been holding for five minutes, what do ya think?" Sims looked up, "If this thing is what we think it is, then he has been around since the big guy said let there be light; so five minutes is like a blink of an eye. I would sit tight until we hear something." Corwin and Phu said cool, and they all sat down for the first time in a long time.

Six hundred yards west of Sims, Dom was working his way quietly toward the tunnel door at the main junction for the outlets to Sammy's Diner, Jimmy's Gas and the way to John's cabin.

Dom stopped and leaned against the left-hand wall and asked Hoss, "Is it still really quiet at the Hole?" Hoss said, "Not for long, in eight minutes Jimmy is going to turn on every light in town and flood the speakers with music from our mardi gras games last year."

Dom smiled, "I was honored to take Marko's place in the games; it was a fun time." Hoss replied, "Well this isn't gonna be fun, from about a mile away Mitchell is going to put a couple of Hellfire missiles into the doughnut shop just to empty the basement for Phu."

Dom wasn't smiling now, "I've got to hump it if we are going to make it out of the way." Hoss said, "We are going to start the party at 1:40 am, best hit it, boy." Hoss only heard the word shit and Dom was off the line.

Chapter Fifty-Three

1:33 am
Springhill Suites to the Coffee Hole
West of Jonesborough, TN

Stavros was trying to convince Rameel that what he heard was just the wreckage settling from the pounding he was dishing out. Rameel was sure it came from beneath him and was obsessed with finding out what it was.

Stavros finally ordered him to finish with the control room and move to the back of the store. Rameel crushed what was left of the console, then he ripped all of the wiring from the floor and foundation.

Rameel waded his way through the debris in the control room, and then he tore a path into the dorm across the hall. Stavros was intrigued by the layout of the bunker. He felt there had to be more; so far, he hadn't seen a way to escape from this level.

Twelve feet below, Corwin, Sims, and Browning were standing and listening to the new activity above. Phu was disgusted, "Now that overgrown cherub is wrecking the dorm." Corwin spun around and was now looking down the tunnel, "Somebody is coming."

Corwin and Sims stepped in front of Browning and took a stance pointing their weapons into the darkness. The last of the lights came on and Dom found himself looking at two 9mm pistols.

As they all started to relax, Phu shouted, "Password or die." Dom raised his two hands over his head still holding his MK18, "Trish loves Sergeant Mitchell." Phu spit laughed while lowering his weapon, "Approach." Dom responded, "Approach my ass, we gotta go! Two Hellfire missiles are about sixty seconds out and we have a lot of tunnel to cover to make the bunker."

Sims removed Browning's cuffs and told him to run. Corwin and Dom were further ahead moving fast. Phu yelled, "Sims get his your ass to the bunker, I'll cover our retreat."

Stavros was focusing on the entrance of Phu's quarters when Rameel swung around looking back toward the control room, "I heard something. They have tunnels below I can feel it."

Stavros was about the yell at Rameel when he heard mardi gras music. He had heard it before in New Orleans, "Rameel what is happening?" Rameel was moving toward the front of the shop; Stavros could see the entire town was all lit up, and fireworks and music were coming from everywhere. Stavros panicked, "Rameel you must leave." Rameel was about to argue when…

Everyone in the tunnels was sprinting for the bunker. They had another hundred yards to go when they heard Hoss over the coms, "Mardi Gras has begun you got to hustle."

Dom dropped back while yelling, "Hellfires in thirty seconds. Phu finally came flying by him, "Why in the world would he need two missiles." Dom winded now running behind Phu, "Rouse wanted to save you money on a new basement." Phu breathing hard, "We gotta find a way to kill these pricks."

Rameel heard the loud buzzing of a million bees and knew there were missiles coming fast. He turned to see where they were when he felt the concussion and was airborne.

He struggled to gain control of his wings but he could only ride the wave into the forest where he crashed through several trees and came to rest about a half a mile from the doughnut shop.

Stavros was stunned, how had this happened. Now a whole town was witness to what had happened. It would be talked about, that was how things unraveled. He could not have his name mentioned; he was supposed to be in Greece at the manor.

Dom and the boys had felt the earthquake from the blast; the tunnels had done their job. Hoss opened the door and they entered the bunker.

Hoss went to his field pack, brought out a fifth of sour mash whiskey and handed it to Sims, "Welcome aboard Master Sergeant." Sims opened it, took a long pull and swallowed hard, "Wooo! Man, that is just what I needed."

Sims turned and winked at Browning, "Join us?" Browning was unsure if that was a question, an invite or what, "For a drink or a job." Corwin stepped behind him, "You got a job; he means as a member. Drink now. Talk later; hurry up." After they passed the bottle around twice, Hoss contacted

Glenn and let him know they had succeeded in recovering Team 3.

Stavros felt extremely exposed; things had spun out of control. He had underestimated Hart in so many ways, his people, their efforts, his strategy, and courage. Stavros needed to regroup.

Stavros had never seen anyone attack immediately after losing so much. It made no sense. Stavros had recalled Rameel, they would meet later. He was about to move on to his other business when a thought gave him pause, *What if the woman he killed was not the wife? Did she survive, if so who took her? Where was her body? Was there only one body? Could the Messenger have intervened in some way...Semjaza?*

Hart's words to Rameel came crashing into his mind, *"I am John Hart, I was killed by Semjaza, yet I am alive. You cannot kill me without permission. If you do, Semjaza will come for you."*

Stavros realized that he had pushed this operation too far. In his operation with Zhang Jei, he told him to use blunt force and it cost Zhang his life. Even destroying Hart's world was not enough to break him.

The best move was to move on. He would revisit Mr. Hart another time. He hadn't dealt with Browning either, but he was not a priority.

His real fear was that the Messenger could be behind this whole thing. *Was Hart that special?*

Chapter Fifty-Four

2:11 am
Team 1
Jonesborough Hospital
Jonesborough, TN

John, Adam, and Trish were in a treatment bay of the ER awaiting the results of a CT scan and blood work. They had verified that Adam was intoxicated, did not have a concussion, but they were worried about possible internal bleeding.

Adam was sitting up on his bed after he had been given two tramadols for his pain; he was feeling none of that. John and Trish were sitting in the adjoining chairs with the curtain drawn behind them. Trish was half-asleep with her head on John's shoulder.

Adam looked at Trish, "You got your purse under the chair?" Trish smiled, "Yup."
Adam grinned, "Well, give it up for the wounded worrier." John looked at Trish and shrugged, grabbed his phone and pointed to the exit. As he turned away, he heard the sound of a twist-off cap bringing a beer to life.

John was extremely tired but wanted to know the status of teams 2 and 3. Glenn told him the stories that came forth from the streets of the town. Jimmy was taking all the credit for the sudden disappearance of Ol' Black Eyes. His management of the diversion made Mitchell's job like shooting fish in a barrel.

Glenn and John had a laugh about the condition of the Coffee Hole; it's now just The Hole. In addition, Stavros' pilot had submitted a new flight plan, they were heading back to Greece at 3:30 am.

Glenn told John that the main force was recovering at the compound and everyone would be in the rec room for breakfast at 9:00 in the morning, including all of Team 1 and Molly.

Glenn said he had invited General Rouse and his guests to join in. Rouse thought it would be a great opportunity to meet Mr. Browning. John as an afterthought, "Is Sergeant Mitchell flying them in?" The answer was yes. John said, "It will be nice to have everyone together again, but we keep losing some along the way. John ended the call before Glenn could reply.

John and Trish headed back to the cabin. Adam was being held for a couple of days to monitor the damage to his insides. Trish was asleep with her head leaning against the window.

As John made the turn that started the five-mile straight shot to the compound, he began to wonder about Semjaza. Why had he not shown himself for the last couple of days? Were Stavros and that other thing related to him or were they enemies?

John was lost in thought when the car was shaken by a gust of wind. John looked around and could see little evidence of a breeze. John realized he was only going forty miles per hour. He shook his head and rubbed his eyes, he needed to get moving.

John pressed down on the gas pedal and the Polaris began to slow even more; he cursed under his breath, "I don't need this shit right now." John began to feel a strong headwind pushing against the front of the car; he stomped on the gas and the engine died.

This time he didn't worry about Trish he cussed aloud, "Damn it. What the hell is happening?" He looked to tell Trish what was happening but she had not stirred. John looked back at the road ahead and turned on the high beams. He was not ready for what came next.

Twenty yards in front of the car the wind was swirling the dust-up and in the middle of the lights. John thought he saw the thing from Bill Bennett's road landing in front of them. John's heart was pounding, he shook Trish but she kept sleeping. She was breathing even and relaxed, but would not wake up.

John thought he might be able to keep it from killing Trish if he engaged it out front. He got out of the car and stood between the high beams. John's fear level went to the max as the thing finally landed.

This beast was not like the other one. It was a human-looking man, jet-black hair and was easily twenty feet tall with huge wings. This beast made Rameel look like a child; John could feel the power emanating from it, he was helpless.

As it stopped and tucked his wings behind him, he settled his gaze on John. John kept his head down and yelled, "What do you want?" John fell to his knees when he heard Semjaza's voice in his head, "John, you were wondering about me, I thought we should chat."

John looked up into the clearest and brightest blue eyes he had ever seen. John's whole body relaxed all at once and he went from his knees to sitting on his ass as a result. John thought *thank God* and Semjaza replied, "You could just thank me. I will let Him know you include Him as well."

John realized this was like the phone calls; it would be all mental communication. John felt better just talking anyway. John pulling his mind back to the moment, "What the hell have you been doing?"

Semjaza had to adjust his thinking to human time, "Well, after I saved your wife, and your dog, I gave Barlow instructions to my house. When you got there I let you in, showed you where your dog and wife were, and then let you go home to celebrate. "Oh yes, and the night of Makayla's death, I gathered her remains and have them stored for you. Have I missed anything?" Semjaza could feel John's remorse but did nothing to abate it.

John stood up and took a good look at Semjaza. His body shined like a raven in the car lights. He was massive with long lean muscles and powerful shoulders; his wings had the look of black razors, sharp and glistening. He wore an ebony armored breastplate that matched his waistcoat. His sword was sheathed in black pearls.

John finally spoke, "I am sorry, but we almost got our asses kicked today by Stavros and his beast. We are still raw from what Stavros did to Makayla." Semjaza got down on one knee and was still much taller than John, "I have to apologize as well, I didn't realize that the Messenger kept you a secret after the night of my great failure. I am the only one of the Watchers that knew who you were."

John finally looked away from Semjaza's eyes and looked at his face. Now it was calm and serene but he could see wrath was boiling beneath the surface.

John didn't feel afraid and Semjaza smiled, "Could we work together or will you always see me as a monster? John was astonished by the question, "What are you?"

Semjaza looked over his left shoulder as if deciding what to say. He turned and looked John in the eye, "I am a Grigori, a Watcher. I look after those humans who share the blood of Angels on this earth. I work for the Messenger; the one who performs the will of the Most High."

John was thinking about what Semjaza had said. Semjaza knew what John wanted to ask but he waited. John looked down, "That night you told me I would have to deal with who I was. What is it that you think I am.? "Why didn't that thing kill me tonight?"

Semjaza stood up and surveyed the area, "That thing's name is Rameel. He and Azazel, the one you call Stavros, were under my command at the beginning. Now they have become jealous of the humans and vengeful against their own kind." John started to say something, but Semjaza held out his hand in a stop motion; John shut-up.

"John, we don't have time for me to sit with you for a year to explain what you need to know. So, I am going to speak to you as if you were one of us. Semjaza went back down on one knee and held out his hand. John moved forward and put his hand on Semjaza's.

John's eyes shot open, his pupils were fully dilated and his breathing was short and rapid. Semjaza continued to hold his hand even after John had passed out. Finally, he stood up and looked at the driver's seat and John appeared behind the wheel. Semjaza stepped over, put his hand on the Polaris and it started; then he vanished.

John came to and realized he needed to get moving again; this time he was going home.

Chapter Fifty-Five

2:25 am
Lil' Pine Cabin
Jonesborough, TN

John stopped out in front of his pine cabin. He could see many of the lights were still on and people were milling around out front. Jake from the Grocery and Tackle shop was the keeper of the gate.

Jake took one look at John and started crying, "John, I tried to save them. I really did, I am so sorry." John reached out and took Jake by the forearm, "I know there was never anything anyone could do. We could never have stopped it."

John realized that Jake was looking at Johns' hand and his whole demeanor had changed. Jake nodded and opened the gates; John drove through. As they approached, John shook Trish and she came to, "Wow, am I tired."

Nick was there to greet them and Barlow was standing in the front door watching them get out of the car. Molly almost knocked Barlow over forcing her way between his knees to get to John; it had been too long.

John gave Molly a big hug and in the middle of it, Molly pulled back and looked John in the eye. She could tell that he had been with Semjaza; John could feel it too.

Barlow had moved out onto the porch, Kat joined John, and Jess went to Trish. John looked around, then turned to Nick, "You got Jake on the gate, that was a good idea getting him involved." Nick put his arm around John and asked about Adam; they all went inside.

John entered the living room and saw an exhausted Sims nursing a beer. Sims raised the bottle, smiled then pointed to the kitchen. John and Kat went onto the back patio. John gave her a massive hug and started to cry. Kat continued to hold on and whispered into his ear, "Don't ever pull that shit again mister; are you feeling me?" John started to laugh cry and almost lost control of it.

Trish and Jess had gone straight down to the control room. Trish used the restroom, washed her face and put her hair back together. Jess was standing aside watching, "I thought I lost you today, that monster was within ten feet. My God, how did you manage that shit?" Trish gave her a wide-eyed look, "I am not sure I did, you're gonna have to clean that suit momma."

Jess left for a second and came back with beers. They clanked the long necks and took a long drink. Jess started walking back up the steps and managed to let Trish get ahead of her.

Trish came into the living room and started talking to Kat and John. John looked wasted, tired and like he had been crying. She looked over Kat's shoulder and saw Sergeant Mitchell talking with Jimmy from town. It looked like they were giving each other the business.

Mitchell turned looked right at Trish. He raised a beer and smiled. He started walking her way. Trish froze, she had just seen herself in the mirror, and now Mitch had seen her looking like hell, she wanted to run. Finally, she decided that she was allowed; besides he had seen her lying in the road bleeding.

Chapter Fifty-Six

6:54 am
Lil' Pine Cabin
Jonesborough, TN

Molly came into the cabin from the backyard using the doggie door. She was up and ready to roll but all of the people in the house were sleeping like zombies.

Sims usually slept on the couch but he was nowhere to be seen or smelled. Molly started smelling for someone she knew. Jimmy, Jake, and many others had left around 3:30 am and the couches were empty.

Trish and Jess had been sharing the second bedroom but Molly was confused by the smells she got from sniffing under the door. They told her that Sims was over again, and Trish would have slept downstairs.

Molly found that the door to the stairs was closed, so she went into her room and nosed opened the closet. Once inside, she put her paw on the black screen and the door popped open.

Molly went down into the semi-dark room. She could smell Trish and someone else she knew but should have left last night. She put her nose on Trish's arm and she stirred, "Molly what are you doing here. Go use your doggie door to pee." Molly nosed her again, this time Sergeant Mitchell sat up and looked at Molly. She gave him a look and he knew she knew, he was quite late in leaving.

Trish looked at her phone, "Oh shit, you gotta go it is seven and we all got the debrief breakfast. Rouse will be looking for his rent a car and the driver; he gets up at five." Mitch, now wide awake, kissed Trish, grabbed his clothes and gave Molly a scratch on the ears, "Molly, don't tell John."

Mitch turned and almost ran straight into John, "Oh, didn't see you." John smiled, "Good morning Trish. Come on Molly, and Mitch you are late.

"General Rouse just called my phone wanting to know if his rent a car was here. I said I had no idea. If you pick him up something on the way to the compound you can say you went out early to get it for him... or whatever."

Trish was sitting up on the bed trying not to laugh. John was still standing there giving her *the what's up* look. Trish replied with a coy smile, "He needed to see my scar, you know to see if it healed right." John laughed, "Sergeant Mitchell, is a very thorough man." Trish fell back on the bed, "You have no idea."

Molly was excited that she had brought everyone together. She thought it meant a bigger breakfast and more grub for her. John looked at Trish, "I'll let you and Molly wake up Sims and Jess. You can share your I am so busted story with her; I'll get the coffee going."

After a red-faced breakfast and many laughs, John conducted a debrief of his own; they finished their coffee on the back patio. Nine o'clock was just around the corner, and John wanted to rally the troops for a counterattack.

After everyone went to get ready for the General's debrief, John sat and replayed his encounter with Semjaza. It was strange that any question he had activated a memory, and an answer as if he had known about it his whole life.

He decided not to dig too deep right now. He would proceed on a need to know basis for now. His eyes were still beet red from Semjaza's late-night lessons. He was most anxious to look into his own history or the history of his own blood.

Chapter Fifty-Seven

8:46 am
Rec Room Hart Compound
Jonesborough, TN

John, Kat, and Molly pulled up in one of the company silver SUVs. Molly jumped out and followed her nose to the rec room. Kat and John went upstairs to check the progress of their master suite makeover. Kat seemed pleased with the designer's efforts and they turned their attention on breakfast.

John went behind the food line, found Sammy and Bev; he slipped Sammy a check and then watched his eyes and smile widened. John needed to pay them for the last couple of day's efforts. They made sure all of those involved in this disaster were fed and cared for.

Kat had joined Jess and Trish in the buffet line. John was about to look for General Rouse when he saw Gavin Tanner, the owner of his manufacturing facility and Jacob, Gavin's Chief of Technology, talking with Nick on the first deck pistol range. John joined them and they all turned and looked downrange.

Nick turned to John, "Gavin and Jacob have your one hundred and fifty dragonflies ready; they just need the operational parameters for the software run. John looked at Gavin, "We just had a meeting last week; it feels like a year ago. Thanks for humoring me. We will know the parameters by the end of the day."

He looked at Jacob and then Nick, "Can we make our tech look like it came from somebody other than us?" Jacob looked surprised, "Will we be leaving any of them behind? That could give our tech away."

John raised a hand, "I know, but what I think I am going to ask you to do with these drones might result in some dragonfly carnage. Can we program them to self-destruct or burn to a cinder?"

Gavin finally stepped closer to John, "What are you planning to do with them?" John looked each one of them in the eye, "I am going to kill Andres Seraph Stavros, and make it look like a terrorist attack."

Chapter Fifty-Eight

9:16 am
Generals Debrief
Rec Room Hart Compound
Jonesborough, TN

Everyone who had watched the network feed last night attended with the exception of George Browning. He was now in a holding cell with Rocky and Bull Winkle.

General Rouse had let Glenn do the review of the last day's events, and explain the role of Stavros and his beast. Glenn showed that their only motivation was to use any means possible to steal the Hart Group's technology secrets.

General Rouse then asked John to update everyone on the current situation and any related information he felt was appropriate.

John was intense and all business, "The current situation sucks. Makayla is dead and Adam is lucky to be alive. As you have seen without Jess' body armor, Adam would have been torn to pieces.

"As for the beast, we are working on an explanation, but it might work out that it is just what we saw; call it what you will. We have experienced some very strange, and, some might say, supernatural events recently.

"Each of these had their origin within the calculated attacks brought against our family." John paused, "I consider this group my family. I finally realize that each one of us is charged with the protection of our group. It is no longer a friendly joke; it is a fact, we are family by design.

"The threats to our family are not over because Stavros and his imp have withdrawn to Greece. They left to regroup, reload and attack again.

"Last night, I learned that the attempt to kidnap Jess, Gavin and Laura was not related to the siege of this compound. Zhang Jei, the mastermind of those attacks was working for Stavros and not the Chinese. He sought to use the siege as a cover for his operation.

"I have said all of this to let you know how I feel about these attacks and explain what has happened. Now that you have been informed, I hope you will understand when I say we are no longer going to wait for the next attack; we are going to do some attacking of our own.

"I will discuss my thoughts with the group and General Rouse to see if we can't send a few of these assholes back to hell or wherever they came from."

As John left to take his seat, there were no cheers, no clapping, just a renewed fire in the eyes of all those who understood they were no longer going to sit by, they were going on the offensive.

General Rouse came to John right after the debriefing; he wanted John to lay out what he had in mind. Rouse, Dunn, and Creps said they would stay at the compound until they could agree on the direction they were going.

John agreed and asked them to make themselves comfortable. He wanted them to join him for a working dinner in the widow's walk at 5:30 pm. He said everyone needed some rest, especially if their work continued through the night.

John left them, went into the living room and sat on the couch facing the front door. Soon Molly had her head in his lap enjoying an ear massage. One by one, people from the town came by, took a seat and talked. At 1:00 pm, John excused himself, he and Kat retired to their master suite and knapped until 4:30 pm.

Chapter Fifty-Nine

5:40 pm
Planning Session
Widow's Walk, Hart Compound
Jonesborough, TN

The widow's walk was John's war room. There John devised the plan that saved their lives, destroyed the compound, and all of Semjaza's plans. In the walk, he could once again take the first step in ending the problems presented by the world's third-richest man.

The widow's walk had been expanded into a medium-sized conference room slash hang out. How you set up the room determined its function. Tonight was relaxed.

This evening ten people would hash out what would become of Stavros. If they could not reach an agreement, John was ready to go it alone without General Rouse. John felt that the General knew from his earlier message that it was a done deal. Nevertheless, John knew he needed his help.

The windows of the room were open and alcohol and cigars were part of the process. There was a nice buffet laid out and everyone was talking about different aspects of the last three and half days, and all were concerned about the force of their enemy.

Creps was shaking his head while talking to Dunn, he asked, "Have you ever heard of the Broadway play called, My Arms Are Too Short to Box with God?" Dunn smiled, "Yes I have and they are still too short." Creps replied, "There you go getting all negative again." Dunn shook his head, "Why, you ready to testify my brother." Creps held up his hands as if to surrender.

John finally got everyone seated and paying attention. John held his beer in the air, "To Makayla." They all soberly spoke her name then drank. John continued, "Second note of business is the processing of NSA Deputy Director George Browning. I understand you all have watched the blackmail video Stavros made that kept Browning in line.

"Personally, I think that it is a unique case and is not something we can share in a discipline hearing. Jackson, how would you even begin a defense, "The Monster did it?" Jackson replied, "Mr. Browning would not see a courtroom based on the video. Even if the court would accept the last part, they would say he was playing himself to defend himself. They would deem him insane and that would be the end of it."

John continued, "Glenn's tracking program can prove that Browning only met with Stavros after he had conducted an assassination, and had already disposed of whomever he had used. Browning would accompany him to business meetings or to his manor in Greece to show the NSA supported Stavros.

General Rouse added, "If we leave Browning in place, we would have a tremendous asset. He could return to duty a critical player in the case here in Jonesborough, and then he could help us as would be appropriate." John looked at Jacob and he left the room.

Rouse continued, "He has only been off the grid for a couple of days. Jimmy did a great job of deflecting Browning's detail. He told them he had to meet with me about a delicate matter.

"He is not due back to his family for another day or so. John let him call home last night and we are all set. Creps added, "This is really our only way to go."

John stood up again, "With that, it is time for a demonstration. I would like you all to go down the stairs and wait for me to call you back up. When you return, make sure you are sitting in a different seat next to different people." As they left, they observed that several dragonfly drones were hovering around the widow's walk looking in the windows.

Before they were called up, they noticed more dragonflies flittering above them; watching them. When they heard John's call to return, they moved carefully as they found their new places.

John began immediately, "You have seen our latest drone technology. The actual dragonfly design is not new but this group is faster, smarter and will never have to be called off station to recharge or refuel.

They may have mechanical problems after two hundred hours on station, but the incremental rotation of the drones, handled by the lead drones, eliminates that problem. John opened the door to the widow's walk and Jacob returned.

Jacob was holding what looked like a remote controller; "I would like to show a few capabilities of these drones." He walked across the room and handed the remote to Corwin, "Corwin was voted the least likely to have never owned a remote toy in our after breakfast pole, so he gets the remote."

Jacob returned to his place, "Corwin would you please push the green button." Jacob turned his back to the group. Within seconds dragonflies started to enter the room via the windows, they hovered on the ceiling; then began to circle slowly. In the next few seconds, all but ten of the drones descended one by one settling in the laps of each of the ten guests, Corwin included; Jacob had ten hovering above him.

Jacob stood and asked Corwin to push the red button; all of the drones shut down but remained in the lap of those they had chosen. Jacob moved over to Nick, "Nick pick up your drone and look at its belly." Nick did so. His dragonfly was about the size of his hand. He held it up for all to see, "It has my name on it."

Jacob, now sounding like a magician in Las Vegas asked, "Would you all do the same." As they did, the room came alive with chatter. Jacob retrieved the remote, punched a couple of keys, the ten extra dragonflies circled the room once and then they all left in different directions.

Jacob held up his phone, "I selected ten other friends from breakfast for the drones to find. When they are found they will call me on this phone and we can inventory our success."

John cut in, "Oh, one more thing." he took the remote from Jacob and keyed in something and hit the green button. "Corwin jumped up and swatted the drone off of his lap, "Son of a bitch bit me." John activated the rest of the drones and they flew out the window into Jacob's van and shut down.

John slowly nodded toward Corwin as everyone settled down. Corwin felt their eyes on him. He was wearing a silly grin, "What?" Jacob laughing asked him, "How do you feel?" Corwin didn't lie, "Much better now, can I have another bite, sir?"

It took a while for things to settle down, but they all understood the point of the demonstration; these things could find you and kill you. As they discussed more of the drone's capabilities, phone calls from all of the other targets verified they had been found and asked that the creepy things return to where they had come from.

General Rouse sat back in his chair, "John I would imagine that all of the previous swarm software and aerosol weapons are included with these things as well. John nodded. General Rouse smiled, "I'll take'm. John laughed, "Not for sale." Jackson Dunn now dead serious, "Then what are they for John?"

John's demeanor slowly changed. He looked much more sinister. Sims, Nick, Glenn, and Corwin moved to his side of the room. John looked at his guests, "I am going to kill Andreas Seraph Stavros, the third richest man in the world, and make it look like a hit carried out by terrorists."

John continued, "Browning says there are thousands of people who would love to kill him." As he finished, the others noticed that Gavin Tanner and Jacob were now standing with the group as well.

Dunn slowly sat back in his chair, "John did you get bit by one of your drones? I think Stavros demonstrated rather clearly that we can't kill them." John continence was stern, "I cannot kill Azazel, the thing that resides in Stavros but I can kill Stavros."

It was dead quiet for about thirty seconds then it began to sink in. General Rouse asked, "What would you gain?" John's eyes widened, "What? The man practically rules Europe and the largest pharmaceutical companies in the world.

John started to pace, "He has no heir. Azazel would lose everything he has built since he took William Clairmore from the crib and made him Stavros.

"He has bought elections in America and other countries. Look what Stavros did to Browning, just so he could gain access to the NSA? We can prove he is preventing the cure for many cancers from being introduced to the world.

"I feel we can change the future of Greece and rid the world of someone we know orchestrated the murders of at least fifty doctors and seventeen men he used then killed."

Corwin waved his hands at John, "What do you mean change the future of Greece?" John pointed to Jackson Dunn. Dunn shifted in his chair then looked at the ceiling, "John is right, without an heir Stavros' holdings in Greece would go to the government.

John stood looking around the room. General Rouse looked at him for a long moment, "How would this work? Azazel or whatever you call this thing isn't gonna stand by and do nothing."

Stavros' DNA is Clairmore's, his fingerprints, retina, and all his security protocols are set up around Clairmore's physical makeup. Once Stavros is dead, Azazel cannot access anything Stavros; his human life will have been terminated. He will have to start over. Our guess is he will take control of one of his big pharma buddies."

Corwin had been sitting quiet, distant and not looking involved. Nick noticed, "Corwin I can see you grinding your gears; what's up?" Corwin looked at Rouse, then Creps and finally Dunn, "So he will take over some guy and then go straight back to his old hobby. He could rape and murder his way around the globe and no one would even know."

John was having trouble focusing, his mind was being flooded by the knowledge Semjaza had downloaded. He realized he needed to ask the question. He was confused by the answer it was vague but positive. John knew he had to talk to General Rouse with his wife and close family. He needed to have a chat with himself as well.

John looked at Corwin, "I think that Azazel may be coming to the end of his run. I can't explain what I mean but I can tell you he is not popular with his peers." Corwin blinked then sat back nodding at John.

General Rouse understood by looking at John they needed to dig into this murder of a civilian deeper and in an environment that was more controlled. The General stood up and excused himself. That, in effect, ended the meeting.

Chapter Sixty

Day Four
8:58 pm
Impromptu Meeting
The Kitchen, Hart Compound
Jonesborough, TN

Molly was lying at John's feet. Kat sat next to John on his right and General Rouse was across from them; they were all poking at their cherry pie; Molly was working on dog chew.

The coffee was excellent, a Sumatra blend, and Rouse complimented Kat. Kat nodded toward John and smirked, "I can't make coffee, John is the connoisseur of all things brewed." Rouse raised his cup to John in appreciation.

Nick wandered in, took a chair on the other side of John and poured himself a cup from the thermal pot on the table. Nick took John's pie and fork and started in. Nick started talking with his mouthful, "Good pie. Are we talking yet?" John shook his head no.

Sims and Glenn half staggered in and were glad someone had made coffee. They said nothing; Kat slid her pie to Glenn who ate it using his hands and her napkin. Sims cut his own slice and Rouse let him have his fork.

John leaned back in his chair and let out a long breath, "I've got some weird stuff to talk to you guys about before we can move on with our operation." Glenn blurted out, "Finally."

Kat turned her face to John, "You sure about this; there's no taking this back once you say it."

John put his elbows on the table and his head in his hands. Glenn whispered, "Oh no."

John sighed and started, "Last night I was stopped on the road by Semjaza in his natural state; he makes Stravros' beast look like a child." I was wondering why he was absent when we really could have used him. At that moment, he landed in front of me on the road.

John watched for their reaction. Sims still a bit wasted, "Did you tell him to get the fuck out like ya did that other guy?" John shook his head.

John started again, "Semjaza has been helping us. His men took Kat to safety, but they weren't able to save Makayla. He has Makayla's remains and is preserving them for us." Kat was tearing up. John continued, "He also fixed Molly and put her with Kat. "I have talked to him a couple of times on the phone in the past. He has tried to explain why he was helping but it was too complex.

Last night he decided I needed to know everything. He told me to take his hand and he would talk to me the way they talk to each other. I took his hand and my mind was flooded with images and data; it was a massive download. It was frying my brain."

"I guess I passed out. Sims whispered, "Vulcan mind meld." John smiled, "When I came to, I was back in the driver's seat with the car running. I drove home and explained what had happened to Kat.

"Now I have what I believe is the entire history of these things and why they act the way they do around me. I also have my complete genealogy." Nick mumbled through his pie, "You know who your mom and pops are?" John nodded with a strange look in his eyes.

General Rouse was not fazed by what he was hearing, "Did he tell you about Stavros?" John nodded yes, "I have to sort that out. I am getting better at gathering the data from my brain, it is a weird process."

Sims still wasted, "So is he an angel or what?" John nodded, "That's what we call them, they have other names in other languages, but yes."

Glenn less ripped than Sims, "We need to get Browning to search all of the NSA files about these guys. I bet that is what the nine-inch finger was about and all those things that were not from around here; you know what I am saying."

General Rouse relaxed, "Exactly, I am tired of asking about what we found and not getting answers." John quietly, "The more we dig the more we may find that what they believe is actually the truth...shit, I don't know, I got a lot in my head right now."

John cleared his throat, "Anyway, Semjaza believes that isolating Azazel from Stavros is a good start. He believes that the higher-ups in his world are just about done with Azazel. I guess all he wants is to destroy humans and punish the earth."

Rouse stood up, brushed the crumbs off his Army sweatshirt. He looked around the table then said, "I have to finalize Browning's legal responsibilities to our nation.

Rouse slapped Sims on the back, winked at Nick and put his hand on Glenn's head, "John, I will give you all the help you need, just figure a way to save Clairmore so he can get back some of the life that was stolen from him." John was struck by Rouse's comment, he smiled and nodded, "We will."

Chapter Sixty-One

Day Seven
12:51 pm
Operation ASS Simulation
The Kitchen, Hart Compound
Jonesborough, TN

Nick and Molly came running through the compound's front door through the living room into the kitchen. Nick slid on the floor like a man stealing second base and smashed into the cabinets, Molly dove on top of him clawing and biting at his hands; he had Molly's ball and was playing keep away from her.

Nick was prevailing when Molly had had enough. She moved her muzzle down to Nick's forearm and went to biting his skin as if she was biting a flea, this was known as the bitty-bite.

Nick screamed and threw the ball into the living room to get Molly off him; she obliged. Nick looked down and he had a little blood blister forming. John and Kat arrived in time to see the maneuver and hear the scream.

Kat was laughing, "Molly does not lose, you give it up or pay the price." Nick rubbing his arm, "She cheats! Molly you are a cheater." A moment later, they all heard the sound of claws clicking on the floor. They turned to see Molly prancing in with the ball in her mouth.

She laid down on her stomach directly in front of Nick. She moved her paws so they were about three inches apart. Molly lowered her head until her mouth was just above her paws, then she dropped the ball softly. Molly watched it roll off her paws toward Nick. The ball stopped right between his legs. She was daring Nick to pick it up.

John said, "You had better not go for it. This game is about seeing who can get it first. You won't win and if you do, your whole hand will end up in her mouth; then the crunching begins. Believe me, you don't want that."

Nick stood up, opened Molly's drink fridge and gave her the fizzy water in the green bottle. By this time, the living room and kitchen were filling up with the rest of those involved in the run through of the upcoming operation. It was now deemed Operation ASS Be Gone.

They had spent most of the day fleshing out their plan by walking through it several times. Sometimes using the dragonfly target drones. Now it was time to relax.

John whistled, then yelled, "Beer and grub in the rec room. The range is now open for high dollar betting. I am betting Sims can outshoot Kill-heel on the sniper's gauntlet."

General Rouse and Jacob were the last ones into the rec room. Rouse had been grilling Jacob about the ability of the dragonflies to handle the winds on the shores of Crete. Jacob was trying to explain that the drones would be starting inland going toward the sea and cliffs as they attacked, and they would ride winds to their targets.

Jacob called Glenn over, handed Rouse off, grabbed a beer and went to the range's rifle deck; Sims was shooting first.

Glenn took out his phone brought up the maps app and showed the General the wind pattern overlays and changed them hour by hour until sunset. Glenn pointed to the screen, "You can see for a billion years the tides have been the same in this region. Note the direction of the wind every day at sunset."

General Rouse was frustrated, "You guys ain't listening. I want to know how you can control them while they are being pushed by a tailwind. It looks like they will overshoot everything before they can engage." Glenn was stunned. He had not thought of the problems aircraft have landing with strong tailwinds.

The sound of .308 rounds being fired snapped him back to reality. He texted Jacob and told him to meet him in the widow's walk and to bring his laptop; they had simulations to run.

Rouse took Hoss aside, "What do you think of John's plan?" Hoss now caught between his friend and his boss, "I think it will do the job, but I'm like you, I don't trust the drones. I am not a big tech guy."

Rouse smiled reading between the lines, "So we are just two old farts set in our ways?" Hoss replied, "Speak for yourself, I ain't that old Sir." Hoss followed up, "He has one hundred and fifty chances to get Stavros."

Rouse looking down, "I hope no one starts shooting." Hoss put his hand on the General's shoulder, "You ever spent any time or should I say sober time, shooting at bugs?" The General smiled, "I just know how creepy and dangerous the Druid is…still scares the hell out of me; it's worse now knowing that bastard is superhuman or whatever."

Hoss trying to be reassuring, "We got mountains with the sun setting behind them. The drones will be flying below the horizon, which will be very dark to the human eye. "When the mountain cuts the sun in half they will come in low; no one will see them until they are right on top of them. It is going to work Jack."

Chapter Sixty-Two

5:33 pm
Confidante, Flight Center
Knoxville, TN

Jacob and Glenn were frustrated. The tailwinds were causing the flittering drones real problems. The worst part of the whole deal was that General Rouse had predicted the problem; they assumed consistent flight from the drones.

They drove back to Confidante, set up the flight simulation lab and worked into the night. Sims and Jess arrived at 7:30 pm. They found Jacob and Glenn staring at their monitors with glazed over eyes.

Sims entered the flight center and asked if the boys had lost any money at the shoot-out. Glenn distractedly responded, "No we only bet Rouse that Corwin would not win; so we win." Jess added, "I took that bet as well, easy money." Sims grumbled, "Corwin whipped our asses."

Jess moved closer, "General Rouse told us you were here and I thought that maybe I could help. We left a little bit after you did. We can solve this; I went through several problems when choosing the shape of the manned drone."

Sims stood close to Jacob and winked at him when no one was looking, "We all left before they started serving dinner, so let's leave all this for later, head to Cracker Barrel, have a drink and eat. You will be better focused after that."

Glenn started talking about staying and working; Sims cut him off. "Glenn I got my ass kicked today on the range, and I haven't had a chance to have a beer because your funny little bugs don't like windy days. So cut the shit and let's go." Glenn held up his hands in surrender. "I am truly sorry that you looked so pathetic with that neon green paint splatter on your headgear; you deserve to have a drink."

After they were seated and the drinks and appetizers arrived, Jess took away their laptops, handed them notepads and number two pencils. Jess smiled, "Now as we talk you sketch or doodle, but no listing; math is allowed.

Glenn pushed his notepad to the side and started on his beer. Jess reached over, put it back in front of him and gave him the look. Glenn was about to object when he took a quick look at Sims and decided to leave it there.

Half way through their conversations Jacob started doodling. Jess started to stare at some skis hanging on the wall; no one paid any attention to her. Glenn was looking at what Jacob was doing and asked him, "What is that?" Jacob said, "It is the way the wind sees a dragonfly wing."

Jess kept staring at the skis. Still, no one paid any attention. After several minutes, Jacob realized that all the talking had stopped. He looked up to see Sims staring at Jess staring at the skis. Jacob looked at his drawing and smiled. Jess looked at him, "Jesus Jacob I thought you would never see them."

Jacob was a bit embarrassed, "So why do you think I needed to see them?" Jess shook her head no, "You tell me why you were drawing them?" He was confused. Jess knew he was getting close, "So one of the laws is that the airflow takes the shape of what it flows around." She stopped talking. Glenn started drawing the same thing.

Jess said, "I am going to ask one more question and if you don't see it and figure it out you guys are paying for dinner and all the drinks we are going have after I tell you the answer."

After a minute, Jacob smiled and started bobbing his head up and down. He asked Glenn, "You ever go skiing?" Glenn said, "Yeah, but I sucked. I couldn't learn how to control…" Glenn stopped dead. Jacob was pointing his finger at him, "Yeah baby, you see it now."

Glenn looked at Jess, "I didn't have the nerve to turn into the hill. I thought I would tip over and roll down the mountain. Once I learned that, I could control my speed and stop on my own." Jess stood up, leaned across the table and kissed each one of them on the forehead, looked at Sims and said, "Let's get a room, we have to be back at the compound early tomorrow. Sims faked a tip of the cap as they left.

Jacob looked at Glenn, "All we have to do is change the software to move the drones across the tailwind to slow down or speed up. If we have the nose of the drone lead the way on every turn, we will be golden.

Jacob sat back in his chair, "I am not going until I have had a couple of beers while staring at the skis." Glenn sat back down, "Jess is hot, yes." Jacob smiled and in a slow low tone said, "Oh yeah."

Jacob quickly sat up shaking his head, "They stuck us with the check! Shit, it is 8:30 pm already; let's just go back to work." Glenn smiled, "John ain't here, Sims and Jess just walked, Nick will be here in the morning; I guess that leaves me with the check. We can stay as long as you like."

Chapter Sixty-Three

Day Eight
11:30 pm EST
8:30 am EET
The Stavros Villa
Isle of Crete, Greece

Andreas Stavros was reading the local newspaper, seated between two open French doors that overlooked the lush countryside.

The morning sun was glistening on the nearby jagged rocks of the Rokogiorges, the mesa of an eight hundred foot high mountainous rock formation. It extended about a mile on either side of the villa to its west.

Stavros was unaware as Dom and Adam drove by the villa. They were surprised by its size. It was much smaller than they had expected. Adam, still in some pain, was riding shotgun while using the laptop.

Adam was reading about the villa. He turned to Dom, "Check this out, the place is some kind of high roller bed and breakfast. Only three rooms with a maximum of nine people allowed. It is booked for years in advance.

"It only closes when Stavros has his quarterly business meeting and dinner party. He shuts it down for a week and it opens again the following Monday. Therefore, we got today to get this recon done. We still gotta arrange everything for the rest of the crew this weekend. Hopefully, this Saturday night Stavros the human will be toast."

Dom pushed the rented Fiat to go a little faster and turned west. Dom looking all around, "The map says this road will work its way behind that half a mountain. We have to verify the area where Trish is going to land with the drones. She is gonna need lots of cover after she sets down."

After they had investigated and verified that Trish would be safe and invisible, they went into the city and checked into what would be their base of operations. When they were in their room, they verified the rooms for the rest of the group, conferred with Glenn, and then went hunting for food.

Chapter Sixty-Four

9:30 am
Hart Compound to Greenbrier Resort
Jonesborough, TN
Sulfur Springs, VA

General Rouse's face filled the monitors in Lab 1 as he conducted the meeting from the Greenbrier Resort bunker. He asked John, "Where is Glenn? I am used to working with someone that is competent enough to handle all of the whistles and bells."

John smiling, "You just want a free winkie cozy." Rouse laughed, "He sent me one as a joke when he created the alert system using that website. He sent an extra-large; my wife was shocked when she opened it. She called me at work and asked why Glenn was only selling children's sizes."

Everyone was laughing too hard to continue and the follow-up comments were even funnier. Rouse continued, "Jess and you girls, I am sorry for such a joke." Jess still laughing, "We actually have found it to be quite encouraging."

Once order was restored, John told the General about the good news from Crete regarding where Trish would be landing and releasing the dragonflies. Rouse wanted to know if Glenn had figured out the tailwind problems.

Jess told Rouse that she and Sims had visited them at Confidante. She moved to where Rouse could see her better, "We isolated them and brainstormed for a while, and then we talked about snow skis and the problem was solved."

Rouse was quiet then, "So you are going to work the wind by crossing into it to slow you down? Jess replied, "Bingo you got it. They are working on splitting the drones into two squadrons that will cross weave their way to the target. This way we can attack from both sides at once; it's pretty cool. We are setting up the big wind tunnel right now for the last of the flight tests."

John said, "Moving on, we want to tell you what we've worked out for Clairmore." John could see Rouse's whole manner change. John continued, "When we take him down, it will appear that he is dead. However, he will be in a suspended state for eight minutes. After that he will start a slow journey back, we will have him completely back after twenty-five minutes.

"This will give Browning and his team time to process him in the field, and then remove the body to an ambulance so he can be worked on. Browning will release photos of the body to the local news and will have him pronounced dead upon arrival at the local hospital.

"Clairmore will then be moved to another ambulance at the back of the hospital where he will be put on board our private jet. We will transport him to the compound where you can pick him up."

Rouse liked using Browning; it gave him standing in the investigation. Rouse was pleased, "Ok let's talk about getting you the hell out of there. I have done some work and the zodiacs can be waiting on the beach to take you out to a submarine and then on to France."

John held his hands up in a hold on gesture, "Jack we are not coming home right away. We will be there as tourists, so we are going to play the part. I am calling it our company retreat. We decided we could use some time away, from time.

"We will be there and set to go in two days. After we scout the area again, see the way the villa is set up for their guests and the actual stage arrangements we will finalize the sequence and bring you online."

Chapter Sixty-Five

Day Ten
6:15 pm EET
Hotel, Base of Operations
Crete, Greece

John wanted to get the group together to solidify their plan and let off a little steam. Moving the operation to Crete had been a major undertaking. He arranged for everyone to eat together in the banquet room of the hotel.

After all of the great comments about the Greek food, John leaned back in his chair, "I want to share some information I gleaned while sifting through the info Semjaza downloaded into my memory.

"He told me that Stavros, or Azazel, has two sidekicks. We have met Rameel and the other is named Asael. They could be at the meeting keeping an eye on things. We must avoid contact with them if we can. Once all the guests are unconscious, these boys will be airborne looking for trouble.

"We must keep an eye on them with the starlight filtered video cameras. Trish you will need to be up high as soon as everyone hits the floor." He turned to Browning, "Your men dressed as local police and medical must come in loud, drawing as much attention as you can. Your presence may be the only thing that will keep Stavros and the boys from tearing everything to shreds.

"They will need to be far away to avoid anyone seeing them. Our use of the starlight scope settings has made them cautious. Semjaza doesn't like this little oddity either. Seems the laws of physics are messing with them as well.

John raised his wine glass, "Here's to the resurrection of Greece. And now Glenn wants to show you a movie." Glenn sat up straight, set down his wine and picked up the remote for the video equipment on the far wall.

Glenn walked to the far wall while the screens came to life, "Jacob and I have created a simulation that mimics how the dragonfly drones will carry out their attack."

The video started to the theme, The Flight of the Bumble Bee (youtube). Jacob stood and pointed at the screen, "Now the simulation will show how their flight will change to make use of the wind to accomplish the mission. Jess, we thank you again for this. It is remarkable."

The two columns of drones became four rope looking lines flying in a spiral-like the threads on a screw. Each set of two looked like a DNA helix squirming its way toward the stage. The movement the dragonfly wings combined with the helix motion was spectacular. The helix of drones moved into the wind and used it to turn back toward the other helix, crossing over as they went.

As the two groups started their attack runs, they became four distinct lines two on each side of the guests. When they were just over the crowd, the individual dragonflies darted to their left or right at a forty-five-degree angle, depending on their side of the guests.

As they flew, they formed a crosshatched pattern above the crowd, and then quickly they dropped onto their targets. At this point, the music was enhanced with the squeaky voice from the movie The Fly, "Help Me, Help Me."

John stood applauding, which got everyone else out of their seats, clapping and cheering, "Bravo." He turned to Jess, "I hope that none of the drones decide to turn on us. Tell us the status of the drones?"

Jess stood up and nodded to John. He turned and said, "Dom and Adam we need you guys to get back to Hoss and Sims first thing tonight. If Stavros knows we are here, his boys might attack the compound thinking everyone is in Greece. Hoss, Sims and the town will be working the tunnels preparing to survive whatever comes." John walked them out.

Jess continued, "The major hurdle here is getting into the site and staying undetected, so Trish, Phu and Lil' Joe will move into position tomorrow night. They will spend the day in hiding until it is time to release the dragonflies. This will be nerve-racking, but our two sniper boys will get Trish through it.

"The combined weight of the dragonflies is seventy-five pounds. Trish will fly them to the site sometime after 1:00 am. "Phu and Lil' Joe will move to the site at midnight. They will establish contact with the mother drone and then work with Glenn to ensure the electronic surveillance is working.

John, returning to his chair, "Phu, tomorrow when Trish has successfully launched her manned drone, you and Lil' Joe will haul ass down the hill and across the road. One will take the left side and the other on the right side of the villa.

"You two will join with Trish in a triangle formation for the overwatch. You guys will have the ultimate angles. Anyone, not our people you will make the call on friend or foe.

"As the crowd falls out and it gets quiet, you will move toward Clairmore to support Browning's people with three-dimensional coverage. Again, if Azazel and his buddies decide to stand their ground we need to back away. There is no real challenge we can bring to bear."

John turned to Browning, "George if you feel things going sideways, grab Clairmore and run for it. If you can't do that, put a bullet in his head. Stavros cannot survive this; the world must know he is dead."

John turned to Corwin, "Corwin that leaves you to free-lance. Start with clearing the villa once the drones start their attack. You can decide what you want to do after the house is dead inside."

Corwin was nodding, "Anything you want double-checked or are worried about?" John nodded, "The worst thing that could happen is we get hit in the ass by one of Stavros' security teams. The other is if Browning goes down we need someone to step in and secure Stavros."

John stepped to the middle of the room, "This has been on everyone's mind but we haven't discussed it, what if one of us is taken over by Stavros or one of his sidekicks. What can we do?"

"I have worked hard to find that answer in my head, but I can't find it. All I know is we will do all we can to get you back. Maybe Semjaza and the boys don't want that information in the hands of humans."

Afterward, John mingled with his team with Kat at his side. Everyone was acting relaxed and happy but John could feel the stress they carried; people could die tomorrow.

He led Kat over to Jess then worked his way over to talk to Glenn. John took Glenn aside, "When was the last time you checked on Stavros' murder squad?" Glenn got very quiet with his head looking at his shoes, "Three days at least maybe four. I have been spending every second on the drones." John put his hand on Glenn's shoulder and led him to the back corner of the room; they had their backs to everyone.

John leaned in, "You are doing everything you can, I know that, and do we all feel good about tomorrow?" Glenn nodded yes. "But," John continued, "I have a feeling that if we run the software now we will find Stavros is moving some of his squad here and others to the compound." Glenn's eyes went wide, "Shit."

Chapter Sixty-Six

8:45 pm EET
5:45 am EST
Crete, Greece to Jonesborough, TN

Sims had just reached The Town with No Name and was parking in front of the Coffee Hole in the Ground. He smiled when he saw the huge army tent in the vacant lot next to the crater that once was the Coffee Hole.

Hoss and Adam had made the coffee and Sims and Molly were bringing the doughnuts. Even though the rest of the Coffee Hole Gang was in Greece, they carried on in their honor. On this occasion, Sheriff Barlow and Sergeant Mitchell attended.

Sammy and Bev had worked with Hoss and General Rouse to set up the mess hall; Sergeant Mitchell had flown in all the supplies needed to feed a dozen soldiers indefinitely.

Sims set down the doughnuts and Molly went to say hi to everyone else. He had just grabbed his coffee when his phone went off. He answered, "Glenn the Greek what is up?" Glenn told him about the party and all that went on. Sims was interested in what Jess had to say but Glenn ignored him saying, "John pulled me off to the side last night. He has a feeling that I need to start scanning for Stavros' men again to see what was up. He thinks Stavros might know we are up to something and the position of his men would tell us that."

Sims was now awake, this was a cool idea; he held up his phone, "Guys get over here and listen to this. Glenn, I am putting you on speaker. I have Hoss and the boys here, tell them what's up."

As Glenn was speaking Sims could see the lights coming on in the heads of his sleepy cohorts. While they were listening to Glenn, Sammy brought by scrambled eggs and bacon. Molly escorted him to ensure his safety; she charged him two strips of bacon and a bite of eggs.

Sammy listened as he paid Molly and arranged the food. He stopped and turned toward the phone, "Hey Glenn, did we tag those devil dudes we're holding in the compound?" Glenn a bit flippant, "Yeah, what's that got to do with anything?" Sammy a bit indignant, "Well, if it was up to me I would let those fools go and follow them. Those guys are dumb enough to take you straight to whoever is gonna be making the trouble around here."

Everyone was quiet for a few seconds; Sims was smiling, "Exactly, why I wanted Glenn to repeat what he told me. Glenn, if I were you, I would light up everyone you got and see what this chessboard looks like; tell John he is a genius. Glenn started to say he was the one who…at that point Sims hung up.

Sheriff Jeffery Barlow started speaking with his mouth half-full of doughnut, "I could pick them up from the compound and tell them we are going to send them to Guantanamo as terrorists. Then we go to the Corner Cup, get some lunch and then leave the doors unlocked; they escape, we have a good lunch and Glenn can watch 'em." Hoss took a bite of his doughnut and mumbled, "Brilliant."

Hoss got everyone together inside the tent so they could brainstorm. Molly reminded them that the food would go bad if they didn't eat it all; they agreed and gave her the job of cleaning up.

They needed information that would provide them a much-needed advantage if the shit should actually hit the fan.

Chapter Sixty-Seven

9:45 pm EET
The Stavros Villa
Isle of Crete, Greece

Stavros was leaning back in his recliner receiving good news from his team in South America; they had eliminated another of the doctors who had discovered key ingredients for formulating a cure for various cancers. It appeared that he had been bitten by a venomous snake.

So many simple solutions to the cancer problem lay in plain sight around the world, it amazed Stavros that so few sought them for cures. Thousands of ancient remedies had been cast aside.

Stavros had observed humans for over a thousand years and to him, cancer was a new disease. It resulted from laziness and need for instant everything. The loss of the cooking culture and the mass manufacturing of food had lit the fires of cancer.

The greatest money-making machine in the history of the world was the selling of hope to dying people. They would pay incredible amounts of money to live just one more day…easy money…he smiled.

With the help of the media, Stavros and his pharmaceutical friends had convinced the people of the world that doctors and pharmacies were the only true answers. All other avenues were considered fringe or uncontrolled treatments.

He roused himself and shuffled out onto the veranda overlooking the grounds of the villa. His catering crews hustled back and forth putting together his quarterly meeting. It would be another good night.

He hoped that he and Browning would be able to announce the acquisition of the three Hart Group vendors. They had worked hard and shed much blood but it was not to be.

Although the recent failure upset him, there something else bothering Stavros. He had felt the presence of the Messenger twice in the past week. At first, he thought he was imagining it, but then the second time his blood was agitated it was seeking the source.

Stavros laid down again and contacted Rameel. He told him to take Asael with him to Jonesborough and prepare their people to destroy Hart's compound.

Afterward, he made sure that his elite team of hitters would be present for the meeting. He needed security to be tight. Maybe he had been feeling Hart's blood; he wanted to be ready.

Eleven miles away in his hotel room, John was focused on Azazel. He was racking his brains for help from Semjaza. He was getting nothing. John knew Azazel's reaction would make or break the day for his group. They were fully committed; this bastard had killed Makayla, and in his mind, for more than a day he had killed Kat.

Chapter Sixty-Eight

10:35 pm EET
7:35 am EST
Crete, Greece to Jonesborough, TN

Glenn was carefully setting up the parameters for his search. He was not taking any chances he was tracking everyone right down to their gate identity. His phone started dancing across his makeshift desk; he could see it was Hoss.

"Hoss, glad it is you. Sims is getting to be a complete wise ass." Hoss let out a long sigh, "I know, Jack and I are at a complete loss, he is no longer in the military so we can't just order him around. Then you guys go and make him a full owner and now there is just nothing you can do with him." The whole time Hoss was talking to Glenn he was smiling at Sims.

Hoss continued, "I wanted to let you know we are going ahead with Sammy's idea; we are gonna let these guys go. Barlow is going to tell them he is taking them to General Rouse who is going to fly them to Guantanamo Bay.

"Barlow is going to stop in town to get some lunch and leave the cars unlocked so they can run. We want this to take place in about two hours, but we are not going to do anything until you say you can track'em." Glenn answered, "It would be better if lunch was after 1:30 your time, that way I will have consolidated the data by region and will be able to pick them up easier."

Hoss turned away from the others, "Glenn are you guys ready for your operation?" Glenn sighed, "We are, but there are a lot of variables we don't even know how to deal with; if you know what I mean." Hoss came back, "Those are some scary variables. We are hoping none of that goes down here." Glenn now distant, "At least you guys are getting Dom and Adam back; they should be there in thirteen hours or so. I got to run this stuff." Glenn hung up.

Hoss turned to everyone, "Two more for coffee in the morning; Dom and Adam are on their way back." Now let's get this operation started. We need to fake some prisoner exit interviews and prep these guys so they want to run.

After they finished eating, they figured out how they were going to proceed with the prisoners and then headed to the compound. Sergeant Mitchell was called away by General Rouse with the agreement that Hoss could get him back in a hurry.

Hoss, Sims, Molly and Sheriff Barlow headed down to the makeshift brig to roust the devil's dumb asses. They walked past the four cutters from the van and started with Rocky and Bull Winkle. Molly decided she would keep an eye on the other four in the first cell. She sat at attention drilling them with her black eyes.

Rocky stood up cocky as ever, "Finally, they made you dicks let us go; so hurry up." Barlow said,

"That is fine with me. I can't wait to hand you over to General Rouse."

Bull Winkle stood up to his full size, "What the hell are you punks talking about? You better quit screwing around and get us out of here." Sims pulled out the keys to the sliding doors, "Step back while I open the door." Both Rocky and Bull Winkle stepped forward. The other four prisoners started nodding their heads and egging Bull Winkle on. Molly growled and they retreated quietly.

Sims started laughing, "Hoss they are all yours." Hoss walked up to the door right in front of Bull Winkle. Hoss let him feel all of his six foot six and two hundred and ninety pounds. Bull Winkle was staring right where Hoss' neck would be if he had one. Neither of the devil's dumb asses noticed that Sims had quietly unlocked the door. At this point, the four guys in the other cell had moved into the furthest corner away from the action.

In defiance, Bull Winkle started to move his face closer to the glass just as Hoss ripped the door open and grabbed him by the throat. Barlow jumped straight up, "Holy shit, no one that size should be that fast." Sims started to giggle. The other prisoners were murmuring in fear. Molly moved closer to them.

Hoss picked up Rocky with his other hand and held them both against the back wall; Bull Winkles feet were well off the ground and Rocky was showing his fear of heights.

Hoss put his nose about a quarter of an inch from Bull Winkles nose, "You murdering pieces of shit are not getting out. General Rouse has arranged lifetime memberships for you to the Guantanamo Bay Club; no one will ever see you again."

Hoss then dropped Rocky. He pulled Bull Winkle's head away from the wall then smashed it back into the wall just hard enough to get his attention and keep him conscious.

Hoss turned to Sims and Barlow, "Would you guys take Rocky here down to his interview while I speak with this thing in private?" Bull Winkle was screaming for them to come back as they left with Rocky. Hoss threw him across the room, stepped out into the hall and locked the door.

Hoss stopped and looked at the other four idiots, "You guys cool?" They all nodded slowly while looking at Molly. Hoss arrived in time to see Rocky eyes getting teary; the term terrorist had done it.

They processed all of the devil dudes. After reading the charges, they were now viewed as enemy combatants. Their hands were zip-tied in front of them, and then Barlow escorted them to the sheriff's cars parked just outside the kitchen exit.

Halfway back to Jonesborough Barlow opened the radio channel between both cars, "I don't know about you boys but I am hungry. I am thinking a hoagie from the Corner Cup, coke and fries."

One of the deputies cut in, "What no beer?" Barlow laughed, "Gentlemen we are on duty and as highly trained law enforcement people we are forbidden such pleasures." You gonna let these mutts mess up our lunch?"

Barlow sighed, "Ok, ok just one or two then we got to get these guys to the General. They got rooms reserved at Guantanamo." A sullen voice, "Oh shit, bye, bye baby."

They arrived at the Corner Cup at 1:47 pm, then ate and drank until their cars were empty.

Chapter Sixty-Nine

5:35 am EET
1:45 pm EST
Hotel, Base of Operations
Crete, Greece

Glenn was uneasy about the time the program was taking to acquire all the tags. He knew that asking for verification of each tag using gate evaluations was going to add time but now he was getting worried.

John was up and moving around and he had less than an hour to get it together. John brought Glenn a cup of coffee and sat on the couch in Glenn's room.

John sat quietly, it was driving Glenn nuts, "John I am sorry this hasn't come together yet, but it should be anytime now." John waited for a beat then, "It is my problem, Glenn. I told you to drop everything and focus on Rameel and Stavros.

"I realized when I made you lead on this, that you would have to let somethings go. Managing the entire group as well as our unwanted guests i.e. the TJAGs and Rouse, that's a tough ask."

John looked at Glenn then realized he had been talking to himself. Glenn was diving down the rabbit hole; something had grabbed all of his attention; John stood up and slowly moved to look over Glenn's shoulder, "Are those tags here? I mean are they at the villa? Glenn!"

Glenn jumped, "Sorry, almost all of Stavros' murder squad, is either at the villa or on their way. That's thirteen killers reporting for duty." John was already ahead of the game, "How fast can you reprogram twenty of the thirty sentry dragonflies to become active killers against these dicks?"

Glenn was still staring at the data. John yelled this time, "Glenn get with it. What the hell are you staring at." Glenn waved him off, "It appears that they are setting up hard locations in the front of the villa to defend an assault. From where they are located they might see the dragonflies a good six to ten seconds before they can cover the crowd and take out Stavros."

John was getting pissed, "Glenn get over here." John moved to the middle of the room. Glenn was moving slowly looking back at the monitor the entire time. John put his left hand on Glenn's chest, which caused his head to turn toward him.

John made eye contact with him then, "What the fuck are you doing?" This got the six foot four inch Sasquatch mad and focused on John, "What do you think I am doing?"

John kept looking him straight in the eyes, "You are the lead on this. Quit looking at the problem and start solving it. I asked you a question, now give my answer." Glenn shook his head, "What question?" John gave him a look like Glenn had frozen under the stress. "You didn't hear a thing I said." Then John restated the question.

Glenn didn't blink he just turned away back to his computer, looked at the numbers and the arrivals again. He looked at the time and then the activity schedule of all the drones, "Jacob can get it done it the next three hours."

John not letting up on Glenn, "What is your assessment of the operation right now; are we still a go?" Glenn controlled and arrogant, "Yes, but we are gonna have to cut Trish loose and use the manned drone as an offensive weapon. We will have her stay low, go down the back of the mountain then come in from the south and take out the front positions at the villa.

"After that, she could return to her spot on top of the hill. Once she releases the drones, she will have the time to move behind the hill before the drones have taken up their formation.

"The key is when she attacks. If they don't respond to the drones until they are right on top of them, then everything will go as planned. If they engage early, then someone will have to take out Clairmore immediately.

"John I think we should release the drones that are assigned to Clairmore earlier so they can work around the villa unnoticed. They can take him down as the others arrive. You should be in the crowd ready to make the call, or even take the shot, should the drones not reach their mark.

"This will not change Browning's efforts only Trish's. If you stay out of the crowd you should take Lil' Joe's spot. Lil' Joe becomes the sniper, Trish is in front and you could slip into the villa to help Corwin; he has thirteen hired killers hanging around inside. If by chance Stavros makes it inside the villa you two need to kill him without becoming him."

John sat on the bed, "Let me recap, Trish releases a few drones, then a few seconds later the whole cluster, and then she goes to the front. Lil' Joe stays in the hide as the sniper. Corwin starts on the roof and drives them down to me.

"If Stavros avoids the dragonflies, Corwin and I mop up if we are still alive. The final cluster of drones will wipe out any of Stavros' killers as they work their way toward the crowd" John stood up, "Ok, send it to everyone now.

"Glenn, make sure Jess, Kat, and Trish are dead cold ready for what they have to do; kick Jacob in the ass right now." Glenn grabbed his phone and turned back to John, "You and I need to do this again in three hours." John smiled, "Yes Sir, see ya then." John left the room and Glenn collapsed into his chair.

He needed to change the formulation for the dragonflies that were going after Stavros' killers; it had to be lethal. Glenn's phone brought him back to focus. It was Sims. He didn't take it. He needed to talk to Jacob first, then check Jonesborough's tracking and see if he could find the escapees. He wanted to have something to tell Hoss.

Chapter Seventy

7:48 am EET
4:48 pm EST
Jonesborough, TN to Hotel base
Crete, Greece

Sheriff Barlow, Sims and his deputies were a bit hungover but couldn't stop for that. They had responded to two car thefts and a robbery at the Jonesborough Wine and Spirits. The descriptions matched their escapees.

Hoss had been feeding the data to Glenn, but he was not hearing back. Hoss knew that if Glenn was too busy, that it meant trouble. It seemed like their plan was breaking down.

Hoss was in the kitchen and Molly was in her bed. He finally had some time to think. He decided it was time to get proactive.

He felt that none of the prisoners knew about the confrontation with Rameel at the cabin. They felt the cabin was still their rally point and they would head for it. They would never believe that someone could chase off Rameel. Hoss called Sims and asked him to find out if they had indeed headed that way.

Hoss finally heard from Nick. He and General Rouse had been working in Washington D.C. with the Joint Chiefs. They were telling them about Browning and trying to get them to believe what had happened in Jonesborough. Trish's camera work had saved them.

Later Creps and Dunn were consulted. Nick played the footage of their part in the confrontation of Rameel. After much head shaking and calls of bullshit, they agreed that Browning had played a major role in flushing out Stavros, and had supplied information that had saved lives. Ultimately, after watching Rouse debrief him at The Greenbrier, The Joint Chiefs agreed to a temporary reinstatement of the Deputy Director with conditions after the actions in Greece.

Hoss was finishing up with Nick, "So Sergeant Mitchell is bringing you home?" Nick sounded tired, "Yup, we should be to the compound in about an hour or two."

Hoss said, "That's good, 'cuz we need him to swing by Tri-Cities airport and pick up Dom and Adam. They missed their exchange in London, adding another three hours to their trek home." Nick agreed and was gone.

Hoss was thinking about his conversations when Molly put her cold nose on his forearm; she needed to pee. He started through the living room to the front doors when his phone went off again, "Glenn are you guys alright?" Glenn filled him in and then changed up the conversation, "Look, Hoss, I got a bad feeling that all of Stavros' hitters are here because he is sending Rameel and his buddy Asael your way.

"John says that Semjaza and those guys can feel each other's blood when they are near. Then he turns around and says that he thinks that Stavros can feel him and might be ready for our attack. What do you make of that shit?"

Hoss took a deep breath, "All I can do is connect the dots. Stay with me; think back to the compound and all the research you did that night. Think about John's dreams how they lined up. Now think about how John died and Semjaza brought him back to life…" Glenn cut him off, "I never believed that part. That is impossible."

Hoss ignored him, "Why would Semjaza bring him back? Why would he care? He could feel his blood; shit, all of them felt his blood at the same time. Don't you believe that Rameel felt John's blood? Rameel backed away after feeling it when John told him he was protected by Semjaza. Glenn accept the fact, regardless of what you believe, these boys believe John has angel DNA coming out his ass.

"Glenn that is why they are coming here; John won't be here. There is no protection for us. John feels it, but he sees it as Stavros knowing he is there. What he is feeling is that Stavros is taking advantage of John being on Crete."

Glenn deflected, "It appears from all of the updates you guys have sent in, that your escapees are heading back to their original rally point." Hoss smiled, "That's good, now we can verify all of the data so you can monitor them."

Glenn got quiet, "We won't be able to do that, John has everything focused on the villa." Hoss intense, "Here is what is going to happen, General Rouse is going to get you coverage and you are going to monitor our guys and our situation. Jacob can handle that even if the shit hits the fan. You don't bother John about this, you just do it; you are the lead. If he bitches, you say exactly this, "As the lead, it is my responsibility to protect the entire group." Hoss hung up.

Chapter Seventy-One

Day Eleven*
10:48 am EET
7:48 pm EST*
Jonesborough, TN

Hoss checked his watch then called Nick back, "Nick sorry to bug you again but is Mitchell there with you?" Nick laughed, "Oh here we go are you giving him a message from his lady in Greece?" Hoss shook his head, "Can I talk to him or what?"

Hoss could hear Nick tell Mitchell he was in a bad mood as he handed Mitchell the phone, "What's up Master Sergeant?" Hoss stated, "I am not in a bad mood, I am in a hurry. So are you guys leaving right now?" Mitchell replied, "We are fifty yards from the chopper and closing."

Hoss hesitated, "Mitchell do you have a thermal pod in that thing?" Mitchell stopped walking, "No, but I can have one installed in fifteen minutes what's up? Hoss was relieved, "I want you to do a fly over the cabin where we met Ol' Black Eyes. I think our escapees are headed there.

"I would rather that Sims and Barlow stayed away. Right now they are on their way to check out the area." Mitchell agreed, "Roger that, I am on it. Hey Sergeant, I will have to refuel after flying all the way back and picking up Dom and Adam; should I replace my Hellfire missiles while I am at it?" Hoss sarcastically, "Sounds like vigilance to me." Mitch handed the phone back to Nick.

Nick felt something was up, "Hoss what is all the fuss, these guys are minor leaguers?" Hoss sounding tired, "Glenn and I believe that there is going to be an attack against the compound that is going to coincide with our attack on Stavros' villa. All of Stavros' hitters have been called back to the villa so Rameel and some other creature can come down on us."

Nick was quiet, "I should talk to John about this and see what his plan is." Hoss stepped in, "Glenn and I would appreciate it if you waited on that. I have a lot to share with you when you get here. Things are changing in Greece by the hour. We are stretching our resources and calling for more; let's talk first."

The phone was silent for about twenty seconds, "Ok Hoss I will wait. What is Rouse's position on this?" Hoss smiled, "I have no idea, but I am about to call the Deputy Director of the NSA and ask for a couple of his best Glenn type guys." Nick tentative, "Sounds like you believe we are in real trouble?" Hoss sighed, "I hope not, but this could be the shit we dare not think of." Nick hung up.

Hoss called Sims and told him to stay away from the cabin that Mitchell was handling it. Sims was relieved, "Cool now we can get some lunch.

Barlow yelled over Sims shoulder, "You want me back at the compound or what? Hoss thought about it, "If I was Sheriff, I would be looking for strangers in my town. Calling my lookouts and posting a watch; new people lead to new problems." Barlow nodded, "Glad to do it." Hoss hung up.

Hoss was not used to hanging out with Molly. He returned to the kitchen. Molly was sat at attention in front of the refrigerator and barked. Hoss winched, she had not eaten since she ate almost all the food at the breakfast.

He dialed Browning's cell while he was fixing Molly cold steak leftovers. He said hello to Browning as he set down Molly's dish, "Deputy Director I am glad to hear you have been reinstated. I hope you are enjoying your current assignment, now I need your help."

Browning listened carefully to what Hoss was saying. He agreed to send him his best two-man team to work at the compound so they could react immediately to Hoss's needs without a middleman.

Hoss could tell they were both leery of giving too much access. He decided that the bullshit had gone on for too long. He told Browning to send his best to the compound and he would set them up in the now famous shooting station 3.

Hoss needed some time with Nick and Sims. They needed to plan for the defense of the compound. He wasn't sure when it would happen, but it felt like it would start as Stavros took the stage in Greece at 6:30 pm EET and 3:30 am EST.

Hoss called Glenn and told him to focus on their operation that he had figured a way to handle monitoring their end. He kind of apologized then hung up. He was now clear to use Browning's guys without Glenn snooping around.

Chapter Seventy-Two

10:48 am EET
7:48 pm EST
Hotel, Base of Operations
Crete, Greece

Glenn had called everyone into the banquet room for another status meeting to establish a clear sequence for their attack based on the various contingencies. Most of the tables had been made into one large conference table about twelve feet long.

Glenn sat in the middle and John at the head to Glenn's left. Glenn jumped right in as everyone sat down, "Jacob you have been busy; tell us." Jacob leaned forward elbows on the table, "I have sixteen drones assigned to our new guests and the aerosol darts have been upgraded for their pleasure. They have been reprogrammed and tested within our simulation; it is simple and clean.

"There were six drones assigned to Stavros and we are releasing three of them before we release the sixteen killer drones." Jacob leaned back in his chair.

Jess was next, "Kat and I have worked with Jacob and Glenn and realized we could give Trish more time by releasing all the drones and let them leave the swarm when they were cued up. Kat and Trish have worked out a firing sequence for the frontal attack and for her final sweep after the action.

"Trish can take her time going down the back of the hill and around to face the placements in front.

If the drones do their job, she should be able to retake her initial position above the hide with a clear look at all the festivities. If not she will light up the front and it will be go-time right then."

Phu's face appeared on the room's monitor, "He added, "What Trish does will determine what Lil' Joe and John will do. If the drones work on the front, I got right and Lil' Joe goes left and we work around the villa to the stage. If the drones get mixed results out front, I will go right and John will take Lil Joe's spot on the right. Lil' Joe will become the sniper for Clairmore."

John stood up, "I have talked with Corwin and we have worked out how we can best clear the house. What Trish does, will determine how we proceed. If she engages the front, many of Stavros' men will move to help.

"That chaos will give us the advantage, otherwise when Stavros goes down they will all jump into the barrel and will be drone bait or worse. If Stavros goes as planned I will enter the villa from the left as Lil' Joe takes my place. I will clear the lower floor as Corwin works his way down from the roof. We will have to decide on the fly what to do as these guys react.

Glenn leaned back, "So we release all the drones and Trish works her way around the hill. The first three dragonflies go and seven seconds after that the sixteen killers are released and seven seconds after that all hell breaks loose as the rest of the dragonflies do their jobs. That is what we want; Stavros goes first then it is game on.

Again, we cannot control what happens after Clairmore is down and Stavros has left him. He and his buddies could go off or they leave when Browning and public services get there.

Be careful watch, your lines of fire and take care of yourself. We go at 6:30 pm, Stavros will be giving his welcoming speech. If he is delayed, we just sit tight and we will pull the trigger when we are ready.

Chapter Seventy-Three

1:44 pm EET
10:44 pm EST
The Stavros Villa
Isle of Crete, Greece

Stavros was met at the base of the steps of the villa by the host of the night's events. He walked around the front of the villa looking at the marvelous rock formation that sat askew of him on the westerly side. He always had enjoyed how the mountainous formation acted like a shade being pulled down as if to announce the end of the day.

Stavros turned his attention to the four security pods in the front. They were tinted, bulletproof glass allowing for three men each. They were chic and modern but the message was clear, nobody was going to cause a problem tonight.

He followed the host to the rooms they had prepared for his special guests. He approved their late-night menus and asked to walk the grounds. The host took him to the eating area. It was set up in the middle of the olive trees, and the place settings were rustic but stylish. He approved the food and the sequence of its presentation. He gave himself ten minutes to welcome the guests and motivate them to push for higher earnings, only the finest quality drugs, and customer satisfaction.

They called for his driver and he told the host he would return at five o'clock to meet early with a few clients.

Chapter Seventy-Four

10:44 pm EST
Hart Compound
Jonesborough, TN

Sammy and Bev were at the compound to barbeque steaks, veggies, and taters for those who remained. Molly wasn't much of a taters girl so she stayed with the steaks. Everyone went easy on the beers at dinner thinking it could be a long night.

Dom and Adam asked Sims to call shooting station 3 and tell the NSA team of Justin and Zack to come to dinner. Justin was tall with an Ichabod Crane kinda vibe, and Zack was medium height but soft and round with white hair; they were both in their thirties. Hoss tagged them, Sherlock Holmes and Dr. Watson.

They both had cut their teeth in Afghanistan. They were pounded with questions while they ate and they gave back as good as they got. Sims actually declared them human beings that were decent folk, and all was well.

Nick, having just returned with Dom and Adam from the airport, had talked to John about how they were going to take down Stavros. Afterward, he joined those fearing the 6:30 pm EET time. They would have to be set, awake and ready for a 3:30 am EST reckoning, a real balancing of the books.

Nick starting to eat said, "Earlier when Sergeant Mitchell flew over the cabin on Bill Bennett Road, we picked up eight signatures; six warm humans and two cold humans, or as I say the others category. Holmes and Watson verified the video confirming all the humans, and others, in the cabin were not moving around and probably sleeping."

After dinner, Barlow dropped by with some disturbing news. Jake from the Groceries and Tackle store had gone missing in the middle of the day; his store was left unattended. In addition, Brian, one of Barlow's men was missing. They found his car down an embankment. He was gone but his seatbelt was still buckled.

Nick sat back looking around at everyone, "The others category is looking real." Barlow sat down while Molly and Bev brought him BBQ and a beer.

As they were beginning to focus on available defensive actions, they heard Sergeant Mitchell fly over and land in the middle of the lawn by the south fencing. Bev and Molly headed back to see Sammy about more BBQ.

Sergeant Mitchell sat between Sims and Nick and across from Hoss, "Two Hellfire missiles locked and loaded and scopes with Starlight for all. He turned to Sherlock and the Doctor, "Did Hoss show you boys the starlight filters for your surveillance equipment?" They both nodded in unison. Mitchell looked at Sims and whispered, "That is some bubblehead shit right there."

Hoss stood up; he motioned with his arms and said, "Huddle up and pay attention." He was now Master Sergeant Hoss Cartwright.

Once they all moved closer and sat in a way they could see each other he continued, "We have got some decisions to make. I am sure that at least six men and their pets are going to come for us this morning around 3:30 am.

"We have to find a way to destroy or distract them to defend this place. I am sure they want to kill everyone and flatten or destroy everything. If we secure ourselves in the tunnels, we should survive. "We were able to recover Sims and the boys the other day. Rameel never rematerialized or whatever into the tunnels after them, so maybe we will be safe, or we try to fight'em."

Sergeant Mitchell raised his hand. Hoss nodded, Mitchell continued, "When that beast was in the Coffee Hole and I hit it with the Hellfires that thing was gone. I know it didn't die, but we didn't hear from it for a while."

Mitchell winked at Hoss, "Now we won't know where it is, so I suggest we wait until it is tearing the shit out of Sims' house and then clean it up with the missiles." Mitchell felt a sharp jab to his ribs from Sims.

Nick was serious and a bit dark, "I don't really care all that much how we do this but I want those six guys that cut up Makayla dead by the end of the night. If they don't come here, then later we kill them in their sleep."

Dom and Adam looked at each other and smiled. Dom said, "Why are we waiting for them to come here why don't we take them out in the open. "Shit Adam shot four of them in two seconds the other day. Better they chase our asses out there than destroy everything here trying to get to us…ya think?"

Hoss and Nick looked at Mitchell. Mitchell smiled, "Better to fly than walk into battle." Adam smacked his forehead with his hand, "Dah, we got a chopper, let's blow their ass out of bed then see how they react. Only a couple of people need to go and we are guaranteed that those six boys are gonna burn as they should." Mitchell was going to add something but Hoss gave him a look; he nodded slightly and was quiet.

Hoss looked at Nick then Sims, "That would leave us with a Hellfire in the bank. Mitchell was excited, "Just let me contact the General and we will be good." Hoss looked at Mitchell and said, "Call sign Hawk." Sergeant Mitchell stood, saluted the Master Sergeant and headed for the chopper.

Nick asked, "What the hell just happened?" Hoss looked at Nick with a very serious look, "I just cut out the General. Hawk is an emergency order to save lives. It is how we saved Trish and Jess at the crossroads.

"Sergeant Mitchell is relieved of all responsibility and all the weight goes on me. The only problem is that Mitchell must stay with the chopper until the order is carried out.

"I will relieve him later, but someone should take him his dinner and a beer." Barlow gathered up Mitchell's food and headed toward the kitchen. He was going to warm up his dinner and get him an extra beer.

Molly was sleeping in her bed and Sammy and Bev had long since left for home. Barlow gathered up the leftovers, nuked them in the microwave and bagged it up with two beers. He was walking across the large grass lawn when he stopped. Barlow felt he was being followed. He continued on a few more feet then turned quickly to face his enemy. All he found was Molly sitting at attention looking all around; he swore he could hear her whistling, and saying nothing to see here, move along.

Barlow laughed and started running, the next thing he knew Molly was running around him having fun playing. Barlow faked as if he threw her a treat. When she bolted, he sprinted to the chopper. They got to the chopper at the same time; Molly jumped in the back and sat in the gunner's seat staring out the cockpit.

Barlow handed the bags of food to Mitchell, pulled an ammo box out of the chopper and sat on it. He looked at Molly who was playing it cool, "Good luck eating your food, the meat shark followed me. She stayed back some sixty feet. She was very quiet; if I wasn't freaked out about tonight I would have never felt her there."

Mitchell slipped her a piece of steak, "She is tough but she knows when it is too dangerous for her or anyone else. If she hides bad juju is on the way."

Barlow probing, "So, Hoss sent you to your room cuz you wanted to tell the General?" The Sergeant laughed, "No he read my expression and enthusiasm properly; I was hoping he would make the call to go to Hawk." Barlow grinned, "So we are going?" Mitchell chewing and talking, "Above my paygrade, ask Hoss."

When Barlow returned to the patio, he could hear some raised voices. As he sat down, they ignored him. Sims was demanding to go on the run to blow up the cabin. Nick disagreed, it was personal he needed to go.

Hoss listened to another round of it then raised his voice, "You guys don't get to make this decision. I am in charge of the facility at the moment whether you like it or not. You would never under any circumstances get to choose who flies in my chopper, so get over yourselves and listen up."

Sims and Nick could not believe that Hoss took control of their compound. They owned and ran the place not him. They looked at Hoss both ready to say something. Hoss stood up and put one foot on the picnic table's bench and leaned in with his head tilted, "Well gentlemen what's it gonna be?"

Sims knew Hoss represented the General and he was putting his ass on the line with the Hawk call; he looked at Nick then back at Hoss, "Sorry you are right, make the call.

Hoss walked a few steps and leaned against a post. "The soldiers will go unless they are an owner of the Hart Group. Therefore, Adam, Mitchell, and Dom will fly out there, blow-up the cabin and run like hell. At that point, we will be at war with Stavros."

Nick asked the ultimate question, "If we go now, will Stavros hear about it and change something or will he shrug it off, knowing that his two boys will be fine?" Sims replied, "He ain't gonna worry about losing the losers." Hoss noted no one said a thing about Jake or Brian.

After much discussion, Hoss deferred to Nick and Sims; they deferred to Stavros' arrogance and said, "Let's fly."

By the time they loaded the chopper, they lifted off at 12:26 am EST or 3:26 pm in Greece.

Chapter Seventy-Five

> 12:32 am EST
> 3:32 pm EET
> Hart Compound and Hotel Base
> Jonesborough and Crete

Corwin was trying to take a nap like everyone else, but he was too worried to sleep. Something was not right. He sat up with his back to the wall grinding on the operation; it seemed clean. He settled on the point he didn't trust the dragonflies. There was a knock at the door.

Corwin opened the door to find John and Browning. John stepped in, "Something is bugging the shit out of me and I need to talk it through." Corwin pointed to the chairs, "I was just struggling with the same gut feeling; something is wrong."

John sat down and motioned to Browning who was sitting on the edge of the couch, "The reactions of Stavros' men is what worries me. We are counting on them being stunned before they are drugged by the drones. I don't think that is what is going to happen."

Corwin stood up snapping his fingers three times, "You are right, Clairmore's body is Stavros' most prized possession, his men will be trained to retain it at all costs. If he goes down, there will be a battle for the body."

John looked up, "I missed it. Now we have given them three more seconds before the drones hit the front. All of those guys could be moving through the house in two seconds and would not turn back until they found the body."

Corwin was excited, "We just need to delay them a bit. Let's do both. Let's attack the front when the dragonflies are actually on Clairmore's face. Lil' Joe can call it from his scope; then we all just let it rip to ensure Browning gets him to the ambulance."

John said, "Then what?" Browning looked at Corwin then to John, "This is going to happen so fast the next part will be dealing with Stavros' men as they dodge the drones and take fire from us. It will get quiet fast; the drones won't stop until it is done."

Corwin, still skeptical of the drones, "What if they get swatted down or miss?" John raised his eyebrows, "We got one hundred and fifty of them that's about four each." Corwin shrugged, "Still…ya know?"

Across the globe in Jonesborough, Sergeant Mitchell put the chopper down in a field about eight miles from the cabin. He took out his cell phone and called Hoss. Hoss picked up on the second ring, "State your business." Mitchell replied, "Can you have Sherlock give me a call and then get me a frequency we can all chat on?" Hoss was still in hearing distance of Sims, "I can do that, but leave me out of it I am busy." Mitchell paused, "I am going to make them chase me and I will blow the cabin after I do a bat turn. That will guarantee that Jake and Barlow's boys aren't in the cabin."

Hoss was quiet, "How much might it cost me?" Mitch smiled, "About fourteen point six million, but it will ensure the Hawks will live." Hoss winced, "I got to go. I don't want to know." Five minutes later Mitch's phone rang.

Mitch answered, "Holmes or Watson?" the caller replied, "This is Zack." Mitch tried again, "Holmes or Watson." Zack replied, "Watson, what can I do for you?" Mitch got to it, "I was told you two guys were the best of the best, from outer space to boots on the ground you are the guys…yes or no?" Watson now a little pissed, "Yes, what can I do for you?"

"I need you to hack into my chopper and fly it back to the compound after we jump out of it into the forest and if needs be, blow it up. Do you have that in your kit?" Holmes responded, "We need to know what your expected outcome is and see if we are cleared for what you want." Mitch now a little put out, "Ok Holmes and Watson listen up. The Deputy Director put you under our direction. He chose you because you have the ability to operate in pressure situations.

"You are about to enter into one of those situations and your performance may save or kill eleven people in the next hour; so, no you don't check in with anyone. By the end of the night you will have seen and done things none of your watercooler buddies could dream of; so let's get to work.

"Can you do what I ask and remember there are no rules? If you must, steal what you need you are cleared to do so." Watson jumped in, "What kind of chopper do you have?" Mitch looked at Dom and grinned, "Ok, we got us an S-97 Sikorsky Raider circa 2017." Holmes said, "This might take a while."

Mitch a little pissed, "You have all the time you want as long as you get it resolved in the next five minutes. People, you screw this up and you won't ever work for us again.

"I have done side jobs for Mr. Hart and let me tell you your bonus will be about ten years earnings if all of this works out." Mitch was now yelling, "So tighten up your shit and tell me what you are going to do."

Watson's voice, "Ok, the Sikorsky platform is a modification of an unmanned combat drone, made by Northrup named The Scout. The Scout has all the remote software. In fact, we both worked this drone identifying high profile targets in Afghanistan. This should work."

Mitch was excited, "Ok patch it together and start my chopper as your test. I am sending you the pan number of the chopper now." Holmes said, "We have to find and authorize the use of this…Mitch cut him off, "Sherlock get on board or go home.

"Use your access, find the software, copy it, patch it in and then start this fucking chopper or I will have Master Sergeant Cartwright shoot you for treason.

"Gentlemen you are sitting in the blackest part of any black site. You are bound by your oaths; get it together."

Sergeant Mitchell looked at Adam and Dom, "Too much?" Adam shook his head, "They are only a couple of miles away, we could go hold a gun to their head; it might be faster." Dom laughed, "Chill, I am not looking forward to jumping from a crashing blender." Adam nodded.

Ten minutes later, Watson's voice, "Here we go." The motors started to whine, the rotors turned, and everything came online. Mitch winked at Dom, "Ok who is flying this thing?" "It's me, Watson." Adam talking to himself, "I love it when they finally give in to their nickname and own who they are."

Mitch smiling again, "Ok my dear Watson, take us up to three hundred feet and hover." The chopper wound up and climbed straight up to three hundred feet and hovered." "Great job, now rotate thirty degrees right and back to zero then thirty left and back to zero." Watson performed perfectly. Mitch asked for control of the chopper and got it; he headed for the cabin.

"Watson you passed with flying colors. Holmes, you need to pull your head out of your ass. You will be on the cameras. I want you to see this shit up close and personal.

"You remember the X-Files Sherlock?" Holmes sounding bored, "Yes Sir," Mitch with even more energy, "Well that is like Sesame Street, compared to what we are dealing with tonight. I have to put my life in Watson's hands. I hope to God that he gets this right so he can collect his medal for doing so.

"Sherlock, keep recording every inch in high definition with the best sound you can get; I am going full cameras now."

Chapter Seventy-Six

4:17 pm EET
1:17 am EST
Stavros' Residence
Isle of Crete, Greece

Stavros was resting in his favorite chair having a chat with Rameel. His humans were all resting up for the attack on the compound. Stavros was double-checking a few points, "I want you to wait until you know I am giving my greeting before you take Hart's compound.

"I imagine they will hide in the tunnels like children. You will have a free hand to destroy everything. I hope that you can cripple his ability to respond in any way against our holdings. If they decide to fight, rip them apart and then feed them to that mutt of a dog he loves so much. When you are done release your humans into the forest so they can tell the others of our victory."

Stavros relaxed, even more; tonight was going to be a great night. He would celebrate all his victories. He had exterminated another threat to the plague of cancer; it would continue to rage on fueled by the accumulation of toxins distributed in the drugs he spread all over the world.

He needed to downplay the recent rash of deaths and deformities that resulted from many of the wonder drugs of the past. It was a game of leapfrog; you release the latest drug to take the place of the one that was no longer trusted; sometimes it was as easy as changing the name.

Stavros knew that time was running out on the drug scam, he needed to take control of all the world's arms manufacturing. He would use various companies and technologies tied together like a ball of snakes. Stavros would own them all, but no one would be able to make heads or tails out of it.

Stavros knew the key lied with John Hart and his people. War machines needed incredible amounts of power, and John Hart had all of it. Stavros had not come close enough to understand how it worked.

The fact that so few people knew it existed made it even harder to deal with. Tonight, he would take the next step into finding out. If Rameel could make it into the tunnels, he might find their prototypes.

Chapter Seventy-Seven

1:42 am EST
4:42 pm EET
Hart Compound
Jonesborough, TN

Hoss, Nick, and Sims had taken Molly and moved up to the widow's walk suite. They felt better being high up with a 360-degree vantage point. They were watching the feed on the monitors. Holmes and Watson were handling the audio and video production quite well.

Nick looked at Hoss, "I took three of the dragonflies to Washington with us to sell the simulation of our attack. They should still be in the chopper. Hoss picked up his radio, "Hawk 2 this is Hawk 1 Big Hawk wants to know if you still have three dragonflies on board?"

Dom and Adam looked at Mitch, "We got drones?" Mitch smiled, "Affirmative Hawk 1, I have Holmes and Watson working on the software and such. We will do a complete Trish on the cabin to see what we got." Hoss all business, "Roger that."

Mitch gave Dom his phone, "Get those guys on that." He looked at Adam, "Dig the drones out of the ammo box and fire them up so Holmes can play the dragonfly video game. I totally forgot about those, maybe we can adlib a new outcome."

Dom looked at the drones then to Mitch, "They found Glenn's flight guides. They are looking for starlight but can't find it." Mitch grabbed the phone, "Sherlock, they are not under the modes icon, they are with the camera filters...good, yup. Do you have the source maps up so you can fly them into the area? There is a 3D working model of the cabin in Glenn's files...cool, so we are set." Mitch shook his head, those two guys are good, they just pulled my ass out of the fire."

When Mitch got within a mile, he came down to the tree line and called Holmes and Watson, "Ok boys are you ready to go to work." Holmes with attitude, "We have been doing most of the work." Mitch laughed, "That was playtime. Now everything you do will have consequences."

Mitch turned on all the microphones and cockpit cameras, "Ok, we are going to hold a drone out the window, when it starts to flutter we will drop it. Adam moved to the chopper's side door, "This one is a dash three." Holmes repeated, "Dash three." The wings began to move and Adam tossed it out the door. It corrected itself and was lost in the darkness. After all of the drones were flying, Adam told Watson to hover the overwatch and circle with the others.

Sims was impressed with the picture and sound that was coming through, "Just like Glenn's work, these guys are good." Hoss humphed, "Remember these guys are using Glenn's stuff and so far they haven't screwed it up." Nick pointed to the screen, "Look." The drone's images of the cabin were coming through.

Barlow entered the widow's suite, "Did I miss anything. I had to put Jonesborough to sleep." Nick waved him over, "Look at the screen; they are all around the table eating something and talking to Jake and your guy Brian."

Nick was reaching for his radio when the picture went to starlight and Ol' Black Eyes appeared. Sims started pacing, "I don't care whose body he is in that Rameel dude is ugly."

Mitch had just told Holmes to go to starlight when it came on the screen they were looking right at Ol' Black Eyes. Mitch smiled, "Hey Holmes you remember the X-Files?" Watson voice, "What the hell is that? It is like someone's head is under his face…shit."

Mitch again, "Holmes I asked you a question boy." Holmes sarcastically, "I thought you were full of shit Master Sergeant, now I see I was wrong; you are not completely full of shit. You gonna tell us what that is." Mitch said, "That is classified, you will see for yourself in a minute.

"Now that we found Jake let's move the third dragonfly toward the other window and see if we can find Brian." Holmes aligned the third drone with the window on the other side of the cabin and found a police officer with solid white eyes with no pupils.

Barlow was shaking his head, "Brian is looking jacked, they have gone all Johnny Winters on him; not a good look." Nick looked around the room, they all had their mouths hanging open, then they just lost it laughing. Adam's added, "Now Brian is the undercover albino brother."

Mitch serious now, "Nick these drones have the armed aerosol darts right?" Nick thinking, "Yeah they have the ones Jacob demonstrated in the widows walk a couple of days ago. I think its hash oil; Mexico's finest. Corwin liked it." Mitch was smiling to himself, "Perfect."

Mitch's voice seemed to change, "Sergeant Major Cartwright, we are going to engage the cabin. Our first pass will be a strafing run from the rear. It's designed to get Ol' Black Eyes and Johnny the albino to come out of the cabin. Holmes will then have the drones shoot Jake and Brian full of weed. At that point, the beasts should dump their bodies and give chase.

"We will then do a stall turn and come right back at the cabin and blow the shit out of it. Our boys will be outside and away from the blast. We will then evade them by hiding behind the blast.

"How we get home from there will be a matter of luck. Watson you ready, Holmes don't miss. Here we go." Nick looked at his watch it was after 2:00 am.

Mitch looked at Adam and Dom, "Put your phones down your pants so when we hit the ground you won't lose them." Dom said, "When we hit the ground." Mitch grinned, "We ain't gonna out fly angels bro. We gotta make them think we are dead."

Mitch took the chopper straight up. He made sure everything was online and working. He flew way wide right of the cabin and circled around to the back of the forest and came around hard and fast heading right for the back of the cabin. He was as close to the treetops as he could get.

Mitch kept gaining speed as they approached the cabin. Dom could not see the cabin when Mitch opened up the Gatling guns and blistered everything except the cabin as they flew by. He kept accelerating for another two miles then yelled, "Status Watson."

Watson came right back, "All the hot signatures hit the deck and the two cold ones are moving to the front. Turn on your running lights now." Mitch checking, "Holmes you ready? "Yes, I am hoping they come out and keep moving forward while following your lights." Adam to Holmes, "Either way, you got to hit'em. Holmes a bit pissed, "I got it, let me work."

Mitch was almost three miles out when he yelled, "Hang on," and climbed straight up. The G-force slammed Adam and Dom deep into their seats. Mitch could feel the chopper struggling then he let off the gas and tipped the chopper to right and let it fall toward the earth.

He feathered the throttle and the S-97 Raider came to life. Mitch accelerated again, pulled up as hard as he could, bringing the chopper to level and heading right at the cabin. Mitch now had twice the speed he could normally get; the stall turn had worked.

Nick looked at Hoss, "Holy shit that was insane." Hoss pointed at the screen, "Now watch how much faster he is traveling when he levels out."

Dom yelled, "Status damn it, status!" Holmes' voice, "Jake and Brian are stoned and heading into the woods and those two things are pissed. They are standing a good forty feet into the front yard."

Mitch turned to Adam then Dom with a weird look on his face, "Watson follow along with me. I am going to put one missile on the two beasts and the other in the cabin…got it?" Watson confirmed. "Then I am going to fly by at top speed then slam on everything to bring it to a hover for a second at twenty feet while we jump and then you fly the bird. You are going to get above the trees and haul ass. Then you will pull up, drop all the gas at once and then land the bird like an airplane; you follow me?" Holmes voice, "You know all that fuel is going to catch fire right? Watson's yelled, "Damn right, and they will think you guys are crispy."

Dom yelled, "Watson, don't get in a hurry give us a second to get unstrapped." Mitch quickly, "Don't listen to that shit, we will unstrap as we run it. Coming up on it now are we ready?"

Mitch didn't wait for replies, he fired the two missiles at the same time each screaming toward its target. Mitch kept it full throttle, as they arrived the cabin exploded. The chopper was going so fast the explosion felt like a speed bump, but the chopper almost came apart as Mitch forced it into a quick stop and hover.

Sims jumped up, "Damn, that is too fast he ain't ever gonna stop." The cameras were showing trees, sky, ground and the sky and finally settled on the canopy of the forest. Then it took off over the canopy gaining speed.

Nick called for the overwatch drone images of the crash. It showed an overhead view of the chopper flying right through the explosion and 360-degree spin stop to a hover some five hundred yards into the forest. The zoom showed Adam leap out on the right then Mitch on the left.

The drone followed as it took off then climbed long enough to dump the gas then nose to the ground and skid into the forest. They never saw Dom jump.

Mitch yelled, "Go now!" Adam was out the right side door and gone. Dom was hesitating. Mitch was about to jump when the chopper lurched as Watson took the controls. The ammo box went flying out the side door.

Watson was heading out at max speed. Mitchell knew what was up and just threw himself out into the air. He looked back as he fell and saw Dom come out way late. Dom probably had a fifty-foot fall to deal with. Then Mitch hit something hard, thought he smelled gas and was out.

Hoss yelled, "Holmes, show us the cockpit cameras now." They came up and Hoss realized that no one was in the chopper. Hoss yelled, "Watson where are they." Holmes voice, "He is flying the chopper right now and is in the middle of…The screens returned with the rearview from the chopper. It appeared to have landed. Then they saw a ball of fire raging toward it, heard a loud explosion and then the camera as it was engulfed in flames.

Watson's voice, "I engaged the fire suppression system at max coverage and launched the countermeasures at the same time. Mitch wanted the beasts to think the chopper had exploded. Holmes will get all three drones there now, and those two things saw the crash and took off toward Johnson City."

The screen split into thirds. Shown in the middle screen was the chopper surrounded by fire. The fire was held back ten feet, showing the suppression system had done its job. The left screen showed Adam, dragging Mitch into the forest and away from the fire. The right screen showed Dom hanging upside down in a tree with the forest fire about to move underneath him.

Hoss grabbed his phone and dialed Adam. Nick yelled, "Holmes get those cameras right on top of our guys." As the drone zoomed in on Adam, they saw him reach down his pants and pull out his phone, "Hoss, holy shit did you see what Mitch pulled out of his ass; damn he can fly." Hoss broke in, "Dom is east of you about eighty yards. He is hanging in a tree and the fire is almost right under him. Get his ass down and out of there." Adam replied, "On it."

Adam made sure Mitch would be safe and then he had to figure out how to get on the east side of the fire. He started sprinting toward where he thought the chopper had exploded. After about sixty yards, Adam started laughing, "Get the drones over here, the chopper is fine. It is surrounded by fire but it looks good. Great job Watson."

Adam jumped through an opening in the fire and stood next to the chopper, "Holmes have a drone guide me through the wall of fire to Dom." Adam was looking around when a dragonfly with its target laser flashing, showed up above him.

Adam waved to the camera, "Let's go." The drone climbed a bit then headed back right of the chopper. Adam had to run through another wall of fire but was good after that. The drone rose again and went further into the trees. Adam yelled, "Dom, let me hear you." Adam stood still then heard Dom's voice off to the left.

He came into a small clearing and looked up. Dom was hanging from his left ankle, which was quite broken. He was situated so he could not get to it himself. Dom was a mess. He was bleeding from a scalp wound, his chest was bleeding into his torn shirt and he was barely conscious.

Adam moved to where Dom could see him, "Why did you jump so late?" Dom stuck his arm out, "I didn't want to land in a tree." Adam would play along, "So how did you get in the tree." Dom with the arm again, "Cause I jumped too late."

Dom seemed like he was light-headed, "Umm you gonna get me down before this becomes a literal weenie roast?" Adam smiling, "Yup, I am going back to the chopper and get some rope and tools." Dom groaned, "Choppers gone man it blew up." Adam gave Dom the good news and then asked for Mitch's status.

Hoss said, "Mitch is sitting up for now. He called us and we told him to sit tight; we are sending people in to get you; the bad guys left."

Once Barlow had contacted the State Police and fire departments, he dispatched his deputies to bring the boys to the Jonesborough emergency room.

Watson came on the line, "Sergeant Cartwright, we have sequenced the entire chopper run from the drones and chopper cameras. We now can see what those two beasts saw, and why they left. Would you like me to run it now?"

Hoss motioned to the screens and waited for Barlow to join them, "Ok let it run." It started with the strafing run. The power of the Gatling guns was impressive, but Mitchell's accuracy was frightening. The chopper's camera footage from the stall turn made their stomachs flip as they fell out of the sky toward the forest and pulling up at the last second.

They were traveling so fast, the forest canopy looked like the road they were driving on. Then the view from the overwatch drone they had already seen. They loved the part when the two drones from front yard followed the chopper through the explosion then showed a spin, stall, go again and then disappear.

In place of the chopper, came a wall of fire, then the fireworks of the countermeasures launching phosphorus balls into the air. The fake crash was capped off by the ammo box exploding. It looked like a crash that no one could survive.

Sims looked at Hoss, "You planned this didn't you; you and Mitch?" Hoss laughed aloud, "You heard me tell him I didn't want to know, and I told him to leave me out of it. This was all him. Too bad they can't give medals for this kinda shit."

Nick was sitting quietly, "We put a Hellfire missile right in their face and they turned around to watch the show. Now they're really pissed off. We freed their hosts, and killed their buddies. In about an hour from now they will be coming to kick our ass." Everyone was still.

Chapter Seventy-Eight

2:21 am EST
5:21 pm EET
The Stavros Villa
Isle of Crete, Greece

Trish, Phu and Lil' Joe were getting antsy, they had been in the hide for almost twenty-one hours. They had an hour left and the winds were picking up a bit. It was the same direction and was within the parameters used in the simulations so they felt good so far.

The mother drone had been on station for forty-eight hours and was recording and downloading like a champion. The mother drone would become their most important piece of technology once things got moving.

They had run through all the possible scenarios and felt good about their capabilities. They trusted their instincts and knew once the operation started events would dictate success or failure as well as life and death.

Glenn and Jacob were sitting in Jacob's room at the hotel. They had done all they could do. They were looking at the thermal image of Stavros and his friends having a conversation concerning drug sales and their latest assignation of the doctor in South America; Glenn was seething. Jacob kept reminding Glenn that in a few minutes Stavros was going to be homeless and poor in his home country.

Jess, Kat, and John were in John's room trying to pass the time. Kat was worried about John going into actual combat. His performance scores were up there, but he had no real experience. John was well aware of this himself.

He could not compare himself to real soldiers like Phu and the boys, let alone Sims. They respected him greatly, but that had nothing to do with his fighting skills.

Kat and Jess would run Trish and the manned drone from Jess' room, John and Corwin each had different paths to walk to their positions. They would need to be dropped off soon so they could hike their ways to the villa.

Browning was in a large garage on the coast of Crete eight minutes from the villa. Staged in the garage were the ambulance, a fire truck, paramedic-based vehicles and all the first responders. They were ready and anxious.

Glenn did another pass with the mother drone. Stavros' hired talent was taking their places out front. Stavros' meeting was breaking up and the last of the place settings on the guest's tables were being taken care of.

Stavros' invited all of his business guests to stay if they liked but most of them had other places to be; Stavros had planned on that. He needed to go to his room and check-in with Rameel before he changed clothes and started his evening.

Rameel bragged to Stavros how he had destroyed Harts team of assassins and their chopper. He went into detail of how it had exploded, killing all those aboard. Neither of them discussed the four humans that were killed inside the cabin. Sims was right they didn't care about them.

Rameel told Stavros he and Asael were going to fly into Sims' house and destroy it. Next, they would look for the adjoining tunnels and rip their way up to the main house. Afterward, they would move on to The Town with No Name and dismantle it as well.

Stavros smiled, "Rameel you have done well; greatness awaits us. It is 6:00 in the evening and I must go. Send me your images of the destruction when it is done."

Chapter Seventy-Nine

>3:28 am EST
>6:28 pm EET
>Hart Compound
>Jonesborough, TN

Sims and company decided they would start the battle in the widow's suite as a matter of perceived luck. As the clock wound down, they began to feel naked up in the sky. They realized the only thing between them, and hell was glass.

They all put on their night vision gear and switched it to starlight. Nick took out his phone and pulled up the app for the compound. He killed all the lights and locked down everything except the areas that made up their escape route into the tunnels.

Sims' big worry was whether the doors that sealed the three-way tunnel access from his house to the compound would hold against what was coming. Hoss was about to complain about all the waiting when Molly whined and headed down the stairs and out of the widow's suite.

Barlow was in the middle of saying, "Oh shit." when Sims' house exploded. It wasn't the sound of a bomb; it was the result of a high impact. Remeel and Asael had arrived. They flew full speed into the house and imploded the entire front façade. Using the starlight mode, Hoss and crew could see the two creatures ripping and pulling at the house.

Holmes and Watson yelled through the com, "What the hell was that?" Hoss replied, "The two boys from the cabin have arrived and they are quite pissed. They are ripping Sims house to shreds and will be moving on to us soon. Make sure you get all this video in starlight mode." Sims cut in. "We have you locked down so follow the protocol book, strap in, shut up and you will be fine."

As Sims finished, his house exploded, and flames shot high into the sky. They lit up the entire expanse between the house and the compound. Nick shook his head, "Damn it, we got to go.

Everyone was heading down the stairs when Barlow looked back one last time; he could not believe what he was seeing. He yelled, "Oh my God it's Molly, she is out in the front." Everyone returned immediately.

They watched in horror as Molly continued to inch her way toward Sims' house. She was crawling on her stomach, just as she was trained to avoid detection in the dark; now she was exposed by the fire and in plain sight.

Sims' entire body began to shake; he would not allow Molly to be taken by these assholes. Sims started toward the stairs. Barlow turned, "Sims stop, leave her alone." Nick got in Barlow's face and started to say something.

Barlow pushed Nick into Hoss and in a low growl, "Leave her alone. I was there when she had torn herself apart and I was there at Semjaza's place and saw the new Molly. I think she is trying to save us. Now shut up and let her do it."

At that point, all the noise stopped; Rameel and Asael had seen Molly and they were working their way out of the wreckage of the house. As they freed themselves, they stood and looked as if they were deciding what to do with her.

Hoss reached for Barlow to toss him from the widow's suite, "We could have saved her now look at her you…" Just as Hoss touched Barlow, they all heard the worst agonizing, primal and visceral howling moan of pain any of them had ever heard from any animal or human, instantly they were in tears.

They didn't want to look but they did. Molly had her nose between her paws while still on her stomach. Sims pleading, "God, we cannot sit here and watch her die. Barlow began to speak as they all leered at him, he spoke anyway, "Look she hasn't moved neither has Rameel. I still think she is trying to do something." Just then, Molly gave an even more raw and desperate cry; this time none of them could hold their emotions. Nick was calling Molly's name hoping she would get up and run to him.

All but Barlow were calling Molly to get up and run; then Rameel and Asael started walking her way. Everyone one but Barlow frantically started to run down the stairs to save her. Barlow watched, praying he was not wrong.

As Rameel came within thirty feet of Molly, Barlow felt he was wrong and began to weep; maybe they could have saved her. He looked down at Molly and noticed the wind was blowing the grass and the smoke from Sims' house began to swirl.

Rameel stopped walking and looked up and behind him. There was a flash of complete darkness and then as if a spotlight had been shined on each of the creatures they stood out in the night.

There was what sounded like a sonic boom and both of the creatures were flattened face down to the ground by an invisible force. Barlow noticed that Rameel wasn't on the ground he was pressed into it.

Sims came around the side of the house just in time to hear the sonic boom and see Rameel and his buddy planted into the ground. Nick and Hoss stopped behind Sims and stood in awe as they saw two creatures land and put their right heels on the necks of Rameel and Asael.

These two were also of the angel looking breed, but they were larger than Rameel and Asael. As they stood dominate over their prey, they were looking kindly at Molly and then into the night's sky. Soon the wind picked up and the earth began to shake. At this point, Molly got up and sat at attention with her tail wagging.

Barlow let out a cry of relief when he saw Rameel and Asael slammed into the ground. When he saw Molly snap to attention, he knew who was coming. Right on cue, Samjaza landed. He dwarfed his two sentries who had bowed their heads. He moved over and stood next to Molly and she leaned into him looking up and smiling.

Semjaza took a knee next to Molly and then looked at Rameel. The sentry on Rameel stepped back, bent over and pulled up Rameels head so he could face Semjaza. Then the same was done with Asael. Semjaza stood and motioned with his hand and the sentries and captives became four streaks of light, disappearing into the darkness; the sonic boom this time shattered the windows of the compound. Lights started coming on in the neighborhoods of Jonesborough and Johnson City.

Semjaza and Molly shared a moment then he turned to face Barlow in the widow's suite. He bowed his head like a tip of the cap, petted Molly and vanished. Barlow started down the stairs to join the rest of his friends.

When he came around the corner of the house, he saw Molly surrounded by the others, so he stopped and watched. He was so glad she was alive; she didn't need saving, they did.

Molly was excited by all the attention until she saw Barlow. She broke out of the group and ran to his side. He kneeled, petted her and then stood up and like a perfect ending; she leaned into him. Hoss, Nick, and Sims all smiled and nodded.

Hoss pulled out his phone and called shooting station 3, "Holmes and Watson did you guys get all that cuz ain't nobody gonna believe what happened here tonight. Watson was crying in the affirmative.

Hoss turned to look at what was left of Sims house, "Hey Sims, look it's just like Mitch said." Sims gave him the finger then pointed. Hoss and Nick turned to see two Sheriff's cars bringing Mitch, Adam, and Dom back from the hospital.

Nick looked at his watch it was 3:25 am. He knew that John and his team were deep into it in Greece; maybe it was all over.

Chapter Eighty

Day Twelve
6:28 pm EET
The Stavros Villa
Isle of Crete, Greece

Everyone had made it to their marks undetected. John was on the far left of the stage and Corwin was hidden on the roof; all their weapons now fitted with silencers. The sun and the winds were cooperating thus far.

Glenn, with a little crack in his voice, "Six-thirty time to go. Start the dragonfly sequence; get them up. Lil' Joe you got the mark; call it when Stavros steps out on the patio." Phu was helping Trish get ready to react if she needed to hit the front of the villa. All one hundred and fifty dragonflies were fluttering just below the face of the rock in the shadows, as the sun came into perfect position; they were invisible.

Stavros stepped out on to the back patio of the villa and faced his guests. There were sixty people seated in the well-dressed olive orchard. He was handed a microphone and he started walking closer to the middle to present his speech. Lil' Joe said, "He is in play let them go."

Glenn started the attack-software for phase one and three dragonflies left the hovering swarm of menacing-looking drones. Glenn double-clicked and phase two started as sixteen of the swarm were launched just four seconds behind the first three, "Chaos is upon them; good luck. Let it rip." Glenn said as he released the rest of the swarm.

Stavros was just starting his comments when he was distracted by what looked like a small bird fluttering to his left. As he turned to look, he was hit twice in the neck by the other two dragonflies. The third dove on him as he hit the ground; Clairmore was out cold and Azazel was…?

The people in the orchard stood to see what was wrong with their friend. Then they noticed what looked like sunspots coming out of the glare of the setting sun. Immediately they were engulfed by fluttering and biting insects; they had nowhere to run.

Out front, the gunfire had begun; Stavros' men were in disarray as they tried to fight off the drones. Glenn decided quickly, "Trish, come mop up in the front. Lil' Joe, you stay and keep them off Clairmore. Phu, you should be seeing his men on your side now. John, get in there and clear the place for Browning and his men.

Trish came from behind the rocks on the right side of security pods. She locked onto three pods and fired her missiles. The front of the villa exploded in flame and debris. Trish strafed pod four and then the entire front of the building. She pulled up and hovered; the entire area was quiet.

Corwin had started early because two of Stavros' men came to the roof to watch the crowd below. When Stavros went down, they turned to go but Corwin redirected them to the afterlife.

Corwin stepped into the doorway leading off the roof and spotted two more men with weapons running for the stairs. He shot them, and then stepped over their bodies, peeked around the entry to the stairs and went down to the next floor.

John had made his way to his side of the patio and was working his way to the door Stavros had just used. As he was about to reach for the lever of open the door, two men burst through heading to help Stavros. Before John could react, both men were shot and lay dead in front of him. John looked to where he knew Lil' Joe was and gave him thumbs up. Lil' Joe reported, "John infra-red shows you are clear to enter." John flipped the door open and was inside.

Phu had seen John avoid the two men and Lil' Joe kill them both. Just as Glenn had predicted, he saw five men making their way toward Clairmore. Phu no longer had to worry about killing civilians, they were all down and quiet. It was eerie in the soft quiet sunset hearing the fluttering of the hovering dragonflies above the sleeping crowd, and the sporadic pops and spits as the battle developed.

Phu had the advantage of cover amongst the olive trees and tables, whereas his enemy was in the open and distracted by the remaining dragonflies. Phu decided it was just like the contest on John's Sniper's Gauntlet. He would keep moving forward picking up points with each target he destroyed.

He stepped into the open about fifty yards from the patio he killed two before he started his forward movement then opened up on the rest. As they turned to engage him, one was bitten by a dragonfly and two more returned fire.

Phu decided to charge the last two and end it right now. He flipped his weapon to fully automatic and was releasing burst after burst as he ran. He felt a bullet graze his vest's collar and that was enough. Phu stopped planted his feet and killed the last two with two rounds. He shook his head, "*I guess I am no Kill-heel.*"

John was greeted by three men running from Trish's onslaught. They came bursting into the villa's main entrance leading with their weapons; he had no time to think. John killed the lead man then darted across to the opposite wall and killed the other two. As he hit the wall, John realized he was not breathing; it took a second, but he found his breath and gasped, "Son of a bitch that was fast."

Trish was hovering over the patio at a hundred and fifty feet scanning the front and back of the villa. She had cleared the way for Browning and his men. They had parked on Phu's side and were entering the back from the same side as the men Phu had killed.

John moved and began to clear all the rooms on the lower floor when he ran into Corwin at the base of the back stairs, "All clear, how 'bout you?" John nodded and they moved to the door leading onto the patio.

Corwin went out first. As he stepped out, he locked eyes with Phu; right then he knew Phu had been taken. His chest exploded and the lights went out. John ducked back inside, "Phu what the hell are you doing?" John heard Lil' Joe in his ear,

"Starlight, starlight I got Azazel in Phu. Azazel is in Phu."

Glenn and Jacob were ready for this phase. They had preloaded secondary targets in each of the dragonflies that were assigned to the crowd. Jacob said, "Ok I got Phu." Glenn responded, "On speed kill…go!"

Phu who seemed to be standing ready to fight kept looking left and right like he was trying to figure which way to go. As Browning and his men jumped on the stage, Lil' Joe was yelling for them to stop; the next second three drones drilled Phu in the face and he went slack but did not fall.

Lil' Joe and Trish were warning everyone that Azazel was standing right in the middle of the patio and his head was above the villa, "This son of a bitch is a monster."

Azazel flexed his wings in a show of force, stood tall and ready for battle; his eyes were fire in black sockets. Azazel was not as tall and lean as Semjaza; he was shorter and built like a fireplug. Like Semjaza, he was blackened by his time in outer darkness but his body looked like he was wearing urban camouflage. If Semjaza was a scalpel, then this guy was the hammer.

As Browning and his men stood awaiting orders, they tried to focus on Clairmore. Everything went quiet with only the buzzing of the drones; everyone could hear their own heartbeat. No one had noticed that John had worked his way up onto the roof.

He was standing in the doorway looking across the roof at Azazel's back and wings. His monocle allowed him to see clearly.

John moved a little closer, "Azazel the Unrighteous, it won't be long, Semjaza is on his way." Azazel turned his head slowly, "Mr. Hart, you finally got out from behind your desk. This is quite the operation, what did you hope to accomplish?"

John's brain now screaming for Semjaza, "Oh, we are done with the main part. Nevertheless, you have screwed up everything else by not running away as you always do.

"We know we can't really deal with you and your kind…" Azazel cut in, "You mean our kind John, our kind. Did you know that Semjaza was the first to combine his blood with the blood of a human woman?

"The daughters of Adam were so beautiful…well; eventually we all gave in to them. In a way, he is the father of your entire family tree. I have no relatives left on this earth."

Lil' Joe saw John approaching Azazel from the back and shouted into his com, "John, don't start any shit with this guy. He is stone cold; he doesn't care about anything. Get off the roof."

Everyone started talking in John's ear. Kat's voice sliced into his head, "Damn it, John, we just talked about this; get your ass off the roof."

Jess needed to move Trish, "Trish move eye to eye with Azazel but stay back out of reach. Trish a bit freaked, "Stay out of reach? So, I am thinking of

Alaska." Trish made her move and caught Azazel's attention.

Azazel pulled his eyes off John, "John, what does this toy do?" John's eyes intense, "It is recording the entire day. I heard from Browning you like to document your deeds like some sick voyeur. We got you in full HD so we can show the world that flying assholes do exist."

Azazel smiled, "Well, I haven't gone on a good blood lust in a long time; I am feeling like this could be the day. I could take your little toy and smash everyone's head in with it; how does that sound?" His voice grew more and more agitated as he spoke. John spoke quietly in his com, "Time for us to leave; start to back out now."

John knew he should be leaving, but he was growing tired of putting up with all the weird shit in his life. He stood looking at the ground; John made a decision.

He looked at Azazel and started walking straight at him with his weapon leveled. Azazel turned completely around to face him. To clear his wings, he had to back up. As John continued forward, he was saying, "Clear the patio, clear the patio."

Azazel was smiling at the stupid human with a gun until John reached the edge of the roof, looked down, found Clairmore and put two bullets in his forehead. Azazel howled as he swatted John from the roof, sending him toward the front of the villa. In a complete rage, he turned on those near the stage.

Kat watching what took place screamed John's name. Jess screamed for Trish to climb. Glenn instincts took over and he sent the mother drone in a straight vertical climb.

John felt like he had been hit him by a train. In a nanosecond, he realized he was airborne, he started to panic thinking where he might land, and then he looked up and realized landing was least of his problems.

He saw the sky crack open like broken mirror glass. Seeing that, he was pretty sure he was already dead, all time seemed to stop.

Azazel raised his arms in rage just as the shock wave from the sky cracking above crushed him into the concrete below him. He shattered the patio, sending Phu, Corwin, and Clairmore into the orchard, landing amongst the unconscious guests.

Barlow and his men were flattened and unable to move. Lil' Joe was knocked out when his head slammed into his rifle. Glenn and the others in town lost their feeds for a few seconds then the mother drone started sending images again.

Glenn spoke when he realized what he was seeing, "Jess, anybody seeing this?" Jacob came on, "I have control of the mother drone and I am zooming in."

From the mother drone's view, it looked like everyone was lying dead on the ground. The images were showing glimpses through the cloud of dust and the now swirling wind. Glenn was stunned, "Is everyone dead?"

Jacob was not responding then, "Holy shit, Glenn let me play what I found. The mother drone never stopped recording, you won't believe this. I am starting the replay; it will take us up to live as it ends."

Jacob had turned the sound up as he hit start. As they watched, they saw a flash then heard the blast when the sky was broken, the mother drone losing altitude rapidly, and then held its position before it snapped back into a sharp climb.

As it climbed, they could make out the sequence of destruction that followed the blast. The center of it hit Azazel and flattened him and everyone else. It looked like they all had been killed.

Jacob voice calmly, "Look at these next few seconds, starting with the flash. Jess started to yell at Jacob when she saw something large flash by mother drone and toward the ground. Immediately the image was blocked with what looked like a white linen cloth.

Jacob's voice, "I am going to replay the flash in ultra-slow motion. Here we go." They could see what looked like a huge hand going by followed by its arm. Finally, the cloth appeared showing the back of the shoulder.

The cloth started to flap allowing them to see small portions of the earth below. They were astounded to see the cloth pullback followed by the arm and in the hand was a crumpled and listless Azazel. The image cleared and they could see everyone lying lifeless on the ground.

Glenn voice, "We are back to real-time; Jacob bring the mother drone down and find me Trish." Jacob speed talking, "I am bringing her in closer now. Glenn, did you see that hand? Was it just like the one…?" Glenn cut him off, "Jacob its ok. Let's just get a line on all our people. Make sure we save all of these images and keep them locked up."

Chapter Eighty-One

3:53 am EST
6:53 pm EET
Hart Compound
Jonesborough, TN

Nick and everyone else hustled into the rec room and put on the European news channel. Holmes and Watson had been recording what was happening at the villa while they were fighting for their lives. They informed the team that the phone services on Crete were disrupted; all the phones were offline.

Watson took the recording back to where Glenn had announced the beginning of the operation to kill Stavros. Nick spoke to Watson, "Make sure we leave the starlight filter on the entire time." Watson replied, "Already done."

They enjoyed watching the dragonflies takedown Stavros and the crowd. Trish's feed showing her purging the front of Stavros' men was encouraging; it all seemed to be going as planned. Mitch was smiling as Hoss elbowed him in the ribs, "Trish is a badass."

Then Lil' Joe's feed of him killing the two guys coming out the door and John going inside the villa was not showing Azazel until Phu came on to the patio. Then Phu's eyes went red as Corwin came out the door onto the patio. Phu turned and shot Corwin point-blank in the chest. They heard Lil' Joe's voice warning everyone that Phu was now Azazel. Corwin was still not moving when the dragonflies took down Phu.

Hoss and Sims were pacing feeling helpless as they saw Azazel appear via starlight on the patio. He was large and intimidating with his red eyes. Nick saw Browning moving onto the stage but then stopped when John started telling everyone it was time to pull back.

It wasn't until Azazel turned to look at John that John was visible to the cameras. He was taunting Azazel then it seemed John had had enough of the whole situation. He raised his weapon and started toward Azazel. When he came to the ledge, he leaned over and fired down twice. It appeared he had killed Clairmore. Mitch stood up, "Oh shit, run John."

It got deathly quiet when Azazel backhanded John and sent him flying backward a good twenty feet in the air and out of sight of the cameras. Nick just stood staring at Sims, "Shit, did John just die?" Sims was frozen; he could only shake his head. Molly was sitting at attention looking at the screen.

Barlow was still staring at the screen when he saw the camera dive then return showing everyone lying on the ground. Barlow yelled for Holmes to find Trish's video feed to Glenn. Holmes ready, "Got it cued it up from where John came on the roof."

Trish's feed was much closer and at eye level with Azazel. Trish had swung a bit left to pick up John coming out of the door and moving toward Azazel. When John got to the ledge, Trish backed out and recorded him shooting Clairmore clear as day.

The image rocked a bit then Trish started to climb with Azazel in the middle of the frame. He swatted John, then turned and looked up. There was a loud noise when they saw Azazel slammed into the concrete; the patio exploded from his impact. It looked as if something snatched Azazel out of the concrete, and with a white streak he was gone.

Trish's feed began to rock back and forth. They saw the ground covered with people, and then just dirt. Mitchell turned to look at Hoss, who would not make eye contact.

Nick a bit lost, "Holmes and Watson, I want you to piece together all the feeds and sequence them as you did with Mitchell's chopper run. Try to get the most recent feeds and add them to the sequence." Nick turned and found Molly looking him in the eyes; she too needed answers.

Chapter- Eighty-Two

4:33 am EST
7:33 pm EET
The Stavros Villa
Isle of Crete, Greece

Browning was able to move on to his hands and knees. He crawled over to Phu. He could tell that the drugs from the dragonflies had done their job; he was resting nicely. He looked back and saw that his men were starting to stir; most of them looked like they were fine.

Browning tried to stand but collapsed, "Crawl it is" he mumbled. He set out to find Clairmore. He crawled over Phu to where he had seen him last, but he was not there, nor were there any signs that he had been hurt. There should have been a lot of blood where Browning was looking.

Trish awoke to Jess screaming in her ears. Her head hurt; she saw some blood on the harness.

Trish gave herself a parts check and found she had cut the back of her head. She couldn't remember why she had not bailed; she was still strapped in and still recording. She finally responded, "Jess I am here. I think I am fine. What the hell was that...did the sky break open or what?"

Jess was relieved, "Thought we lost you; where did you end up?" Trish finished climbing out of the harness and was standing on the west side of the villa in a small tilled area. She looked back to where Lil' Joe was. "I am between the villa and Lil' Joe; I am working that way. Do you think we will find John?"

Jess had been too focused on finding Trish, "Kat and Glenn are working the coms trying to find everyone; I will let you know." Jess tired, "I will tell Glenn you are fine. Let us know about Lil' Joe he has not responded yet."

As Trish approached Lil' Joe's position she could see he was talking. She went into the hide and sat down; Lil' Joe was talking to Glenn and Jacob. His nose was on the wrong side of his face and there was drying blood all around his mouth and chin leading to the front of his vest. Lil' Joe smiled at her and gave her thumbs up; he was fine.

Corwin's first thoughts came to him in the darkness that had taken over his mind. He could tell he had been hurt; he could barely breathe. Corwin was not entirely aware of any one thing except his chest felt like it was caved into his spine. He wondered if he was in the final throes of death. He remembered his vest and then wondered if Phu had been using special rounds; he wished he could see.

His thoughts slipped sideways. Corwin visualized several men he had seen die. Many panicked when they lost their sight; realizing they were heading into death.

Corwin's thoughts landed on the face of his training officer on his first day of special operations training, "If you find yourself slipping into the darkness, feeling you are going to die, realize that you are still alive. So, if you are still alive, then you are obligated by your oath to continue fighting. So, get off your almost dead ass and kill someone."

Corwin worked hard to get his eyes to open and when he did it was still dark, but a different dark; he smelled perfume. He decided he needed to rotate his head and try to crawl. As he started to move his right hand, he felt dirt and fabric he realized he was laying on a body.

Corwin's realized since he was trying to solve his problem, his mind must be working; he knew he had to inventory his situation. He moved his left hand and could feel his toes wiggle in his boots but his legs above the calves were asleep. He knew something was crushing his back and thighs.

He pulled his right hand all the way to his neck. He could feel the com was still near his face, "Hey Glenn is anybody still alive?" He realized he practically whispered what he said when Jacob spoke into his ear, "Corwin, you're alive. Holy shit, where are you?"

Corwin instantly knew he wasn't dead, and either was Jacob, "Ok, I am alive, cool. I have no idea where I am, except I am pretty sure my face is buried in some lady's ass."

Jacob laughed, "That means you are in the crowd in front of the stage. Something destroyed it and took Azazel." Corwin confused, "Did John make it?" Jacob subdued, "We don't know, he got smacked by Azazel. We have no idea where he landed."

Corwin yelled, "Get me out of here. I need to find him." Corwin could feel the blood coming from his mouth. His chest started to spasm he gurgled, "I need help."

Browning had heard Jacob and Corwin's conversation. He was trying to gather enough men to follow him into the rubble and crowd of slowly waking guests.

Trish was cleaning up Lil' Joe's face as they heard Jacob and Corwin's exchange. Lil' Joe looked at Trish then pressed his com button, "Glenn, why can't we let the drones find John? They can be like bloodhounds give them a sniff and let them go." Glenn looked at Kat who was nodding yes, "Lil' Joe we are starting on that right now. Can you help Browning find Corwin? Right now we have no idea where Clairmore is." Trish and Lil' Joe started moving down the hill toward Corwin.

Trish looked at her watch. It had been fifty minutes from the start of their attack and now she was hearing sirens and klaxons coming their way. It was almost completely dark.

She heard Glenn working with Browning they had found Corwin. Now he could move his men out front to control the situation. Trish saw Browning's men carrying Corwin on the stretcher intended for Clairmore.

Browning directed all of the first responders to the side of the villa he had just come from. He set up a small outpost underneath a large tree by the road. It was a perfect spot to triage his resources and control the narrative of what supposedly happened.

As Trish and Lil' Joe reached the road in front of the villa they heard the swarm of dragonflies rallying to Glenn and Jacob; the search for John was about to begin. They walked on until they joined Browning by the tree.

Glenn was handing the drone search off to Jess when his phone rang. Apparently, the problems caused by the broken sky incident had subsided; Glenn saw it was Nick; he didn't want to take the call.

Chapter Eighty-Three

4:51 am EST
7:51 pm EET
The Villa, Isle of Crete

John's mind could not lock on to anything familiar, not a speck of place or time; it was awash. John's awareness returned when he heard someone speaking to him. He was not bothered that he could not see who was speaking; it just seemed natural that they were.

"Mr. Hart," the voice in the darkness spoke. John stated, "You are the Messenger." After a pause, "I have been asked to consider your life.

"You have just killed an innocent man knowing that by doing so you would be killing yourself." John nodded. "You and your group recently killed several other people these past days, including one of your own townspeople.

"I must weigh this in light of your lineage and those aspects of your blood that have brought you to me. Mr. Hart your blood contains the most Angel blood that currently exists in a human. When you were of age, this is what brought on your visions." John became uncomfortable.

"Your dreams would have driven most humans to suicide or an institution. However, you kept your visions inside; you shared very little and with very few. Somehow, you and Molly managed to keep your mind intact. This, I found astonishing.

"When your visions came to pass, you were relieved and moved on; it was the drugs you said.

Now you have been shown your lineage by Semjaza and it has given you pause. You now understand that the drugs were not the cause.

"Your bloodline is indeed quite unique. What you have done with your life, in spite of your circumstances, makes you remarkable." John felt a little better about things.

"However, you have murdered many others to advance yourself and your colleagues. Your yearly ashtray ceremony reminds you of those who came against you and failed.

"You believe that policing yourselves is your right. You consider what you have created a great advancement for your kind, and that alone justifies your actions." John was beginning to dislike this guy.

"But alas Mr. Hart, you are a murderer, same as Azazel. He too felt justified in his actions. What am I to do? How should I view your life when I write my judgment against your name?"

John felt the judgment; he didn't like it. He knew why he did what he did, "If saving the ones I love costs me my life, then so be it. I will never stop doing so. I don't care if you understand that or not."

John's mind faded and was slipping again, and then just before his head ricocheted off a tree he thought he heard, "I understand John."

The downward force created by the cracking sky deposited John's body deep into the branches of a tree. He could not be seen unless you flew directly over his position.

Kat ran up onto the roof of the villa to watch the dragonflies search for John. Jess returned the swarm to their original starting point and then introduced the original attack program with only one target, John. Their orders were to locate and hold their position.

It was eerie to watch the drones serpentine their way toward the villa, then fly over the roof, as they continued past the patio and into the orchard. The drones formed a new swarm and they were working hard to access new info from the mother drone.

Jacob noticed, "Jess, these guys did this to us at Confidante, they are lost, have no target and have covered their grid." Jess let out a long sigh, "Ok, I am going to attack in another direction." Jacob smiling, "You mean retreat?" Jess frustrated, "Exactly."

Jess wasn't going to wait for them to serpentine their way back to their starting point, so she just ran the rally program and they all turned and headed for Trish's and Lil' Joe's hide.

The rally program told the drones to get home, nothing more. There were no restrictions, just fly back. As the swarm broke up the dragonflies came out at a hundred and fifty different angles and then started to gather as they flew back over the villa.

Kat was worried that they had not picked up anything on their first pass. She started thinking that maybe they took John and Azazel to God knows where.

As she turned to watch them, she noticed several of the drones were holding their position over the large tree by the road. She saw Browning and screamed into her com, "John is in the tree. He is in the tree!"

Browning, Trish, Lil' Joe, and many others looked up into the face of the unconscious John Hart. Upon seeing his pallor and twisted torso, they feared the worst.

Browning spoke to all channels, "We have John, he is in the large tree in the front area of the villa. I need a ladder team and the EMTs here now."

Glenn heard the news but had to wait a few minutes longer before he would call Nick. He wanted to tell him John was alive; right now, no one was counting on that.

Chapter Eighty-Four

5:21 am EST
8:21 pm EET
Hart Compound, TN

Nick was pissed that Glenn was not picking up. He had had enough staring into space and checking his phone; he wondered where everyone else had gone.

He found standing up to be a challenge. He was beginning to feel how tired and battered he was. He moved from his chair outside onto the small arms deck and looked downrange at shooting station 3.

Nick decided he would find a bunk upstairs in the shooting shed, get an hour or so of sleep and then try Glenn again. When he got to the top of the stairs, all the lights were out, and he heard snoring. Hoss and the crew had lost their battle with fatigue; Molly was not amongst the victims.

Nick figured Molly was worried and retreated to her bed in the kitchen. He thought she needed to smell John on her ball. Nick was struggling while making the trek to the kitchen; Molly was not there.

Nick began to worry and collected a night vision headset on his way to the front door. He turned out the porch light then opened the door. The sun was just threatening to bring on dawn as he stepped out and took in the view.

Smoke was still rising from the wreckage of Sims' house. He saw Molly sitting where she had been lying when she had summoned help from above.

Barlow had gone home so Nick was wondering, but then it came to him. He smiled while putting on his night vision gear; Molly was sitting next to the Angel of her choice. Nick went inside and laid down on the couch, pulled the afghan over him and slept the sleep of the anguished.

Chapter Eighty-Five

5:26 am EST
8:26 pm EET
The Villa, Isle of Crete

Trish, Jacob and Lil' Joe were walking the property with their flashlights. They were assessing the fiasco that had started at 6:30 pm and had gone south almost immediately.

Clairmore was gone, Phu shot Corwin in the chest, Azazel swatted John into the hospital, then he was scooped up into the sky, and now half of the Isle of Crete had descended upon Stavros' villa.

They thanked God for Browning's NSA team of first responders. Calls from the Joint Chiefs to the Government of Greece had kept the media at bay. Now, they needed to salvage the operation.

Glenn, Jess and Kat followed the GPS to the address Browning had given them. They pulled into Crete's version of a strip mall and found suite #146. The mall looked dead in the darkness.

The name on the mirrored entrance door was Dr. N.S. Alverez. Kat and Jess thought they had come to the wrong place, but the name on the door told Glenn this was the place.

They all took a long look around to make sure they had not been followed. All they saw was an older looking man sitting on a bench under a light four suites to their right.

Glenn pressed the doorbell and a voice answered, "Do you have an appointment?" Glenn, "Yes." The voice again, "Name." Glenn smiled,

"Swordfish."(Marx Brothers, Swordfish YouTube) The door buzzed and then opened.

Glenn went to the desk for John and Corwin's room numbers. The agent at the desk commented that they were lucky to be alive and that he was pulling for them.

Jess asked, "Is this mall always this empty?" The agent smiled, "That is the point, we own all the shops." Jess puzzled, "So the gentleman sitting on the bench is one of yours?" The agent seeming upset, "No he just showed up twenty minutes ago and won't leave; says he was told to wait for Glenn."

Without saying a word Glenn bolted out the door; the man was still there. As fast as he could he got to the man and looked at his face, "Mr. Clairmore, I am Glenn, please follow me quickly." They were inside in a matter of seconds.

Kat and Jess needed an explanation, but Glenn was a bit busy, he turned to the agent, "Bring up the front view." Glenn had worked his way around the desk and was now looking over the agent's shoulder at his monitor. After another fifteen seconds of watching, Stavros' SUV entered the mall and slowly drove by every shop looking for Clairmore.

Glenn looked at Jess and Kat, "I think you know William Clairmore." Clairmore looked around to see whom they were talking about.

Glenn and Kat went on to John's room, while Jess called Browning so he could arrange a safe place for Clairmore. It took a while to move

Browning past the whole I saw him die thing, but eventually, Clairmore was resting quietly in a maximum-security room.

Jess found Corwin's room and stepped in. He was sedated with tubes going into and out of his chest. At first, she didn't notice Phu sitting in the corner to the right of the bed. She went to him and they hugged; she reminded him it was not his fault. Phu knew that but it didn't help, his special rounds were for Stavros' men, not Corwin.

Corwin's doctor told Jess the next two days would tell if he was going to live. He also said that if he lived, it would be a long road back. He explained that the vest had indeed spared him thus far, but the special round went far enough through the vest to shatter his sternum. The loss of the sternum, allowed the force of the bullet to collapse his chest into his lungs, causing massive bruising.

When Jess joined Glenn and Kat, they were sitting in the dark watching John breathe. He had been unconscious since he had been hit, almost two hours.

John's doctors didn't know why he was still breathing, "Based on what we are getting from his scans, nothing is working, yet his body continues to function, and he has brain activity. Look he is hooked up to the monitor, but we are getting nothing but flat lines; there see he just took another breath. I have no explanation for you." Glenn trying to lighten the mood, "So he is only mostly dead?" The doctor dropped his head and smiled, "Yes, he has been mostly dead all day."

Kat half laughed, and then was sobbing when they left John's room. Glenn was smiling as he looked at Jess. Jess thought she knew why. She looked at Kat then at Glenn, "John said that Azazel could not kill him that he was protected. Is that what we are seeing?" Glenn shrugged his shoulders.

Kat had fire in her eyes, "We talked about all of this before we started the operation. He said he wouldn't do anything stupid he was gonna let them take care of Azazel; he should have waited. I am gonna kill him when he wakes up. I am serious."

Jess and Kat sat in the lobby while Glenn tried to get the agent's attention. The agent pushed Glenn aside, ran to the door and opened it.

Browning and three other agents rushed into the lobby with a gurney. One of them appeared to be a photographer. Jess looked outside and saw the ambulance from earlier. Behind it was their silver SUV with Lil' Joe at the wheel.

Browning shook Glenn's hand, "Follow us we need to make this happen now." Glenn disappeared into the small hospital. Kat and Jess went to talk to Lil' Joe.

Glenn found himself in Clairmore's room. Clairmore was sedated and redressed with what he was wearing when he was dragonflied. A make-up artist was working hard to make him look dead.

Phu and Glenn found it creepy that they had to put two fake bullet holes on his forehead where John had put real ones. Phu went to see Kat. Glenn stayed with Browning.

The second the make-up was done, they moved Clairmore to the back bay of the building. The photographer arranged him so he was lying on concrete with a pool of blood behind his head.

They took several photos before they loaded him on the gurney and into the ambulance. Browning turned to Glenn, "Now we are back on track. Tell Rouse that his package is on the way."

Glenn thanked Browning for saving the operation and then jumped into the SUV with Jess, Phu and the others. He looked at Lil' Joe, "There must be a liquor store on this rock. Let's find us one before we get back to the villa."

As they approached the villa, they saw more order than chaos. The NSA had a grip on things. They were selling the elaborate murder of Andreas Stavros as a terrorist attack. The media was running with juicy stories of murderous drones, headshots and no terrorists killed or captured. Several local meteorologists were calmly explaining the thunder and freak lightning strike that destroyed the patio.

Trish and Jacob were leading the way. They had a handle on everything, but it looked as though they could use a beer.

Chapter Eighty-Six

7:26 am EST
10:26 pm EET
Hart Compound, Jonesborough, TN

Nick was startled when his phone rang. As he came back from the darkness of fatigue, he remembered why he was sharing his pillow with Molly.

As the sun rose, Molly nosed her way on to the couch and snuggled up to Nick. He responded by adjusting the afghan to keep her warm as well.

Then Molly changed Nick's life, she turned her head and gave him a lick on the nose and then buried her head in the pillow. It was the strangest thing Nick had ever experienced; he knew right then that John was ok; he went back to sleep.

Glenn started telling Nick what the doctor had told him about John's condition. Nick locked eyes with Molly, "That doesn't really surprise me after what we saw here tonight."

Glenn told Nick the operation had succeeded in spite of what went wrong. Glenn said he needed to call Rouse with the news about Corwin, John and the operation as he signed off.

Nick called Sammy wanting to have a breakfast set up at the compound. Bev answered the phone, "We thought you and Molly were going to sleep all day. Everyone is down here at the Coffee Hole in the Ground; get you asses here right now mister." She hung up before he could respond.

Nick looked at Molly, "I need some coffee how about you?" She barked then started spinning around with excitement. Nick got dressed then went looking for Molly. He found her sitting shotgun in John's Polaris.

He felt John as he started the car. Smiling, he was about to put it in gear when Molly barked at him then sniffed the GPS. Nick laughed while shaking his head. He felt weird about it, but he did it; he activated the GPS and said, "Coffee west of Jonesborough."

Molly's eyes were gleaming as she looked ahead and then she barked twice. Nick turned to her, "Ok, I am going already; I am sure they will have plenty of food for everyone."

As Nick approached the Coffee Hole, he noticed that just about everyone from the town were either in Sammy's diner, in the mess hall or walking between.

He noticed that they were huddled in groups by the TV's that had been set up like a gaming center. The coffee and various other beverages were flowing, as were the stories of last night at the compound, and the news coming in from Crete; the mood was festive.

The international news was hyping the terrorist attack at the villa of Andreas Stavros the third richest man in the world. Large cheers would breakout whenever they showed the picture of Stavros with the two fake bullet holes in his head. Molly used these diversions to her advantage and pilfered herself a great meal.

Nick saw Hoss with Barlow and joined them. Hoss looked past Nick, "Where is Sergeant Molly Malone?" Nick looked back, "She is collecting the spoils of war."

Nick looked Barlow in the eyes and shook his hand, "You are so much more than our Sheriff. I underestimated you, Jeff. For that I am sorry." Hoss reached over and put his hand on Barlow's shoulder, "You got that Semjaza mojo man; stay close my friend."

Sims, Mitchell, Dom, and Adam were sitting with Sammy and Bev at the diner. Holmes and Watson were at the table next to them. Holmes was about to ask Sammy a question when the TV grabbed their attention again.

The newscaster was saying that several of Stavros' security detail had been killed by manned drones out front of the villa and others in close quarters combat within the house. Stavros had been shot when he came out to speak to his guests. That was when the battle ensued.

The newscaster had another note related to the American communications entrepreneur John Hart who had attended Stavros' gathering. Apparently, he had been thrown into a tree as the patio exploded. Two other Americans, tied to Hart's security detail, were wounded as well. Hart and his men had been hurried away to a private hospital.

The newscaster put his hand to his ear, "I have been told that the body of Andreas Stavros has been seized by the Government of Greece pending the search for any family he may have.

"Those who have followed Stavros know that he bragged many times he had no parents after age seven, and he knew of no brothers or sisters; truly a self-made man."

They showed the photo of the dead Stavros and the cheers went up again. Sims smiling, "That will never get old."

When Nick came into the diner, he was welcomed by boisterous cheers. He was about to say something when he realized they weren't looking at him. He turned to see Molly greeting all her fans, accepting their charity. He turned back to see Sammy, Bev, and the entire table laughing at him while cheering Molly. Nick just lowered his head and made his way to the table.

Nick was about to join them when his phone rang, it was Glenn and he sounded a bit drunk. Apparently, he had been drinking beer since Clairmore was packed up and sent on his way to General Rouse.

Glenn needed to report that John and Corwin were going to be put aboard the USS Abraham Lincoln and would be home in a few days; their wounds prevented them from flying. The Abraham Lincoln was the fastest warship in the fleet.

Glenn was still coming down from their day, "Once Corwin and John are on the boat we are out of here. Browning has arranged for all of our stuff to make it on the boat with John and Corwin. We will sleep on the flight tonight and probably be at Tri-Cities in about eighteen hours."

Nick asked, "Did John wake up yet?" Glenn, "Not yet, but the doctors don't know what to do. They say he is dead, but he is breathing, and they can feel his pulse, but the machines say nadda." Nick frustrated, "They are full of shit…what do they know?"

Nick sat down with Sims and the gang and finally ate some food, He started sipping Jack Daniels, he looked at Adam, "I am about to get serious about still being alive." Molly came and laid at Bev's feet.

Nick motioned to Sergeant Mitchell and he stepped toward the men's room, Mitchell followed. Nick had three envelopes in his hand, "I want you to be the one to pay Holmes and Watson. Make sure they know we are going to cover their pay with the NSA per our contract.

"This money doesn't exist, so it won't ever show up anywhere. The only problem will be if they declare it. So, get them schooled up on the concept of private contracting. The other one is for you. We also put in a little extra for your headstone should you ever fly like that again."

Nick left the diner then stuck his head in the tent and waved to Barlow. Barlow nodded and joined Nick outside and they both walked to Barlow's cruiser. Nick turned back and looked into the windows of Sammy's Diner; he saw Holmes and Watson opening their envelopes. Mitch was laughing at the look on their faces. Barlow and Nick drove to the Corner Cup Café.

Nick had called the owner's wife after Barlow had heard that she didn't want to run the café. She had no children that were interested either. Nick was there to buy the café and set her up for life.

Earlier Barlow had explained that her husband was kidnapped and murdered by the same people who murdered Makayla. He told her they were killed resisting arrest.

When Nick stepped into the café, he saw a neat and modern establishment that met the needs of old Jonesborough and the millennials. The product was top drawer and it was staffed properly.

She was asking seven hundred thousand for it and the goodwill. Nick wrote her a check for seven million; seven hundred thousand for the café and the rest was just old fashion goodwill.

At seeing the check, she wanted a coffee with a little Jack Daniels. Nick told her he uniquely understood her situation and the money was very little in light of what she had lost.

It was almost 9:00 am and Nick was operating on three hours sleep. He had Barlow drop him off at the compound and he asked if he could tell Sims to bring Molly and the Polaris back when he returned.

Chapter Eighty-Seven

Day Fifteen
7:40 pm
Hart Compound
Jonesborough, TN

Sergeant Mitchell and Sims had gone out of their way to make sure they were the ones to pick up the members of the Crete operation at the Tri-Cities airport.

With Sims' house being destroyed, that eliminated the bed and breakfast and the four bedrooms that went with it. That left John's little pine cabin, the extra bedroom at the compound and the bunks above the rec room.

Sims thought since Trish and Jess had been placed in the pine cabin before the operation that took care of Sims and Mitchell as well. Hoss had room for Dom and Lil' Joe went home. Phu had wrangled himself a cot on the USS Abraham Lincoln.

When Nick called Sims to follow up, he pointed out that when Kat returned from the hospital in DC, she should not be left alone. Nick reshuffled their arrangements putting all the women in the pine cabin and Sims and Mitchell in Corwin's bungalow.

He would hold down the fort with Molly, with the caveat that they all would meet for breakfast at 9:00 am every day if possible. He instructed everyone to lay low until he was sure the operation in Crete was completed. Sims agreed and hung up.

As soon as Sims put the phone in his pocket, he, Jess, Trish, and Mitch jumped into Sims' SUV and headed to the pine cabin. Hoss and Dom dropped Lil' Joe at Adam's house with a six-pack of beer; he and Adam had a long drive to DC to visit Corwin. Dom stayed the night with Hoss and then flew home to Rockford, Maine the next morning.

That next morning, Hoss showed up at Sammy's Diner at 9:00 am. He found Nick and Molly in the back; they were alone. Hoss plopped down into his chair and coffee appeared. He said his good mornings to Bev and she and Molly went to see Sammy.

Nick thanked Hoss for showing up in a sarcastic tone. Hoss laughed, "Did you expect those boys to sleep at Corwin's? Nick trying not to smile, "I guess not; besides they had been on opposite sides of the world for a while."

Hoss leaned back in his chair, "So the boys docked late yesterday what is the word, did they both make it?" Nick put his feet up on the chair next to him, "Turns out Corwin wakes up and Phu is standing next to the bed. Corwin freaks, thinking Phu had just shot him a second ago, and now there he is. I guess they all had a good laugh about it, but Corwin was not in any condition to be laughing like that."

Hoss picked up his menu, "So, any good stories about John?" Nick started reading the back of Hoss' menu, "On their last night at sea, Phu decides he was going to sleep through the night in his own quarters. So, about 1:00 am Phu gets up to pee and he finds John in the chair sound asleep.

"Phu wakes up John and asks what he is doing there. John says he was there to keep Stavros from coming back. Then he walks back to his room and back to sleep. John remembers nothing. But the whole point was John was up and walking around."

Hoss was still staring at Nick, "This weird shit is not going to stop is it?" Nick shook his head, not saying anything. Bev and Molly returned so Hoss and Nick could order.

After they had received their food, Nick got a call from General Rouse. It was only a few words and Nick hung up, "John and Corwin walked into Walter Reed on their own power; Kat was quite relieved to see him."

Hoss made eye contact with Nick, "Glenn wasn't on the plane. Any comment?" Nick squirmed just a little, "This may be the weirdest thing to have happened thus far, Glenn is meeting with Browning, General Rouse, Holmes and Watson in the NSA's New York field office."

Hoss just kept staring at Nick, "He hates the NSA, why in the world would he do that?" Browning wants Glenn to help him track down the murder squad. Glenn wants to go after any connections to big pharma; he wants to bring it all down.

Glenn feels if they can bring the doctors together and provide for their safety, they could share their work on a secure network and finalize cures for the various cancers.

If they become a protected government entity, they can farm out the manufacturing and vet their vendors. Then they can set the prices and help on a global scale.

It would mirror the allied defense systems of the major countries. It is the same premise; provide new and better weapons to defend your way of life. Cancer would be their first common enemy.

Chapter Eighty-Eight

Day Seventeen
8:45 am
Walter Reed National Military Medical Center
Bethesda, MD

John had a good night's sleep and was having an even better breakfast with Kat in his room. He was in the wing where the Presidents had their physicals and he was being treated like a VIP.

He was most thankful for the hug he was finally able to have with his wife last night as they settled him into his room. John had felt disjointed and ungrounded since he gained consciousness; now he felt human again.

Later that evening, they hooked John up to the machines and they were getting readings. It was the first time since he was hospitalized that any machine had produced a reading of any kind. He looked at Kat, "Thank you for bringing me back." She looked puzzled but smiled.

This morning he was feeling strong and fit. He could see clearly, and everything seemed to be in high definition. Today he was going to receive a battery of tests. They hoped to get a CT scan and an MRI. Those two tests would take up the bulk of his day. Kat decided she would see Corwin then do some shopping at shops the first ladies of Washington haunted.

Corwin was sitting up eating breakfast with Adam, Phu and Lil' Joe when Kat walked in. They caught up on the latest info and she gave them the latest on John. Kat was glad to see that Corwin no longer had tubes protruding from his chest. He said he could almost take a regular breath. She said her goodbyes and left them.

Adam got up, shut the door and closed the blinds. He lifted up his Hawaiian shirt revealing a flask of prominent size, "I brought my friend Jack Daniels along with me, he has the gift of healing." Corwin smiling, "Amen brother and with any luck, he will interact well with my drugs."

Adam looked over his shoulder then passed the flask to Corwin, "Careful, just a little at first you don't want the Jack hack from a burning throat." Corwin's eyes opened wide as he understood, "That would hurt to no end."

Right as Corwin was about to swallow Lil' Joe told Adam that Nick told Sims and Mitch that they had to sleep at Corwin's place. Corwin could not control his auto-laugh reaction; the Jack was halfway down.

He wanted to scream it burned so bad, but he just cringed with his face distorted in pain and just one eye open. Finally, he took a deep breath with both arms crossed hugging himself from the pain in his chest. Phu pointed at him, "See its working already." Phu and the boys snuck out just before dinner with plans to continue the next day.

John was tired when he had finished his days testing. He and Kat had dinner and later she went to her hotel. John was looking forward to early morning rounds; he wanted to know his test results.

When the nurse woke him and checked his vitals, he felt refreshed and ready to go. He finished his breakfast just as the doctor arrived.

Doctor Moore sat in a chair on the left side of John and began to ask questions, "Do you remember what happened before your fall?" John did but was not sure what General Rouse would want him to say. John responded, "I am not sure, only bits and pieces."

Moore was miffed, "Let's try again. General Rouse would like to know if you remember anything before you fell." John said, "Yes I do, it is exactly what will show on the video from the mother drone." Moore smiled, "Nicely done."

Moore moved on, "When did you break your right arm just above the elbow?" John responded, "I have never broken one of my arms or legs, just fingers, and toes."

Moore, now pissed, looked down at his clipboard, "John you have evidence of several breaks in your arms, right femur and two vertebras in your lower back. These all appear to have happened several years ago and at different times. How do you explain that?"

John was locked in a blank stare, "I could only say they happened a few days ago and ah...I don't know." John looked Moore in the eyes, "What did General Rouse tell you to expect when you talked to me?"

Moore stood up, "What he said was bullshit and now I am getting the same thing from you." John still on the offensive, "So, other than old injuries, is there anything wrong with me right now?"

Moore with his hand on the doorknob, "Well, three days ago it appeared you were killed when you were blown up and landed in a tree. All the machines said you were dead, but you continued to function despite what they said.

"Now you sit here with evidence of bone fractures throughout your body from years ago and are trying to tell me they are from three days ago." John now pissed, "Hey doc, other than the fact you think I am a liar, what else is wrong with me?"

Moore turned to open the door, "There is nothing wrong with you Mr. Hart, not a damn thing. You are a walking miracle; rise up and walk." Moore left the room, threw his chart on the nurse's station and kept moving.

John called Corwin's room, and Phu answered, "Corbin's room. John started laughing, "You morons are getting drunk in there. John heard Adam's voice in the background, "Jack Daniels is healing all those who will come and be baptized in his greatness. You missed getting healed yesterday; don't disappoint Jesus today young man."

John asked Adam if he could use one of their phones, he wanted to make some calls. Lil' Joe came on the phone, "Is your navy duffle in the room?" John looked around, "Wait; let me look in the closet."

John opened the closet and found the duffle on the floor. He brought it to his bed and grabbed the phone, "Got it, now what?" "Rip out the bottom of the toiletries case; your phone should be there."

He found it, "Thanks, don't get Corwin wasted it might mess him up." Phu sang his answer in the background, "Tooooooo late."

John needed some answers and he hoped his phone could help. He took his phone, went to the video applications and found what he was looking for. He closed the blinds and turned off the lights; it wasn't dark enough.

He thought for a few seconds then went into the bathroom and turned out the lights. He put the phone on video record, placed his face in the middle of the frame and let it record for several seconds.

He turned on the lights, found his way back to his video apps and selected what he wanted. He brought up the video he had just recorded, hit play and then starlight; John was dazed by what he saw.

He staggered from the bathroom; he didn't understand what was going on. John dialed Semjaza's number and Semjaza voice came into his head, "Still, you use the phone?" I haven't figured out how to get to you yet."

Semjaza laughed, "I got your call when you were on the roof. I got Molly's emergency call from your front yard the other night; what does a guy have to do."

John cut him off, "My eyes are deep emerald green like yours are blue." Semjaza did not respond for what seemed like forever, "Semjaza are you there? Semjaza finally replied, "Yes, I was just absorbing the weight of your comment."

John now almost hyperventilating, "What do you mean?" Semjaza a bit distant, "Deep emerald green signifies something entirely new. Only three of us have deep emerald green eyes; you might know them; Mikey, Gabe, and Raphy. Look'em up in the book."

Chapter Eighty-Nine

Early Morning
The Hart Compound
Jonesborough

Twelve weeks later, Molly was awakened by her need to pee. This was the second time her urge had disturbed her slumber; it was time to wake up John.

She was not happy with the recent changes in her sleeping arrangements. She had to sleep across the foyer in what used to be the dream room, while John and Kat slept in their nice new master suite.

She had already been scolded for scratching the paint on the door and barking. She was now at an impasse; pee on the bathmat or find a way in.

The last time she had been in this type of situation she had to escape creatures that were hunting her and John. She had become separated from him and hid in the dream room. Molly eventually had jumped into and slid down the laundry shoot. She came out right next to the Polaris, which was parked by the kitchen elevator.

This time was different; Molly had to get into the master suite and needed to do so quietly.

She went and stood in front of the master bedroom door, no new ideas. Molly decided to sit at the front door where they went out to go pee and play ball; this was the right spot.

She remembered they had come down from the master through the walk-in closet, then down and out the foyer closet door, and then out the front door. She sat in front of the foyer closet.

Molly sat scrutinizing the door when she saw the flat, shiny, black biometric plate on the right side of the door, above the handle. Molly could open regular doors with levers, the ones with knobs tasted nasty but she could do it. This one was like the one in the cabin, but a different type of deal altogether.

Molly stared at it running through all her thoughts and memories. She decided she could not bark, but Molly needed a closer look. She stood on her back legs, put her paws on each side of the plate and looked closer.

Molly knew if she could sniff it and get a small bite of it, she could figure it out. She sniffed all around the edges then decided to feel it with her nose; with a small pop, the door opened. Molly giggled to herself and fetched her ball; she was going in.

After a moment of indecision, she realized she had to set her ball down to nose the door open; then get the ball. She headed up the stairs to the back of the walk-in closet where she set the ball down, jumped up, nosed in, picked up her ball and snuck into the bedroom.

The new master was much larger than Molly's dream room. Kat's designer had included all the amenities. There was a vanity, reading nook, a headboard designed for reading or working in bed and very lavish draperies and floor coverings throughout.

Molly appreciated the plush carpet as she belly-crawled her way across the room toward John's side of the bed. When she was finally aligned with John Molly sat up.

She wanted a direct line of sight so she could stare into his eyes when they opened. Molly put the ball in her mouth and slowly moved it to within three inches of John's nose. She placed her chin on the bed and began the Molly mind-meld.

She stared and concentrated as hard as she could, *"Open, open, open your eyes.* After a minute, John stirred and opened his eyes a crack and saw Molly smiling at him, *"See boss, you can't keep me out."* John smiled and then got on one elbow. He reached over and scratched Molly's ears, "I knew you would figure it out. Good job Molly girl, very nice."

Molly started to move as if it was time to play but John gave her the settle down signal, and she sat quietly. John motioned for her to come closer and he whispered near her ear, "Momma Kat is going to have a puppy; you will have a full-time job now. You must make sure the baby and Kat are safe."

Molly looked nervous for a second then she moved slowly around to Kat's side of the bed and lay down. John finally got up and took Molly to pee.

In the months to come, Molly never left Kat's side. Molly comforted Kat after the funeral and sat up proudly for her Bride's Maids photo.

Sometimes Kat would get frustrated with Molly being so protective. When she did, she was reminded of what had happened when they prevented Molly from doing her job; they never should have left her in the car.

Kat and John formalized their marriage at the compound with the party to end all parties. It was an open house so the people of Jonesborough could finally see what was behind the fences.

Made in the USA
San Bernardino, CA
16 August 2019